ALWAYS AND FOREVER

WENDY LINDSTROM

rustic studio
PUBLISHING

ALWAYS AND FOREVER

Lindstrom, Wendy
Always and Forever / by Wendy Lindstrom
ISBN: 978-1-939263-28-5 (pbk.)
ISBN: 978-1-939263-21-6 (Kindle)
ISBN: 978-1-939263-21-6 (e-pub.)

1. New York — History — 19th century — Fiction. 2. Victorian America — New York. 3. Mail Order Bride — New York — Fiction. 4. Death and Grief — Fiction. 5. Sawmill and Lumber Industry — Fiction. 6. Family Relationships — Fiction. 7. Love stories. 8. Historical Fiction.

EBook design by Rustic Studio Publishing
Cover design by The Killion Group, Inc.
Published by Rustic Studio Publishing
www.wendylindstrom.com/contact

From the New York Times bestselling author of the Grayson Brothers family saga comes the first novel in a riveting Historical romance series about unforeseen love, hard choices, and healing second chances...

ALWAYS AND FOREVER

**A Mail Order Bride He Doesn't Want—
A Woman He Can't Resist.**

CHAPTER ONE

Always and Forever is the SWEET edition of
When I Fall in Love (Grayson Brothers series)

A s Hal Grayson angled his gouging tool and created a shallow arc in the lid of an oak chest, he tried to lose himself in the scraping, rasping sounds from his carving tools. The rhythmic motion of carving and sanding wood, and the earthy smell of the old barn that housed his woodshop, usually calmed him after a hard day's work at the sawmill. But tonight nothing could soothe the anger churning inside him.

With an agitated groan, Hal braced his fists on the workbench and dragged in a hard breath, trying to settle his frazzled nerves. He had to finish carving the lid and staining the chest before he could line it with cedar, but his hands were too unsteady to work.

His brother had completely lost his mind.

Hal and his brother John Radford had experienced their share of disagreements over the years, but they always talked it out in the end. That's why Hal believed they would have a successful partnership in the sawmill business, but John's latest decision made Hal question that possibility.

What was John Radford thinking ordering a wife like one might order a piece of furniture? And why hadn't he talked to Hal before making such a foolhardy move? He was thinking only of himself, that's what. He wasn't thinking about Hal, and he sure as heck was not considering the future of their mill.

Hal tossed aside the gouge and slammed his fist on the workbench. The whole idea was absurd. They couldn't afford the responsibility and expense of another person. That's why they hadn't hired a man at the mill. They were trying to build a business, and Hal was going to remind his thick-skulled brother of that fact as soon as John Radford returned from making their last delivery of pine planks.

How could John have done something so irresponsible and thoughtless? Their sawmill business was just beginning to show a profit, but still not enough support them. The money Hal made building furniture for Addison Edwards was barely enough to cover their monthly payment on the mill and their house. How could John not see that they couldn't afford a single added expense. They ran the mill until dark and built furniture in his woodshop until the wee hours of the morning. They were already working around the clock and couldn't physically work more hours if they had them. They were exhausted. What they needed were extra hands at the mill, not a woman to warm John's bed.

Shaking his head, Hal inspected the chest lid, eyeing the sweep from his last pass with the gouge. He took up a veiner to add finer detail but had to stop several times to take a calming breath and relax his tensed hands before he ruined the piece. Not even the fragrant scent of cedar, his favorite wood, could unlock the tension between his shoulders.

Hal loved his brother, but he could literally throttle John at the moment. Barely a year apart, they were usually lockstep on every-thing. But just two hours ago John had flippantly announced that he'd found a bride and made an agreement with her. Hal had stood staring at him, open-mouthed and stunned. He still couldn't believe it.

Even now thinking about it made his chest cramp with anger. What a fool-brained and inconsiderate decision.

Hal had told John in no uncertain terms that he needed to break the agreement with the woman.

John just laughed and promised Hal that he'd soon be thanking him for bringing in a lady who could tend their house and put some decent meals on the table. Then he said he needed to deliver the lumber and drove out of the mill whistling a happy tune as if their conversation was over and Hal's opinion didn't matter.

Oh, no, it was a long way from over.

Hal blew out a breath and flexed his fingers. He needed steady hands and a clear mind for carving such a detailed piece. One wrong arc with the gouge could ruin the whole lid of the chest. But his head felt ready to explode and concentrating on the intricate detail proved impossible.

The sound of the barn door banging closed signaled his brother's return.

"John! Get in here," he hollered. They were going to have it out and get this problem resolved so Hal could clear his mind and get back to work.

When Thomas Drake stepped inside, Hal's irritation jumped a notch. Not because he didn't like the man. Drake, a dark-haired some-what stocky man about Hal's age, was becoming a friend. Hal liked and greatly respected his competitor, but he wasn't interested in leasing his sawmill to the man.

Hal tossed the veiner tool onto the workbench and raised an eyebrow. "I suppose you're here to bend my ear about leasing the mill?"

"I wish I were," Tom said quietly. Hal expected to see a grin light Tom's face as their back and forth was becoming a bit of a friendly debate that Drake seemed to enjoy. But there was no light in Tom Drake's face. All Hal could see in the man's eyes was pain. "There's been an accident, I'm afraid."

Hal's heart started pounding.

"The axle on your wagon broke and —"

"Is John all right?" Hal asked stepping toward Drake. "Has he been hurt?"

Tom's shoulders seemed to deflate. "I'm sorry, Hal. Reggie Orwald found him beneath the wagon, and it was... it was too late."

An ocean roared in Hal's ears. He heard Drake talking but felt as if he were floating in thick liquid that made it difficult to move, to breathe, to understand.

"The front axle broke and the wheels snapped off. We suspect John was thrown off the seat. The crash surely startled horses and... well, it seems they pulled the wagon over top of him."

Hal backed away from the words that were pelting him like shards of ice.

His back slammed into the workbench, jarring his tools, shattering his composure. Crushing pain gripped his chest. His breath came in ragged gasps. He couldn't get enough air.

"Your brother is at Doc Kinley's house."

Hal shook his head. "This is a mistake." He glanced toward the door, expecting his brother any minute. "John was delivering a load of pine planks. It can't be him."

Thomas wrung the black cap he held in his hands. "Reggie didn't know John and thought he might work for me, so he came by the mill to let me know. I went to Doc Kinley's to make sure my suspicion was true before I came to see you. I'm sorry Hal, but it's your brother, John Radford."

Gut-punched by the news, Hal sagged forward, his back against the workbench, his knees barely able to support him. It couldn't be true.

"I'll help any way I can," Tom said, his voice coming from the end of a long tunnel.

A loud buzzing filled Hal's ears, and his body quaked. The smell of cedar wood shavings that he loved so well turned his stomach.

It couldn't be true.

He'd just talked with John. They hadn't even finished their argument.

How could his brother be... dead?

John was smiling when he left the mill. He was happy—and alive!

Oh, God.

Oh, no...

Dear Mr. Grayson,
I will be arriving the Dunkirk station June 2ⁿᵈ at 6 o'clock.
I look forward to meeting you in person.
Your intended,
Nancy Mitchell.

HAL GRAYSON FOLDED the mud-spattered letter and jammed it into the pocket of his dusty trousers. He clenched his fists around the reins and directed his team of rented horses toward the Dunkirk train depot and a meeting he did not want to have.

He should be delivering a load of cherry planks to A. B. Edwards store, not meeting his brother's intended. But his brother, John Radford, couldn't make the trip because he was...

Dead.

Hal squeezed his eyes closed and then opened them wide trying to clear the gut-wrenching nightmare he couldn't seem to awaken from. His brother, John Radford, was really gone.

On any other day, the clip-clopping sound of the horses' hooves and rattle of the wagon would have rocked Hal into an easy state of woolgathering. But today even the singing birds and warm sunshine on his shoulders agitated him. How could life go on as normal when everything was upside down? How could his strong, healthy brother be dead?

Dropping his forehead into his palm, Hal squeezed, trying to force the image of John's inert body out of his mind. "You should have listened to me," he whispered, his throat thick with grief and love. Hal lifted his face to the breeze, deeply regretting that one of his last conversations with his brother had been so heated and upsetting.

But John's insistence that they needed a woman to tend their house and prepare their meals had vexed Hal. It wasn't that he'd disagreed with John that they needed a caretaker for their home. They worked sixteen hours a day, wore their clothes for days at a time before washing them in the creek and tossing them over a sagging clothesline to dry. They barely slept. They ate apples and eggs and bread given to them by their neighbors. Their small house had grown dirty and remained scantily furnished, a sad fact neither of them had time to worry about. They were too busy trying to keep their sawmill business afloat.

That's why Hal wouldn't entertain the idea of John taking a bride because they couldn't afford the expense.

They'd been hunting bigger dreams.

Hal and John were making monthly payments on a small home and sawmill they were buying from Tom and Martha Fiske. They believed if they worked hard they could earn enough money to help their father as well. Progress was slow, but Hal was earning income by carving spectacular pieces for Addison Edwards' store and also partnering with John in their new sawmill. They had made their first whole dollar of profit the week before John died.

That's when John had revealed that he'd advertised for a wife—and that he'd found one.

Miss Nancy Mitchell, a gal from Buffalo, had answered John's advertisement.

Her train would arrive in a few short minutes.

With a snort of disgust, Hal sat upright and turned his wagon onto Central Avenue and headed toward Dunkirk. Leafy maple trees lined the street on either side, reminding him of one of his favorite areas back home in Buffalo.

The irony of meeting his brother's intended made his gut burn.

How could John have accepted a bride he'd never even met? Little wonder that John hadn't a clear thought since receiving Miss Mitchell's letter. That's likely what distracted him from noticing the problem with the wagon wheel until the axle snapped in half.

A flood of regret and anger filled Hal's chest and restricted his breathing. He wanted to shout out his pain and hurl it past the leafy tops of the maple trees. He wanted to howl and rant and force time to move backwards so he could rescue his father's new sawmill from being repossessed by Lloyd Tremont—and save his beloved brother from death.

But it was too late.

And so Hal drove toward the train station because there was nothing else he could do.

Sick to his soul over the whole mess, Hal pulled up at the depot and parked the wagon. Sunshine streaked across the hard-packed yard and bleached the wooden slats on the platform of the depot. Other carriages and wagons were arriving, perhaps to fetch a friend or family member coming in for a visit or to send a loved one off on their own journey. The expressions of anticipation or trepidation on the faces around Hal indicated both. Neither of those emotions were present within him, however. He was too numb to feel anything. And this was merely a bit of business he needed to deal with so that he could return to work.

Still, he wondered what his own expression revealed. Grief? Agitation? Anger?

Dread. That's what he felt inside. His stomach ached with dread as he stepped down from the driver's seat. To even mention John Radford's name wrung Hal's insides. To reveal such tragedy to Miss Mitchell would be gut-wrenching. What would she think of this turn of events? Would she offer quiet condolences and return home? What else could she do?

What else could anyone do?

A howl of grief rose up in Hal's throat, choking him. He sucked in sharp breaths as he strode to the ticket office. Five minutes later, he stood on the platform, fists clenched, waiting to meet his brother's mail-order bride.

———————

As THE TRAIN came to a stop at the Dunkirk station, Nancy turned from the window where she'd been watching the landscape pass and sat up to adjust her hat. Her heart ached, and she was scared and terribly homesick for all she'd left behind. She hadn't wanted to leave. She loved her family deeply and had never thought to run off this way.

But staying would have forced her to do something that would have broken her sister's heart.

Better that it be her own heart she was breaking.

Passengers folded newspapers, straightened skirts, and coats, gathered their children and valises, and began departing the train.

Nancy stood, wavering with indecision, the ribbons on her hat left untied. What if John Grayson didn't like what he saw? What if he decided he didn't want to marry her?

Her stomach rolled, and for the life of her she couldn't seem to draw a full breath.

She was running away.

She was going to marry a man she'd never met.

And she'd lied to secure John Radford's agreement.

Mile after mile she had practiced her name Nancy *Mitchell*, she silently repeated. *Mitchell... Mitchell... Mitchell.* Changing her last name was necessary because... because the Grayson family hated her father.

She had heard her father state this truth to her mother in a recent discussion they'd recently had over supper.

Nancy didn't know much about the Grayson family because they socialized in different circles, but her father knew Daniel Grayson well and seemed to consider the man a friend. Other folks spoke highly of the Grayson family, so when Nancy found John Grayson's advertisement seeking a bride to join him in Fredonia, she grasped his offer with both hands and answered as Nancy Mitchell, using her mother's maiden name.

The lie was necessary, and yet the deception ate at her. Her only comfort came in knowing she would do all in her power to be a good wife and to create a loving marriage with John. She would tell him the truth as soon as it was possible to do so, when she felt he might understand and forgive her this one falsehood.

But withholding information was a form of lying, too, and so it was more than one lie on her conscience.

She'd also lied to her cousin James to get him to deliver her and her trunks to the station.

So many lies! Nancy gripped her stomach fearing she might be sick. The lies bubbled like acid in her gut, eating at her.

A young lady in a stylish blue dress and matching cape exchanged a warm glance with her handsome young escort as they passed Nancy's seat. Their love for one another was obvious. Nancy envied them. Would she and John ever look at each other with that same warmth? Or would he ultimately hate her because she'd lied to him?

Adjusting her gloves and smoothing her skirts into place, Nancy told herself there was nothing to do but to step off the train.

Negotiating her way to the door on shaky legs proved difficult. She used the high seat backs to keep herself upright and moving through the car. As she stepped from the train, she clutched her small reticule and surveyed the milling crowd. Not one face looked familiar. Not one person approached her.

What if he'd changed his mind? What if he'd gone back to Buffalo?

Clasping a palm over her roiling stomach, she scanned the crowd.

Laughter and shouts of joy sounded around her as families and friends reunited. She hooked the wrist chain of her reticule over her forearm and straightened her shoulders. Her legs trembled as she stood on the platform with too many people casting curious, probing looks at her as they rushed to and fro.

Where was he?

As the porter deposited Nancy's three trunks on the platform, she tried to present herself as a confident woman rather than a nervous girl still in her teens—another falsehood. Smoke billowed from the gasping train and made her eyes tear as it pulled out of the station. Her stomach felt upside down and her breath came shallow and fast. The letter she'd received from John Radford was kind and assured her of his character and his intent. Surely, he would be here, so she would just have to wait for him to approach and hope he found her acceptable. And she prayed she would find him acceptable in return because if she didn't... her life would go from bad to unbearable.

One pleasant-looking older man asked if she needed assistance, and for an instant she was hopeful he might be John Grayson. Unfortunately, the man had come to fetch his brother returning from Albany. So Nancy waited while the crowd thinned, observing each man who passed, wondering if this one or the next would smile and announce himself. Not one of them did. The longer she stood alone the faster her heart beat and the stiffer her back grew. What if her intended didn't show?

She *couldn't* go back.

As the crowd thinned, her eyes met the dark speculative gaze of a man on the other side of the platform who seemed to be observing her. With a slight nod, he tucked his dusty hat beneath his arm and headed toward her. He was taller than she'd anticipated—and very handsome.

Her heart beat faster. Her cheeks warmed, and she wondered if the man walking toward her with a confident stride was her future husband.

Another train pulled into the station in a cloud of billowing smoke, blasting its arrival, and shattering her nerves.

"Miss Mitchell?" the man asked, his voice respectful, yet unmistakably strong and commanding.

As she took in his soiled clothing and circles of fatigue beneath his eyes, she nodded to let him know he'd found his intended. She hoped he wouldn't notice her aversion to his dirty, unkempt clothing.

He didn't smile. He didn't extend his hand. He waved a filthy piece of paper in front of her face. "I'm Hal Grayson, John Radford's brother.

I received your letter to John and regret to inform you that he must cancel your agreement because he...because he recently died in an accident."

Stunned, her gaze jumped between the letter and his unwavering gaze.

"I've purchased your passage back to Buffalo," he said, his eyes wrought with grief and... anger? "I apologize for your trouble. I'll load your bags while you board. The train will be departing again in minutes."

Sawdust covered his clothing, and perspiration wet the underarms of his shirt. He towered above her, thin for his height, and yet despite his frown, she couldn't think of another man more handsome... or indifferent.

A few passengers stepped off the train, greeted their friends and loved ones, then gathered their belongings and rushed off.

"You'd best hurry, Miss Mitchell," he said, nodding toward the open train door.

She glanced around her believing there had been a terrible mistake. "But I don't... John promised to meet me here."

Hal Grayson's lips twisted. "As you can see, my brother is not here. He was laid to rest in Buffalo four days ago. While I was there, I tried to locate you after his funeral to save you the trip. But I was unable to find a Nancy Mitchell in Buffalo. I regret that his death has changed your plans, Miss Mitchell. It's inconvenient for both of us."

"Oh, dear... I'm terribly sorry," she said, realizing her words were offensive. "I only meant... I'm sorry."

Her plan was crumbling. Of course, Mr. Grayson had been unable to find Nancy Mitchell in Buffalo, because Nancy Mitchell hadn't existed until she'd answered John Grayson's advertisement. Helplessly, Nancy searched the station for the man she was supposed to meet, the man who had provided a means for her to escape the disastrous marriage her father had arranged for her. But that man wasn't coming, so she turned to the only hope she had. "I can't go back, Mister Grayson."

"I'm afraid you must," he said without batting those long black lashes of his. With a curt nod toward the train, he added, "I'm sorry to disappoint you, but you'll need to board now, Miss Mitchell."

She shook her head and threw herself on the mercy of the only person who could help her out of this predicament. "Please, Mr. Grayson. I had an agreement with... with your brother. I can't go back because I... I simply must stay."

His dark eyebrows lowered in a scowl. "Your services are no longer required, Miss Mitchell. Now please board the train before it leaves without you. I emptied my purse purchasing your ticket. I can't afford to put you up in a room for the night."

"My *services?*" Her temper flared. "I was to become your brother's *wife,* Mr. Grayson, not a servant who provides a *service.*"

He raised his palm as if to apologize for his offense. "Beg pardon, Miss Mitchell. My brother sought a woman who could prepare our meals and tend our home. Those are the services he advertised for in exchange for marriage, yes?"

"His letter said he was looking for love." Nancy retrieved John's letter from her purse and waved it beneath Hal Grayson's arrogant nose as he'd done so unceremoniously with the letter she'd sent to his brother. Thanks to years of debating her father at every turn, she'd grown adept at outwitting a worthy opponent. "He wanted *love,* Mr. Grayson."

Hal's eyebrows shot upward in surprise and then slashed right back down into a scowl that was already becoming familiar. Although he didn't say it, she could tell he didn't believe her claim.

John Grayson's letter had stated that he hoped they would get on well together and both find their arrangement pleasant. He wanted an amicable relationship. That was close enough to love for Nancy. It was far better than the alternative waiting for her back in Buffalo.

She noted that Hal Grayson's hand was devoid of a wedding band. "Forgive my breach of etiquette, Mr. Grayson, but are you married?" Her boldness made her face burn, but she was desperate.

His eyebrows lifted, no doubt surprised by her bold question. "I haven't made a match as of yet," he said.

"Your brother promised that I would have a good home here and be treated kindly," she said. "I left everything for him, Mr. Grayson. I can't go back. I'm truly sorry about your brother, but in his absence, I must place myself on your mercy and beg your assistance."

"I'm afraid there's nothing more I can do, Miss Mitchell."

"But you can't just leave me stranded here."

"I've purchased your passage back to Buffalo. This train is heading to Buffalo."

"I told you I can't return. It's out of the question, Mr. Grayson. Until we find a suitable solution, I have no choice but to hold you responsible in your brother's stead."

"Me?" He staggered back a step with a derisive laugh. "No, ma'am. I'm not fulfilling my brother's contract. That was an agreement I was against from the start."

"An agreement nonetheless, Mr. Grayson. I have nothing to go back to because of the *promise* your brother made to me. And now I'm stranded in a strange town without any means to support myself. I have no other options. Not one."

"I'm not seeking a wife, Miss Mitchell."

"Well, your brother was, and he made a commitment to me. A man of integrity would honor his deceased brother's debts and agreements."

He drew himself up as if preparing to bodily put her on the train, but it was already chugging out of the station.

Through clenched teeth, he said, "You've missed your train, which was extremely unwise, Miss Mitchell." Releasing a growl deep in his throat, he said, "Wait here," and headed inside the station.

Nancy stood outside and tried to calm her racing heart. Warm June sunshine splashed across the worn planks of the platform, and yet she stood alone and shivering, wondering if she'd just won a battle or made the biggest mistake of her life.

CHAPTER TWO

As they pulled out of the depot, Hal noticed Miss Mitchell looking over at him. "This... awkward situation isn't entirely my fault, Mr. Grayson."

Hal said nothing. He was utterly baffled to find himself carting the woman home. He'd fully intended to put Miss Mitchell back on a train bound for Buffalo. He'd spent nearly every coin he had to purchase her return trip, and yet he'd simply stood on the platform while her train chugged out of the station.

He'd meant to send her back. He really had. But the minute he saw her step down from the train looking apprehensive and even a bit scared, he felt his anger and frustration shift to curiosity and concern. He had expected to meet a self-possessed twenty-year-old woman. He thought she would be plain, perhaps even uncomely, a woman whose only choice for marriage was to answer an advertisement. And while Miss Mitchell seemed poised and composed, she appeared younger and was far from plain.

"What was I to do?" she asked, softly, her dark eyes peering from beneath her stylish hat.

He couldn't look away from those dark eyes of hers. They had ensnared him at the station and made him forget his purpose in coming here. When he'd first seen her, he'd experienced a sense of familiarity sweep over him, as if he were meeting a long-lost friend, and yet he knew with certainty he'd never met the woman. He would have never forgotten a woman like Miss Mitchell.

"Are you so angry you won't speak to me?" she asked.

He braced his elbows on his knees so that he wouldn't have to look at her. He couldn't think while looking into those big brown eyes. "I'm not angry with you Miss Mitchell, I'm just... I'm trying to figure out what to do with you."

"It's a bit late for that, don't you think, Mr. Grayson?"

He sighed. "I have no idea what to think at the moment."

He'd expected a fragile flower, one who would be easily persuaded to return home when faced with the information of John's passing. But instead he'd found a petite, red-haired spitfire, a determined young woman with a sharp mind of her own. Although wildly beautiful and desirable, Miss Mitchell would have been a terrible match for John Radford. He wouldn't have appreciated her forthright manner and intelligence. He wouldn't have known what to do with such a woman. John had expected a passive and plain wife. The spark of defiance in Miss Mitchell's eyes said she was anything but submissive.

Still, when Hal cut his gaze to the young woman seated beside him, he sensed a bit of innocence and naivete about her that elicited a protective instinct in him—a feeling that wholly surprised him as much as discovering her stunning beauty.

Why was a woman with so many assets willing to marry a complete stranger who could offer her nothing? Hal knew John wouldn't have lied about their situation, but had he neglected to tell Miss Mitchell what she'd be getting herself into?

But the more pressing question was why Hal had allowed her to distract him to such a degree that she'd missed her train?

It was a question he couldn't answer, and so he found himself returning to Fredonia with Miss Mitchell by his side, heading to the house he'd recently shared with his brother. Hal had nowhere else to take the headstrong woman.

As they traveled out Liberty Street, they passed William and Mary Tucker's house. His neighbors greeted him with warm waves and curious looks at the stylish young lady at his side. Hal considered throwing himself on their mercy and leaving Miss Mitchell with them, but he couldn't impose on his neighbors. He was already in their debt. While he'd been in Fredonia for a number of months, he and John had only moved in next door a few weeks earlier and were just becoming friends with the Tuckers. Now that John was gone, Mary Tucker and his other neighbor, Martha Fiske, had been delivering Hal's supper each evening. Their generosity and kindness were overwhelming, and he couldn't even think of imposing on them further with Miss Mitchell.

The only option was to put the woman up in his home for the night and then take her back to the station in the morning. She would have to make do with a dusty room and a bed with a lumpy mattress. That's all he had to offer her.

The obstinate woman should have taken the train right back home instead of forcing his hand. John would have wanted Hal to ensure she had favorable circumstances and wasn't left stranded. And Hal did feel a sense of duty toward the woman. She was here because of his brother's foolish promise—and her own bad decision. But that didn't mean he had to be happy with the situation.

Hal's house was badly disheveled, sparsely furnished, and filled with grief. Until now, he hadn't much cared, but when Miss Mitchell stepped into the small foyer, her look of shock made his face burn.

The disappointment in her eyes gouged his conscience for not preparing her, for not helping her understand what she was walking into. But her obstinacy and unwillingness to get back on the train had made him too angry to care. The woman was beyond unreasonable. She'd promised to marry a man sight unseen. She deserved what she got—or so he tried to convince himself.

"It's just for the night," Hal said, by way of apology. "I'll return you to the station in the morning."

Instead of weeping or complaining, Miss Mitchell drew in a steadying breath and walked through the house. Her pretty brown skirt stirred up balls of dust that rolled across the oak floor like tumbleweed. The cut of her stylish dress with its puffed sleeves and fitted waist emphasized her petite figure and told Hal two things: she was a fit, beautiful woman, and her garments alone were worth more than he earned in a month.

She peeked in each room as she circled the parlor and eventually found her way to the kitchen. "Three bedchambers and a cozy parlor will make a lovely home," she said, although she sounded unconvinced.

A *home*? For whom? Hal didn't ask because it seemed better not to know what was on the lady's mind.

She entered the kitchen ahead of him. "The table is large enough for a family and there are... plenty of dishes," she said, as her sharp gaze took in the mountain of unwashed plates and bowls and silverware piled in the sink and stovetop. Nearly every item in his home, including the dishes, had been inherited from the recently deceased previous owner, Harold Crandale, and the man's generous daughter, Martha Fiske.

"Are you hungry?" Hal asked because he didn't know how to excuse the inexcusable mess he and John had created. He gestured toward a wicker hamper on the sideboard. "You'll find eggs, bread, and a crock of butter in the basket. My neighbor William Tucker brought over that crate of last year's apples," he said, gesturing to a wooden crate shoved into a corner. "They're packed in sand and still very tasty. It's all I have at the moment."

"I'm quite content, thank you." She looked around the kitchen and sighed as if preparing herself for an insurmountable job. "Where is your housekeeping staff?"

The idea was so preposterous it made Hal laugh. "*You* were to be our *staff*, Miss Mitchell, had you married my brother."

Her eyes widened as she took in the disheveled rooms and dishes overflowing the sink. "I did not understand that to be the case. I believed I was to tend John's home and direct our staff."

"Well, I'm sorry to disappoint you."

"Not to worry, Mr. Grayson. I shall set about acquiring a suitable staff on the morrow."

"You'll return to Buffalo tomorrow," he said, reinforcing the fact that she would not be staying and that he would not be honoring the ridiculous contract his brother had committed himself to.

She seemed not to have heard him as she examined the heavy cast iron stove standing in the kitchen like an old mule. "Does the stove work?"

"Yes," he said, baffled by the woman. How could such a tiny lady possess such grit in the face of their obvious calamity?

"That's good." She nodded and peeked into the parlor. "The oak floor will clean up nicely, and the fireplace will make the parlor quite lovely I should think."

Hal remained silent. He had no intention of talking about the merits of a house she would not be staying in.

As she surveyed the parlor, her eyes lit up when she spotted the pianoforte. The instrument, a rare treasure that had come with the house purchase, seemed to pull her across the room. Before he could comment, she tugged off her gloves and laid her delicate fingers across the black and white keys sending a discordant trill of sound across the parlor. "It's badly out of tune, but such a beautiful instrument." Her lips tilted upward, hinting at a smile. "May I avail myself?" she asked.

"Whatever pleases you, Miss Mitchell. I'll get your bags and put you in John's room for the night." Hal nodded toward the door behind her. "I'll sleep in the barn so there's no... so you won't... because I'll be up late working." Clearing his throat, he spun on his boot heel and headed outside.

The discordant sound of felt-covered hammers striking the mistuned strings stretched across the soundboard followed him out of the house.

When he returned, Hal deposited her valise on the only bed in the house, a wooden framed thing with a lumpy mattress where John had slept. Hal had been sleeping on the parlor sofa, but tonight he would sleep in the barn loft. He didn't want any question about Miss Mitchell being compromised because he was getting rid of her tomorrow. What had possessed him to bring her home? "I'll return momentarily with your travel trunks and then bid you good night," he told her.

She was so engrossed with the pianoforte she barely lifted her head to acknowledge him.

When he returned, he quickly deposited the heavy trunk in John's room, fetched her second and third smaller but heavier trunks, and then headed to the foyer. "Good night, Miss Mitchell. I'll be in around at daybreak to take you to the station. I apologize that you'll have to wait for your train, but I'll need to get back to the mill as early as possible."

Her delicate hands slipped from the keys, and she turned to face him. "Must you rush out so soon?" she asked, appearing small and uncertain as she stood beside the pianoforte. "It's still early and I thought... I hoped we might talk about our arrangement...."

He planted his hands on his aching hips and looked straight into her beautiful brown eyes. "There is no arrangement, Miss Mitchell. You'll rest here for the night, and I'll take you to the station in the morning."

Hal berated himself all the way to the barn. Nancy Mitchell wasn't supposed to be here. Hal and his brother should be scrambling eggs and wolfing them down with cold coffee and buttered bread. They should be hunched over the scarred kitchen table too exhausted to hold their heads up and yet too excited to stop talking about how they would make the impossible deadline for delivering cherry planks to Edwards. Instead, Hal found himself camped out in his woodshop listening to the distant sound of the out-of-tune pianoforte and thinking about the ridiculously obstinate and painfully beautiful Miss Mitchell.

CHAPTER THREE

J ust before dawn, Hal entered his small home. He hadn't slept much the previous night because his mind had raced with thoughts of his brother, his father, and the haunting eyes of Nancy Mitchell sleeping just mere feet away in his house. He'd known better than to bring the woman home, but he'd been too distracted by her to think clearly and make other arrangements. He would take care of the problem this morning. First, however, he needed to wash up and grab an apple for breakfast before taking Miss Mitchell to the station.

Two steps into the foyer the smell of smoke spiked Hal's heartbeat and sent him bolting toward the kitchen.

He found Miss Mitchell standing beside the smoking firebox, coughing, and fanning her face with a singed potholder.

"What did you put in there?" he asked, trying to peer inside through tearing eyes.

"Wood."

"I assumed that, Miss Mitchell. What wood did you deposit in the box?"

She coughed and pressed a kitchen linen to her nose. "Two chunks of wood from the wood box."

"Did you add tinder?" he asked, already knowing the answer.

She nodded, eyes streaming. "I used a bit of newspaper that was in the box."

That bit of newspaper would have been plenty to build a fire had she used kindling. "You need to start with tinder," he said. "You have to wait until the flames are high before you add the larger wood. And *one* piece will suffice."

She frowned and coughed. "I've never built a fire before, Mr. Grayson. Being privy to that information last evening would have been most helpful." She squinted against the roiling smoke and coughed again.

"I assumed all women your age would know how to set a fire in the firebox."

"Well, I assumed John would have staff to tend to that chore."

Coughing, Hal threw open the windows in the kitchen. "A disappointment for both of us."

"Apparently," she said, her comment muffled by the linen.

Hal took up the iron tongs from beside the stove, locked onto the large chunk of oak and tossed it out the back door. "Keep the firebox closed until I return," he said, then strode through the house closing all the doors behind him to keep the smoke out of the other rooms. How was it possible for a woman of Miss Mitchell's age to have no experience building a fire? How did she cook anything? If she didn't start her own fires, who had managed that task for her? He knew absolutely nothing about the woman. Had John known anything about his intended?

Outside, Hal fetched the smoldering piece of firewood, doused it in a pail of water beside the well, and laid the saturated log aside for later use. When he returned, he found Nancy standing beside the window, her back to him.

"Let's get you out of the smoke," he said. "I hope an apple will suffice for breakfast, Miss Mitchell, because I need to deliver you to the train station now so that I can make that delivery."

"I'm too ill to travel, Mr. Grayson. The smoke has made me feel quite dreadful, I'm afraid."

"Is this a ploy of some sort?" he asked, exasperated by the course his morning was taking. Because if she thought she could manipulate him again, he wasn't having it.

The woman turned from the window, her face ashen, eyes streaming, hands trembling. "Forgive me, but I'm unable to make it to the chamber pot." With a gasp, she turned and hung her head out the window.

Hal stood open-mouthed as Miss Mitchell retched out his kitchen window.

"I... forgive me, Miss Mitchell... I apologize." Ashamed of his own bad behavior, he crossed the floor to stand at her back. "Let me help you to your room where you can lie down for a spell." He waited for her to catch her breath, then tucked her shaking arm against his side and guided her through the haze. "I'm sorry I don't have a clean handkerchief to give you."

With her face buried in the kitchen linen, it was difficult to understand her, but it sounded as if she laughed... or perhaps she'd sobbed.

He opened the bedroom door and nudged it closed behind them with his foot. He led her to the bed and made sure she was seated on the mattress before he opened both windows to let in the early morning breeze. It was a bit damp and cool but refreshing.

"This is highly unacceptable," she croaked, holding the linen close to her mouth as if she might retch again.

Was she was referring to him being in her sleeping quarters? Or that she had vomited out his kitchen window? Or that she had spent a night in his home without a chaperone? It was all unacceptable by his measure.

"Why don't you lie down, Miss Mitchell? If you can manage without assistance, I have a delivery I must make first thing this morning. I'll air the house before I leave, and then I'll check on you when I return."

She flapped a dismissive hand at him. "I plan to spend the day right here, Mr. Grayson, so you might as well go about your business or wherever you're needed today."

Her ashen complexion confirmed the fact that she wasn't fit for travel and that he would be stuck with her another night. "I'll check on you before I head to the mill."

"Do what you will," she whispered, sounding so miserable that his concern overrode his exasperation.

Hal shook his head and set about airing the house. He stumbled over dirty clothing and stepped around misplaced furniture, fully viewing the extent of his mess as Miss Mitchell must surely see the place. For an instant he wished she could have viewed the small home the day he and John purchased it. The pianoforte and some pieces of furniture had been left behind. Hal and John had needed everything and had gratefully accepted the items from the Fiske family.

Neither John nor Hal could play the pianoforte, but Hal's desire to keep the beautiful instrument had provided fuel for John's endless heckling. He'd wanted to know if Hal would be taking up lessons or if he planned to find himself a lady who could play for him. Hal had cuffed John, which started a round of good-natured tussling until they knocked a lantern off the parlor table. They laughed and shrugged off the loss of the glass lamp globe and went about their day. That's how things went between them. They heckled one another. They tussled and laughed and worked themselves weary, but all the while they'd been happy.

Now there was nothing but misery in the house—and a woman Hal deeply regretted bringing home. What promise had his misguided action planted in her mind? He didn't want to imagine what she was thinking.

Already she was laying claim to his home as if it were her own.

She was smoking up his kitchen, lying in his brother's bed, and playing his pianoforte.

Hearing the melancholy songs drifting from the open windows last evening had been bittersweet. In the middle of the night, the distant sounds of her playing woke him, and he wondered if those long lonely chords were a reflection of her emotions. What trouble had driven her from Buffalo and made her determined not to return? He'd seen fear and anxiety in her eyes when he'd informed her at the depot of his intent to send her back. Curiosity had driven him to linger and allow her to miss the returning train. In his defense, because of his brother's promise, he did feel an honest need to do right by her.

Sighing in exasperation—with himself—Hal turned away from the window where he'd been woolgathering. He returned to the bedchamber and cast a final look upon the pallid face of the woman lying on John's bed... in Hal's house. With her long lashes dark against her cheek, Miss Mitchell's gray pallor made her appear more delicate and vulnerable, and it caused an upwelling of pity in Hal's chest. This was exactly why he didn't want a woman around. They twisted a man up inside and were a dreaded distraction. He stepped out of the room and pulled the door behind him, wanting to leave his troubles behind as easily.

CHAPTER FOUR

Nancy buried her face in the pillow and regretted it instantly. The sour scent of unwashed bedding filled her nose and gagged her. Moaning, she rolled to her back. She felt positively wretched... and foolish. She'd wanted to show Hal Grayson that she could run his household. All she'd done was fill his house with smoke and show him how inept she would be as a wife. Now he would surely put her back on that train tomorrow and ruin her life forever.

Unless she died first.

Which she might.

Her gut twisted violently, and she vaulted from the bed and rushed to the open window.

After her stomach quieted, she collapsed back on the bed, too weak to move or care about the soiled bedding.

The sun was setting when a knock on her door startled her awake. Mr. Grayson entered the room.

"I've brought you a bowl of boiled calf's head and cornbread that Mary Tucker delivered this evening. Perhaps a little food will settle your stomach," he said.

Her sinuses still burned, and her stomach churned. "Please don't mention another word about food."

"I thought you'd have improved by now."

"I have. My head is resting on the pillow instead of hanging out the window."

A slight smile lifted his mouth, making him more handsome and almost approachable. "All right then, I'll let you rest for the night. Before I head to the barn, are you in need of anything?"

She wanted comfort and friendship and to be home in her own bed. "I would be grateful for a glass of water."

"I'll fetch it for you." He returned in a few minutes with a glass of water, the plate of fragrant food nowhere in sight.

"Thank you," she whispered, trembling as she tried to push herself upright.

He sat beside her, looped his strong arm around her waist, and drew her up beside him.

She stiffened, unaccustomed to the touch of a man, especially in such a familiar manner. But he seemed oblivious to her reaction, or perhaps he simply did not care.

"You're a bit wobbly, Miss Mitchell." His lips quirked up on one side, making her wonder if he was taking pleasure in her illness or if there might actually be a kinder side to him.

"You find that entertaining?" she asked, her head still woozy.

"I've never met a person over the age of ten who doesn't know how to build a fire."

"Well, now you have. May I please partake of that water before I wilt?"

He gave her the glass.

She'd planned to sip it like a lady, but the first taste of the cool, refreshing liquid had her gulping the cold liquid down her parched throat like her mare used to drink from the stream after a good run. The frigid water soothed her throat... and upset her stomach. "Oh, dear," she said, pressing her fingers to her mouth. "I shouldn't have been so greedy."

"Shall I fetch a bucket?"

"No, I... I just need to lie down," she said, tipping over onto her side, praying she wouldn't vomit.

He lifted her feet onto the bed and draped the smelly old quilt over her legs. "I'll let you rest then," he said.

"Wait. Please." She looked up at him as he stood beside the bed. "Are you opposed to marriage?"

He arched one black eyebrow, and surprise filled his eyes.

"I know it's terribly rude to ask such a thing," she whispered, feeling wretched in every way, "but I... I need to know."

"I'm opposed to marrying a stranger if that's where this conversation is headed," he said. "When I fall in love, I intend that love to last forever."

He did? This man intrigued her, and she found herself asking, "What sort of woman would you court were you interested in seeking a bride?"

Both of his black eyebrows lifted like a raven spreading its wings. "One who doesn't ask so many questions."

Warmth flooded her face for being so bold, and yet to her surprise she could see gentleness and a hint of humor in his eyes. He seemed to find her lack of etiquette entertaining rather than off-putting. The knowledge gave her hope. "I suspect you would be bored by such a lady. You strike me as a man who prefers adventure and lively conversation."

"Perhaps, but I'm not adventurous enough to marry a stranger," he said, and all warmth fled his expression. "I mean no offense, Miss Mitchell, but when I'm ready to take a bride, I'll seek a more mature lady who can make a warm and loving home for our children."

His words stung and swept away all hope, but his eyes told another story that confused her. In those golden-brown irises she saw curiosity and interest... in *her*? Perhaps this situation wasn't as hopeless as she'd initially thought.

"I need to head to work now and you should rest. I'll check in on you later, Miss Mitchell."

"Thank you," she whispered, but he'd already closed the door behind him.

Tears still seeped from her eyes an hour later, but not all of them were caused by the noxious smoke. If Mr. Grayson put her back on that train, her life—and her sister's life—would be ruined. Nancy had nowhere else to go. Her father's men would already be visiting the homes of relatives and friends to find her. There was absolutely no one she could turn to without being found and returned home to a devastating arranged marriage.

She couldn't go back. Nancy levered herself upright. Head swooning, she dug her fingers into the worn quilt. She would *not* ruin her sister's, and ultimately her own, life.

But as Nancy looked around the disheveled room, she saw her trunks packed and waiting for Mr. Grayson to load them onto the wagon and deposit them—and her—at the train depot in the morning. He did not want her here. He intended to send her away.

In truth, she didn't want to stay. But she had to. She had no other options.

IN THE EARLY morning hours when Hal Grayson returned for her, Nancy told him she was still too ill to travel. It was true. She felt sick at heart.

The news clearly disturbed and irritated him, but her pallor and trembling convinced him she was being truthful. And she was, for the most part.

He insisted she try to eat breakfast.

She said she would try hot tea and a biscuit when she got up.

After giving her a curt nod, he fetched a fresh glass of water for her and then left for the day.

Nancy wanted to sag back on the mattress and rest until her head quit spinning, but she forced herself to stand. Her legs trembled, and her stomach still felt queasy, but she staggered into the parlor.

The blue haze had cleared out of the parlor and the kitchen, but the acrid smell lingered, increasing her nausea. She placed her palm over her queasy stomach and made her way to the kitchen.

She couldn't build a fire. So what? She couldn't cook either. So be it. She *could* clean things up a bit and make some improvements to Mr. Grayson's living conditions, which might please him and would also benefit her.

As she sipped a cup of tea and nibbled half a dry biscuit, she surveyed the mess around her.

Soiled clothing littered the parlor. Plates with dried-on egg yolks filled the kitchen sink. The house was in shambles unlike anything she'd ever seen. Did all men live like this? Is that why they all took wives? This certainly wasn't what Nancy expected when she'd answered John Grayson's letter. The Graysons were a good family in Buffalo albeit not as well off as her family. But she surely hadn't expected the squalor she'd found upon arriving. She went to work, determined to make the most of her situation and prove her value to Hal Grayson.

Rolling up her dress sleeves, Nancy started cleaning in the kitchen. She thought about the kitchen staff in the home she'd so recently left behind. Hazel, the head kitchen-maid, would set aside sweets for Nancy. Although Nancy had enjoyed the warm kitchen, delicious treats and Hazel's kindness, she'd never imagined she would be responsible for those same chores one day. But as Nancy surveyed the mess in her new home, she knew she should have paid closer attention to Hazel's efficient managing of their big, busy kitchen.

Rolling up her dress sleeves, Nancy started cleaning in the kitchen. Heaping stacks of dirty dishes were piled *everywhere*. The only soap she could find was a cake of lye soap that had last seen a pair of filthy hands as evidenced by the rings of dirt clinging to it. As she scrubbed dirt and debris from the misshapen lump of soap, she shook her head at the irony of washing a cake of soap and then cringed at the necessity. Cleanliness would be the first lesson she would teach Mr. Grayson.

He could teach her how to build a fire.

But who would teach her how to cook?

She had thought she would manage a household staff. She hadn't been trained for manual labor that would ruin her skin and strain her back and turn her into an old crone before her twentieth birthday.

Thoughts went around and around in her mind as she scrubbed mismatched bowls and chipped plates with a torn rag and lye soap. The more she thought about her situation, the harder she scrubbed, removing layers of dried on beans and scorched beef from cast iron pots and frying pans. Her hands stung and her back ached, but she refused to quit until every plate and utensil had been scrubbed clean.

Eventually, sparkling wet dishes covered the table. When the last dish and pot were finally dried and placed in an old cabinet or returned to a wall shelf, Nancy turned her attention to the soiled walls before she would allow her weary body to give up on the enormous task.

She washed down walls and pulled the worn kitchen curtains off their rods. They smelled of smoke and needed to be laundered, so she tucked them into the large pot sitting atop the stove. She'd seen their maid Clara soak items in a pot of hot water before scrubbing them and hanging them on the clothesline behind their greenhouse. It seemed like something Nancy could manage as well. But she was *not* attempting to start another fire to heat water. She would have to wait for Mr. Grayson to teach her how to build a fire.

Sunlight outside the window dwindled and peepers started singing as she finished scouring the floor. Her back ached and she felt positively filthy. But scrubbing what could become her own kitchen gave Nancy a surprisingly wonderful sense of accomplishment. Tending a home felt good—and hurt so bad.

Releasing a weary sigh, Nancy dropped the thick rag in the bucket of dirty water, got to her feet, and propped her hands on her waist. Arching backward, she stretched and rolled her tight neck. She had planned to do this to please Mr. Grayson and convince him that he needed a wife... that he needed *her,* because she desperately needed him. Instead, she'd merely convinced herself that being the mistress of a house without a staff would take a lot more skill than she possessed. Still, she liked the challenge of learning to build fires and cook meals and turn this messy house into a home. If she could manage all that, would Hal Grayson see her as more than a burden?

A knock at the front door startled Nancy from her reverie. She pressed her raw hands to her hair. Her chignon had fallen out hours ago. She'd been so busy that she'd simply gathered her mass of hair and tucked it away from her face with a few pins. Her dress was wet and badly soiled. Perspiration speckled her face and damped her underarms. Her hands... her sore, aching hands, were reddened and dirty. She was a disheveled mess!

Another knock at the door, louder this time, followed by a female voice calling out "Mr. Grayson. It's Mary Tucker, and I've brought a basket for you."

Fretting, Nancy crossed the unkempt parlor, stepping over strewn clothes and linens, attempting to avoid the clumps of dried mud that had been tracked through the house. That would be something she would change immediately.

She hesitated in the foyer, uncertain what to do. She didn't want to be seen in such a state. And it would be presumptuous to answer the door as if it was her home, but it seemed terribly rude to be present and ignore such a warm greeting. After another few seconds of thought, Nancy squared her shoulders and took the final steps across the foyer, knowing she would seal her fate the instant she opened the door. If Hal Grayson didn't want her answering his door, he shouldn't have brought her to his home or left her alone. With that in mind, she opened the heavy oak panel and presented her unkempt self to the women standing on the other side.

Two lovely ladies with matching expressions of surprise stood on the stoop staring at her. Their lips moved as if they wanted to speak, but neither of them said a word.

"May I be of assistance?" Nancy asked, feeling a little speechless herself. She patted a hand over her unruly hair and then adjusted her stained and soiled dress. She never would have greeted guests at home in her current state. At home she'd have never found herself in her current state. Yet, here she was in this small home in Fredonia, ridiculously disheveled, greeting two proper ladies. Face burning, Nancy tucked her chapped hands in the pockets of her dress.

A pretty lady with black hair tucked beneath a fashionable hat patted the handle of a brown wicker hamper hanging from her arm. "We brought Mr. Grayson his evening meal, but perhaps we're being presumptuous and possibly intrusive as well. We didn't know he had company." The woman pressed her gloved hand to her chest. "We have yet to make an acquaintance although, if I'm not mistaken, I believe I saw you and Mr. Grayson pass by our home day before yesterday. I'm Mary Tucker and I live with my husband William just there across the orchard," she said, gesturing to a white two-story house with a lovely large porch. "This is Martha Fiske, and she and her husband Tom are also your neighbors, although they live in the other direction in the large white house where the road curves."

Martha, a pretty brunette with rosy cheeks, smiled and cupped a delicious smelling apple pie in her hands. "My daddy used to own this house, but he passed away a few months back. Tom and I were delighted when Hal and John bought the house although we're just heartbroken over John's tragic death. Are you a relative of theirs?"

Uncertain how to answer, Nancy could only say, "I'm Nancy Tre —Mitchell."

When she offered no further explanation the ladies exchanged a quick guarded glance.

Martha pasted her smile back in place and lifted the pie a few inches. "Well, we've been trying to help out Mr. Grayson since his brother's untimely death. We know the tragedy left him extremely burdened, and we hope these small gifts help in some small way."

"That's very generous. I'm certain your gifts will be warmly received and deeply appreciated by Mr. Grayson," Nancy said, hoping to smooth out the awkward moment. "The pie smells delicious, and I'm sure he'll be very grateful for your visit."

Nancy was certainly grateful. There wasn't a chance of her providing an edible meal for herself or Mr. Grayson this evening. And now that her appetite was finally returning, the thought of a good meal was most welcome.

The ladies seemed to relax a bit, and Mary hefted the basket on her arm. "This is quite heavy, and you won't be able to manage both the pie and the basket. If you'll lead the way, I'll carry it to the kitchen for you," Mary offered.

Nancy's heart skipped a beat. "I'd be honored to invite you in to wait for Mr. Grayson, but I've not yet finished cleaning, and I'm afraid things are still in terrible disarray. I can manage the basket and leave it in the kitchen for Mr. Grayson."

"Has he hired you to clean his home then?" Martha asked, her relieved expression giving her away. Apparently, she'd seen the inside of the Grayson brothers' house and its obvious decline since they had taken residence.

"No, Mrs. Fiske, I'm not hired help. I was John Radford's intended." Nancy had merely intended to state a fact, but to her horror her eyes welled up. She was ghastly tired, and the knowledge that her life had become a wretched mess simply overwhelmed her.

"Oh dear! Oh, my..." Martha cast a helpless glance at her friend Mary.

The genuine sympathy in Mary's eyes increased Nancy's emotional struggle. "Gracious, I'm so sorry, ladies."

"Why there's no need at all to apologize, Miss Mitchell. It's just dreadful, and I suspect you could use a woman's kind ear right now."

She could indeed, but she had so many chores awaiting her, and it was imperative that the house be in order when Mr. Grayson returned home. Still, in the face of Mary Tucker's compassion, Nancy gratefully welcomed the women inside.

"You must be beside yourself with heartache." Mary slipped her arm around Nancy's shoulders and escorted her to the freshly scrubbed kitchen. Martha encouraged her to sit while Mary poured fresh brewed tea from a jar that she'd tucked into the hamper.

35

While Nancy enjoyed the sweetened tea, Mary and Martha shared more about themselves and told Nancy a bit about Fredonia. They told Nancy about the village and where to shop. Mary talked about her garden and her husband's livery. Mary's husband William sounded like a rascal who was wildly romantic. After only a few minutes of conversation, it was obvious that Mary was deeply in love with her husband. Martha glowed with motherly love as she confessed that she and her husband Tom were expecting their first child. She wanted a girl. Tom wanted a boy. They both anticipated the arrival of their baby with joyful hearts.

The mention of children made Nancy's heart flutter. She knew when she'd accepted John Grayson's offer of marriage that their union would lead to having children. And though the thought of having children was pleasant, her lack of knowledge about the intimate side of marriage put knots in her stomach.

"Gracious, I hadn't meant to go on so," Martha said, her smile a bit sheepish.

"I'm enjoying getting to know you ladies and to share in your excitement, Martha," Nancy said honestly. "I want to hear every detail." And she did because perhaps it would help her learn a bit about marriage.

But before Martha could comment, Mary lifted her nose and sniffed the air. "Do you smell smoke? I smelled it in the parlor and I'm sure I smell in here now and again. I hope nothing dangerous is brewing."

"Goodness, I hope not!" Martha paused and lifted her nose. "I only smell soap and sunshine." She angled a smile at Nancy. "If this is the room you've been cleaning today, it smells lovely."

"Thank you," Nancy said, but she hung her head. "I made a mess in the firebox yesterday morning. I thought I might try to make breakfast for Mr. Grayson. All I managed to do was smoke up the house and make him angry."

Both women gaped at her. "Are you staying here?" Mary asked, her voice filled with concern rather than censure.

Nancy nodded. "When Mr. Grayson met me at the train depot, I was without funds. I hadn't been informed of John Grayson's death. I couldn't go back because... I had no other options, and so Mr. Grayson brought me home with him."

Mary seemed both confused and sympathetic. "Do you have anyone with you? A sibling? Your mother? A chaperone perhaps?"

Nancy shook her head. "I'm afraid not. I had come intending to marry John Grayson immediately. The situation was quite unconventional with Mr. Grayson, *Hal* Grayson that is. We were uncertain what to do with the predicament we found ourselves in. I hadn't a better solution, and so he brought me here."

Mary and Martha exchanged a shocked glance that didn't require words to be understood. Their eyes, one pair green as emeralds and the other forget-me-not blue, were filled with concern, pity, and... outrage?

"Miss Mitchell, it's certainly not my place to meddle, however I simply must speak to you," Mary said. She sank gracefully onto the chair beside Nancy. "I understand that your plans have gone awry and that you were likely uncertain what to do when you learned about your intended, but I fear you've unwittingly compromised your reputation by staying here. I can't be the only one who saw you and Mr. Grayson riding through town alone together when you arrived." She met Nancy's eyes without flinching. "Before this can become a problem for either of you, may I suggest that you stay with William and me until you decide what to do?"

"You will be welcome in my home as well," Martha added, her voice warm and sincere.

Nancy wanted to throw herself in their arms and accept their generous invitations. She wanted to escape her problems and Mr. Grayson's displeasure, but she couldn't. If her father found her, and he *would* find her, he would haul her home and force her to abide by the marriage contract he'd arranged with Stuart Newmaine—one year of courtship followed by marriage. The only way to escape one marriage was to enter another. Hal Grayson was her only hope. "Thank you, ladies, but I'm afraid we were seen at the station and also by several folks in town, some of whom greeted Mr. Grayson by name as we traveled here."

Pity filled Mary's expression. "Oh, dear..." She sat back with a sigh and placed her palms on her knees. "May I ask your age, Nancy?"

"I'm nearly seventeen," Nancy said because seventeen sounded much older than sixteen. She wanted to be friends with these generous ladies, and though they were likely only a few years older than herself, she feared her age would put them off.

"Is Mr. Grayson apprised of your age?" Mary asked.

"No." Nancy shook her head and lowered her lashes. "We haven't talked much."

Mary and Martha exchanged a glance, seeming to offer each other a slight nod of agreement. "There's only one thing to be done then," Mary said, but neither woman had an opportunity to share whatever was on their minds because the sound of the door opening told them Hal Grayson was home.

Nancy's stomach rolled, and she felt breathless for a moment. She and her visitors waited in silence while Hal's boot heels thudded across the parlor.

He appeared in the doorway, dirty and disheveled, rings of exhaustion around his golden-brown eyes. Surprise flashed across his handsome face as he surveyed the clean kitchen and the ladies Nancy was entertaining.

"Good evening." He summoned a slight smile and glanced at Nancy. "I see you've met my neighbors."

"Y-yes," Nancy said, standing, and clenching her hands in front of her. "They brought you supper."

He glanced at the basket and pie on the table. "Thank you, ladies."

"We were just about to have tea if you'd care to join us," Nancy said, because she had no idea how to talk to him.

His attention remained on Martha and Mary. "I'm grateful for your kindness and the delicious meals, ladies. I must, however, decline the invitation as I need to finish sanding several chair spindles to meet my delivery date for Mr. Edwards. You ladies enjoy yourselves, though."

Mary Tucker rose to her feet and stood solidly beside Nancy, who was now bracketed by the ladies. "I quite understand that you're a busy man, Mr. Grayson. Before you leave, though, there is one thing of consequence that we simply must discuss."

As if he knew what was on Mary's mind, Hal's expression flattened. He nodded for Mary to have her say.

"Mr. Grayson, we don't wish to meddle, but I'm afraid we must intervene on behalf of this lovely young gal. She has told us that she's staying here, with you, unchaperoned."

Nancy's stomach tilted sideways, and she thought she might be sick.

"We understand you've both found yourself in an awkward predicament that has compromised both of you," Mary continued. "But you must know this situation is extremely damaging to Miss Mitchell's reputation."

Hal Grayson was a smart man. Nancy was certain he knew what Mary was driving at, and yet he remained silent, saying nothing of Nancy's stubbornness at the station or his intention of returning her immediately to her father.

"I'm sorry to press the issue, Mr. Grayson, but you must know that you have compromised Miss Mitchell by bringing her here."

"It wasn't my intent, but yes, I understand our situation," he said. Nancy detected a weary sigh in his voice.

They were in this predicament because she'd been obstinate and had appealed to Hal Grayson's sense of honor. Although she needed to marry to avoid a disastrous arranged marriage with Stuart Newmaine, Nancy realized in that moment she just couldn't stand by and let Hal Grayson's neighbors think the worst of him. They were both trapped in an unfortunate situation not of their own making. No matter how desperate Nancy was she couldn't knowingly trap Hal Grayson. He was a decent man and shouldn't be responsible for her troubles.

"Ladies, Mr. Grayson is sleeping in the barn," she blurted. "I have not been compromised."

"I beg to differ," Mary said, her words gentle and apologetic. "By coming into his home unchaperoned, you have consigned yourself to marry this man—or to a less respectable life that you surely don't want to endure."

"I'm afraid I must stand with Mary," Martha said, turning to Hal. "I suspect you understand why we're concerned, Mr. Grayson?"

"Quite clearly," Mr. Grayson said, his voice stern.

Nancy wrung her hands, realizing *she* had been foolish and terribly inconsiderate. "Please, ladies, nothing has happened," she said, suddenly desperate to undo the damage she'd done. She'd been trying not to ruin her sister's life and to retain some hope of finding a loving marriage. Now she was ruining Hal Grayson's life. "I should like to avail myself of your generous offer to stay with one of you until I can make a more suitable arrangement. Mr. Grayson is only guilty of being a gentleman. I've not been compromised in any manner."

"For your benefit, dear, I respectfully disagree," Mary said.

"As do I," said Hal Grayson, his deep, cool voice filling the kitchen.

Looking into his eyes was like peering into a black cave that hid everything inside. Nancy could only imagine the anger and possibly even hatred he must feel for her.

He lifted his chin as if facing a herculean task. "I'll visit Judge Barker immediately and request his presence here at noon tomorrow. May I impose on one of you ladies to give Miss Mitchell proper shelter for the night?"

"Of course," Mary said. "And I hope you'll accept our gesture of goodwill as it was intended and enjoy the chicken dinner and fresh pie we delivered.

As if seeing the basket for the first time, he nodded. "Thank you for your kindness, ladies." With that he turned and left the house without a glance or kind word to Nancy.

"What's happening?" She looked up at the ladies who had defended her honor as if she were a daughter or sister rather than a near stranger. "Why is he going to bring the judge here? Is he going to ask the judge to send me home? Can he legally do that?"

Mary sighed and then summoned a light smile. "No, Miss Mitchell. You're getting married tomorrow."

HAL SHOULD HAVE FORESEEN this course of action when he brought the headstrong Miss Mitchell into his home. His decision had been impulsive, yes, but he'd felt drawn to help this woman who had been his brother's intended. He should have taken her to the Tucker's home as soon as he saw them in their yard. But he hadn't. And now they were trapped.

Nancy's remorseful, dark eyes had beseeched him not to abandon her... not to hate her.

He didn't hate her.

He hated himself for making so many bad decisions.

As he headed down Liberty Street into the village, he made his way to Judge Barker's house. The man would be at home now eating his supper as Hal should be doing with his brother.

But everything was upside down now. Hal had walked himself into a situation with only one decent resolution. And that resolution would find him marrying his brother's intended tomorrow. Once again, much like his decision to bring John here and invest in the mill, Hal's impulsiveness had led to disaster. He had nothing to offer Miss Mitchell but hardship. He was struggling to keep up with his work at the mill and with his projects for A.B. Edwards, both of which he desperately needed. His head was filled with problems, his heart filled with grief, and his pockets were empty.

And Miss Mitchell would be the one to suffer the consequences of his sorry situation.

She couldn't have understood the dire circumstances in which he and John had been living. It was obvious by her clothing and lack of domestic experience that the lady was accustomed to a much more comfortable existence. Now she was tied to Hal and his world of problems. And it was all because of Hal's moment of weakness at the station. He should have put her back on the train but had instead sought refuge in her presence and the welcome distraction her beauty and intelligence had provided.

That truth filled him with shame as he finalized the arrangements for their marriage the next day.

CHAPTER FIVE

Numb, Nancy stared out the second story window of the Tucker's home while Mary finished lacing her into what was to be her wedding dress. Martha Fiske had already styled Nancy's hair and was now downstairs decorating the porch with ribbons and setting out covered food trays for after the ceremony.

"I hope you don't mind having us at your wedding," Mary said. "A lady should be surrounded by friends on her wedding day, wouldn't you agree, Nancy?"

Mary had requested that they use each other's given names since they were sure to become great friends. Nancy hoped that would be true, but she couldn't speak past the lump of emotion in her throat. Her childhood dreams had been filled with love and adventure. She'd dreamed of marrying a man of her choosing, taking her vows surrounded by family and friends, and being given away by her beloved father. But when she'd found herself promised to a man in love with her sister, Nancy had realized her childhood dreams were just that. Dreams. Her current reality demanded that she cut her family from her life until she was safely married. She could make friends here and had already begun forging a relationship with Mary Tucker and Martha Fiske, but that didn't salve the homesickness she felt for her family.

"Mary, I... I'm so grateful for your kindness, and I deeply appreciate your friendship because... well, it will be unbearably lonely living with a man who hates me."

Mary turned Nancy to face her. "I can't believe Hal Grayson hates you. Any tension you feel is likely because he's grieving his brother's recent passing. Hal is a good man. Give him a chance. If I thought he harbored ill feelings toward you, I would have brought you home with me and told any nosey townsfolk that you're my guest and that Mr. Grayson fetched you from the train depot as a favor to me. But whether he realizes it or not, that man needs you as much as you seem to need him. She patted Nancy's hand. "I know when I see a romance in the making and your attraction to each other is as obvious as the nose on my face."

Half of Mary's words rang true. Nancy couldn't look at Hal Grayson without flushing from head to toe. She'd always joked with her sister, Elizabeth, that the man she married would be tall, dark, and handsome. Hal Grayson was all of that and more—mysterious, and his touch made her pulse race.

Releasing a long sigh, Nancy glanced in the mirror and smoothed the front of her gown, trying to calm her breathing. "Mr. Grayson has been trying to get rid of me from the moment he laid eyes on me."

"I suspect if he'd really wanted to be rid of you, he'd have put you back on that train. Or he would have brought you to my door. Don't fret, Nancy. You and Hal can create a good, loving marriage. All you need is faith and respect and to trust one another."

It would take far more than faith and trust. It would take a mountain of forgiveness. But Nancy kept her fear to herself as Mary inspected her handiwork.

"Simply perfect." Mary clasped her hands in front of her chest, a warm smile on her face. "You are a beautiful bride. Where did you find such a divine dress?"

Shame flowed through Nancy as she thought about all that had gone into the making of her dress. The concoction of spring green muslin sported exaggerated puffed upper sleeves that tapered tight along her forearms. The skirt, sleeves, and neckline were trimmed with expensive white satin. As the dress was being made her mother had fussed over every detail, especially over the gathered bodice decorated with white lace. Her father had paid an exorbitant amount for the gown believing that Nancy would wear it when he presented his twin daughters at their coming-of-age birthday ball and announced their engagements to the wealthy young men he'd hand selected for them. He'd chosen Stuart Newmaine as her suitor and future husband. When her father refused to consider an alternate suitor for Nancy, which would at least give Elizabeth a chance at happiness, Nancy knew she needed to come up with another plan. And that's when she found and replied to the advertisement for John Grayson's mail order bride.

Nancy planned to wear her new dress when taking her vows with John Radford Grayson. Instead, she would wear her special dress to take her vows with another man... an angry man who did not want to marry her. She'd seen the tempest brewing in Hal Grayson's eyes. He would never forgive her for forcing him into a marriage he didn't want. And if he didn't already hate her, he would when he learned the truth about her.

She hadn't meant for him to become involved in her arrangement with his brother John Radford. But when she'd found herself stranded at the train station with no other acceptable option, she had grabbed hold of Hal Grayson like he was a buoy in a storm.

Now *he* was the storm.

MARY HAD SUGGESTED to Nancy that the orchard would make a wonderfully romantic setting for a wedding. The trees were dropping their pink blossoms and creating a carpet of petals upon the grass. The babbling creek flowed beneath a wooden bridge providing the perfect musical accompaniment for their vows. Under normal circumstances,

Nancy couldn't think of anything more beautiful or romantic than to speak words of love and exchange vows in the midst of nature. But knowing the man awaiting her didn't love her, and might even hate her, tied Nancy's stomach in knots as she waited for the ceremony to begin.

Just before noon, William Tucker escorted his wife Mary into the apple orchard where Tom and Martha Fiske waited with Judge Barker —and Hal Grayson.

Watching from the Tucker's wide porch, Nancy's stomach swam with nerves while she waited for William to return for her. She could well imagine Hal Grayson's expression and was in no hurry to see her betrothed. She directed her gaze to the pink and blue ribbons that Martha had tied around the white porch columns. They fluttered cheerfully and danced around the posts.

Nancy touched her fingers to the back of her head and felt the slack braid Martha had woven and pinned into a loose chignon. Martha had threaded a beautiful green ribbon, perfectly matching Nancy's dress, through her stylish braid. Long spaniel curls framed her face and bounced at her collar bones. The curls gave Nancy a carefree grace she needed but didn't feel.

William Tucker approached the porch with a jaunty swagger and wide grin. He was a shorter and stockier than Hal and possessed boyish good looks and an ever-present playful sense of humor. "Are you ready, Miss Nancy?" he asked familiarly as if she were family already. He bounded up the porch steps with a lightness of heart she envied.

She wasn't at all ready for what awaited her, but it was a walk she knew she must take. "Yes, William, and thank you for..." She inhaled a shaky breath as she struggled to suppress her emotions. She must get hold of herself. What's done is done, she told herself, as her father's words sang in her mind. "I deeply appreciate your friendship and... all of this." She gestured to the festive porch and outward to the glorious apple orchard awaiting them.

William winked and gave Nancy's hand a reassuring squeeze. "Have faith in Hal Grayson. He's a good man, and he'll make a wonderful husband. I'm sure of it."

Nancy nodded, hoping William was right. Hal Grayson seemed to be a decent, hardworking man. But after witnessing the closed expression on his face when he left the house last night she knew he was not at all pleased to be saddled with a wife.

Nancy gripped William's arm as he walked her across the orchard to where Judge Barker and her future husband awaited her. Her legs trembled, but she knew it could be a worse situation. It could be Stuart Newmaine waiting for her. At least Hal Grayson wasn't in love with her sister. That was one thing to be thankful for.

But he hadn't *wanted* a bride. That reality stopped her cold. "Oh, dear..."

William glanced down and squeezed her forearm firmly against his side as if encouraging her to keep her chin up and keep walking.

But she didn't want to keep walking. She wanted to give Hal a chance to walk away if he so desired.

"Come. Your fiancé is waiting," William said, gently nudging her onward.

When they arrived at the bridge where she and Hal would take their vows, Nancy steeled herself for the task ahead. What's done is done, and she must follow through with as much grace and humility as she could muster.

"Who gives this lovely lady's hand in marriage?" Judge Barker asked, a warm smile on his face.

"I, William Tucker, give this beautiful young lady into Hal Grayson's safekeeping," he said, his voice holding a certainty and joy that Nancy couldn't feel. As he transferred her hand to Hal's waiting palm, William added a piece of advice for Hal, "Take good care of this young lady."

Nancy glanced at Hal, expecting him to be cold and curt as he accepted her hand. She expected to see his jaw clamped in anger and his eyes filled with disdain. But he greeted her with a slight smile as if he'd been joyfully anticipating their vows and sharing their lives together.

As he drew her to his side he leaned down and spoke softly to her.

"You are a beautiful bride," he said, his manly voice resonating in her ear and the warmth of his breath raising gooseflesh on her neck.

His comment stunned her and left her reeling and... speechless as they stared at each other.

"Shall we make this official?" Judge Barker said with a delighted laugh.

Chuckles surrounded them as Hal turned Nancy to face the Judge.

"We're ready, your honor," Hal said.

And so they stood before Judge Barker while he spoke of love and what it takes to make a fine, lasting marriage. Nancy looked up at the tall, handsome man standing solidly beside her and wondered if his kindness was real, if he might learn to forgive her and perhaps even one day come to love her.

Hal spoke his vows as if he meant them. Nancy spoke hers as an apology.

When Judge Barker announced they were married, Hal lifted her chin, looked into her eyes, and placed a brief and tender kiss upon her lips.

For the second time that day, Nancy was speechless. Her stomach twirled, and she felt unbalanced. As she struggled to remain upright, she gripped her husband's forearms and their gazes locked.

The laughter of their guests snapped her out of her dazed preoccupation with her husband's handsome face. With her cheeks burning, she turned to their guests, her new friends, and accepted their hugs and best wishes.

HAL STAYED at his bride's side throughout the afternoon. Despite being forced into this unplanned marriage with a girl far younger than she'd admitted, Hal found himself enjoying the day. Nancy seemed less at ease, and he wondered if her anxiety was from anticipation of the wedding night or because she was hiding something from him. Nancy Mitchell—*Grayson* now—was a mystery that he intended to solve. Hal hadn't planned on being married, and now that he had taken vows, he found himself confused how to proceed with Miss Mitchell.

Grayson.

The woman had his thoughts in a spin.

So he sat back and watched his new bride talking with Mary and Martha, listening intently as the women explained how to make their favorite bread or a properly thickened stew.

"Do you fry the beef before putting it into the stew pot?" Nancy asked, her dark auburn brows pinched with concentration.

As Mary answered, Hal could fairly see Nancy making notes in her head as if recording and storing recipes in a ledger in her mind. She was incredibly intelligent.

And magnificently beautiful.

And she was *his* bride.

Unimaginable.

William Tucker thumped Hal on the knee to get his attention. "Tom was telling me that the two of you are discussing the idea of letting Thomas Drake lease your sawmill for a spell. Now that you're trying to run it without... alone that is, leasing it to Drake might yield the highest profit for you. It can't be easy trying to run that old girl alone."

"She's temperamental and doesn't make it easy on me, I'll give her that," Hal said, "but I plan to continue on myself if at all possible."

William arched one eyebrow, but merely nodded. Tom Fiske, on the other hand, leaned forward in his chair and braced his elbows on his knees, his gaze fixed on Hal. "I understand the desire to build your own mill business, Hal, but it would only be a year lease, and it could bring you a tidy profit without breaking your back all day long. Why not think on it a while?"

"I appreciate your insight, Tom, but I just can't commit to something that wasn't part of the plan John Radford and I came up with. Our plan was to build our own mill business, and I still aim to do that."

Tom and William exchanged a glance. Though they didn't speak, Hal knew they were thinking he was being foolish. But what they didn't understand is that Hal couldn't give up on his brother. He couldn't quit because the work was too hard. He wouldn't commandeer John's dream for his own profit. He'd promised to see the plan through, and that's exactly what he would do. For John. He owed his brother that much.

Hal sighed, extended his legs, and crossed them at the ankles. Despite the reason for whiling away the afternoon with his neighbors, he was glad of the break. His body ached, and it felt good to sit and relax a spell. His mind nagged that he should be working, but for once he was able to appease that voice with a valid excuse. It was his wedding day. Hal was among friends and feeling a sense of community he hadn't felt in a long time. And he was enjoying watching his new bride interact with the ladies while he talked business with two men he greatly respected.

Each time his gaze strayed to Nancy, which was every few seconds, Hal noticed a new detail, the soft curve of her cheek, the pretty angle of her jaw, the alluring dip where her neck and collarbone met. Although almost imperceptible, her bottom lip tugged down and slightly left when she laughed. He wasn't sure why noting something so minute about her made him feel as if he knew one of her secrets, but it did. Suddenly, he realized that it was this sort of thing that had entranced him at the station and had made him forget everything else. It wasn't just Nancy's obvious beauty. She was truly stunning, but it was her shifting expressions, the flash of her eyes, the quirk of her pretty lips, the dimpling of her cheeks, the intricacies of her conversation and her plea for help that had snared his attention and reeled him in hard.

Intrigued by his own discovery, Hal struggled to follow the conversation Tom and William were having about the livery and a wagon William was repairing.

They dined on roasted turkey and stewed vegetables and hot bread that Mary and Martha had prepared for their celebration. Hal made a note to return the kindness that his neighbors were lavishing upon him and his bride. Late in the day, they sat on the wide porch and nibbled pies and sweets. Nancy ate sparingly and tended to do more listening than talking, but as time passed and the Fiskes and Tuckers shared some of their funny stories about the early days of their marriage, Nancy began to open up and speak more freely. When she grudgingly admitted to smoking them out of the house two days earlier, Hal found himself laughing with the rest of them. At the time the incident hadn't been funny, but hearing Nancy retell the story brought a level of humor to the event he'd been able to appreciate until today.

The ladies talked about their mishaps in the kitchen and some of their favorite meals, and Hal silently hoped that Nancy could learn how to make some of those meals.

He and William and Tom discussed how Hal might manage the mill without John Radford. Unable to bear the conversation that included such a painful reminder of John's death, Hal got to his feet. "I appreciate the advice, but this is all business for another day, gentlemen. It's time to take my bride home." With that he extended his hand to Nancy. "Shall we?"

The smile slid off her face, and she glanced to her lady friends as if to seek their assistance. Mary smiled and gave a small nod as if to assure Nancy that all would be well.

Nancy placed her hand in Hal's and stood.

He tucked her hand into the crook of his arm. "Thank you all for your generosity and for giving us such a memorable day."

"Y-yes, thank you so very much for... everything," Nancy said, standing beside him, her trembling hand revealing the acute level of her anxiety.

Was she afraid of him? Or was she simply anticipating their wedding night? Hal grasped her hand firmly as much to convince himself as it was to assure his bride that all would be well.

NANCY EXPECTED Hal to march her across the orchard and rush her home where he could privately berate her for locking them into marriage.

But he lingered on the bridge where they had both committed their futures to each other. As he braced his elbows on the railing and stared into the water rushing beneath the oak deck planks, she wondered if his promises had been empty. Had he given any thought to what they might make of a marriage together? Or had he simply accepted their marriage as a duty or penance for making the poor decision of bringing her home with him?

Her own promises had been given with hope for their future and apology for their present. None of their words were given in love or joy. That knowledge burdened her heart, weighing her down as she stood beside a man she barely knew.

Sighing, he turned and leaned against the railing. "I don't know what you're running from, Miss Mitch—Nancy, but I hope it won't come back to cause problems for us or our friends."

His comment stunned her and weakened her knees. If her past found her, they both stood to lose. Her father would crush Hal Grayson if he ever learned that Hal had compromised his daughter. Nancy had knowingly compromised herself, but her father would place every bit of blame at Hal's door. Hal was older. He was a man who should have known better. In her father's mind, it was the man's place to protect a woman regardless of the situation.

"My past will stay where I left it," she said, but that was another empty promise. If her father ever learned where she'd gone, he would commandeer the quickest conveyance to carry him to her doorstep. "I'm more concerned about our future."

"That makes two of us," Hal said, his gaze floating off across the orchard as if trying to see what was ahead of them. "This is a fine kettle we're in."

For several minutes they stood there together lost in thoughts and roiling emotions. Nancy's gaze strayed to the rebellious waves of black hair that meandered below her husband's white shirt collar. His black hair shone in the late day sun, clean and soft and... tempting. Hal Grayson was an extremely handsome man. Even his scowl lent him a rugged and rather dashing look that had her heart galloping.

Heaving a sigh, Hal pushed off the rail. "Shall we go home... *Mrs. Grayson?*"

She couldn't answer him. His dark gaze delved deep into her own as he held out a hand. The breeze ruffled his hair, and she thought of a swashbuckling pirate beckoning her aboard his ship. His eyes promised passion and adventure.

Her tongue felt tied and she couldn't respond.

He seemed not to care. Silent, he lifted his hand to her hair. She felt his fingers gliding over the plaited and loosely pinned braid as he inspected it. "This is... like a piece of art, intricate and beautiful."

Her lips parted on a small gasp.

"It suits you."

His gentle touch raised gooseflesh on her neck and created havoc in her chest.

One side of his mouth tipped up in a half-smile, and he tucked her hand in the crook of his arm. "Let's go home."

Her heart thundered the entire walk across the orchard.

Stepping inside, the mess of clothing and haphazardly placed furniture in the parlor had remained untouched. Having been out of the house overnight, Nancy was now able smell the lingering hint of charred wood that Martha had noticed. Tomorrow she would scrub the parlor clean. For now, though, she sought the nearest chair to relieve her trembling legs.

Grateful the wedding vows were spoken and behind them, she perched on one of the worn parlor chairs. "I'm afraid I don't know what comes next. I must confess I'm... most apprehensive."

"Understandably. Being swept into an unexpected wedding is nerve-wracking." Hal took the chair opposite her. "I suspect we're both a bit on edge."

Their eyes met, but neither of them spoke.

What now? Nancy rubbed her arms, suddenly chilled. *What was a wife to do after the wedding service?* She hadn't thought this far ahead, and now she wished she'd asked her mother or Mary Tucker for advice.

"Are you chilled?" Hal asked.

She sighed and met his eyes. "Perhaps a little."

"I'll lay a fire. You should watch how it's done." With that he got to his feet and retrieved the needed items, explaining how to weave tinder and starter fuel, be it straw, sticks, or paper to create a loose pile. "Always be sure to leave room for the fire to breath," he said. Atop the pile of straw and kindling, he added a small log about the diameter of Nancy's calf. "Notice I've only added one medium-sized log. Once that catches, I'll add another one or two, if needed. Start light and layer the heavier wood only after you have a hot fire or bed of lively coals."

She nodded and watched intently as he lit the stack from the bottom. He sat back on his heels and gently fanned the flickering fire.

Nancy clasped her palms together as she watched the lively flames devour the straw and smaller kindling. "You are an artist, Mr. Grayson!"

"It's simply the smartest way to build a fire," he said, but there was no gloating in his voice. He seemed... tired.

"Well, I shall endeavor to learn this art and spare us another incident like we had my first morning here."

One side of his mouth lifted. "That would be of benefit to both of us."

His grin... his small concession toward softening gave her hope. "If I can master the art of building a fire, why I might even learn to cook," she said, hoping to keep their conversation light and let him know she intended to try to be a good wife.

His smile fell away. "You'll need to learn, Miss—Nancy. I can't afford to provide you with a household staff."

"I know," she said, crestfallen. "I had thought to make light of my shortcomings, not add another burden to your shoulders."

As if he realized that he'd misunderstood her comment, he stood and took the chair opposite her. "I apologize. I didn't mean to be offensive." He nodded toward the blaze in the fireplace. "Warmer now?" he asked.

"Much, thank you." She sat for a moment feeling a little wounded and yet knowing he had every right to think the worst of her. Determined to meet their situation head on and with as much honesty as she could risk, she said, "Thank you for being so kind today. I know you don't want our marriage, but I appreciate you not sharing your feelings with your friends."

"They're your friends now, too, Nancy. We're going to live in this town. I'd like our neighbors to look kindly on both of us."

She nodded. "I thought your anger would show. You're a much better actor than I."

"You were expected to be a nervous bride and I an eager groom. We both played our parts admirably."

"But you're not an eager groom, are you?" she said, stating it as a fact rather than a question.

His gaze roved her face, dipped to her lips, and fell away on a sigh as he leaned back in his chair. "Why didn't you tell me you're only sixteen?"

Startled by his question, she didn't have a ready answer.

Hal pinned her with his gaze. "John Radford believed you were twenty years old and would be adept at being a wife. But our marriage papers indicate you are sixteen. How would John have come to that conclusion unless you lied to him about your age?"

"I didn't lie. He was seeking a bride of twenty years who could manage a household. I simply replied to his advertisement and stated that I'm adept at managing a staff, which I am. I'd hoped your brother would see that and honor his agreement despite my age."

"My brother would have felt betrayed by your omission. He would have sent you straight back to Buffalo. Then John and I would have gotten back to business, and he might have forgotten about his ludicrous idea of ordering a wife."

"I'll be seventeen in just over a month at which time my father felt me old enough to engage in a one-year courtship that would have culminated in an arranged marriage. Ordering a wife isn't ludicrous if you actually want one."

"Well, you apparently didn't want the marriage your father arranged for you, so why answer my brother's advertisement?"

She didn't answer. Instead, she asked him a question that had been burning in her heart all day. "Have you ever been in love? Did you get your heart broken? Is that why you haven't married?"

His bark of laughter echoed through the parlor. "I haven't had time to think about courting much less marriage. My plan was to build a sawmill business with my brother, but that plan has... changed." Hal shook his head and looked at the fire. "You've walked yourself straight into a life of hardship, Nancy."

"Our situation might be difficult at present, but together we can improve our circumstances."

"Do you really believe that?" he asked, cutting his eyes back to her. "We're strangers to each other. You can't cook or even build a fire. How is that supposed to help us prosper?"

His comment hurt, but she lifted her chin unwilling to be a burden to anyone. "I'll *learn* those duties, Mr. Grayson, just as I'll learn to ignore your hurtful words." With that she lunged to her feet intending to shut herself in the bedchamber to escape his harsh comments.

He caught her hand and stopped her. "I'm sorry, Nancy." He stood, towering above her, close... overwhelming her with his manly presence. "My name is *Hal*. Not Mr. Grayson." The flickering flames reflected in his eyes. "For good or bad, I'm your husband now. I'll do my best to be gentle with my words and to support you, but I'm certain it won't be in the luxury you're accustomed to."

"I'm not asking for luxury," she said, her voice trembling from emotion. "Kindness and understanding would be enough." She couldn't finish because there was no easy way to say she wanted love. From where she stood that wish seemed impossible.

He released her hand and shoved his fingers into his hair. "I'm not thinking clearly, and I've been unintentionally harsh. I just... I want you to understand that I can't give you much."

"Simple friendship would be enough," she said. "I hope we might someday become friends."

"Friends?" He laughed and pinched the bridge of his nose, eyes closed as if he couldn't bear to see the truth of their situation. "What a mess John Radford has wrought." He groaned and shook his head. "No. This is all *my* doing."

Their lives were indeed a mess, but stewing in their problems wasn't going to solve anything. Nothing they said seemed to be improving their situation, so Nancy changed the subject. "We're in need of provisions, but I think there's a little of the tea left that Mary brought by. Would you care for a glass?"

"No, thank you." He sat and leaned back in the chair. "I'll leave some coins on the table, and you can fetch some of your needed items tomorrow."

"Thank you. Shall I... shall I prepare for bed then?" she asked, her voice so tremulous and uncertain it came out as a whisper. She had only the vaguest idea of what was expected of her, but she wanted her new husband to see that she was trying to be a good and dutiful wife.

As if she'd stuck him with a hot poker, Hal shot to his feet. "No! I mean, if you wish to retire, then please feel free. I have work waiting for me in the barn. I'll be late. Don't wait up for me."

"But—" She gazed up at her husband, a stranger and yet a man she felt drawn to. "It's our wedding night. That is... shouldn't we spend the evening together?"

He towered above her, a dark, brooding look in his eyes. "You're sixteen, Nancy." As if that statement answered every question she could pose, her husband bid her goodnight and left the house.

Alone, she sank onto the armchair, vowing she would find a way to pry open Hal Grayson's eyes and his heart. He had openly admitted he'd never been in love. His heart wasn't spoken for, so she would claim it for her own. She might only be sixteen, but she'd spent her life dealing with her strong-willed father. Hal Grayson was about to see what kind of woman—yes *woman*—he'd married.

CHAPTER SIX

As Hal trudged to the barn, his mind swirled with thoughts. For better or for worse he was now married. He was determined to make a good life for himself and for Nancy, but how to do that eluded him. He stepped into his woodshop and sighed at the unfinished projects strewn across the shop bench and out into the barn. He sank down on a nearby crate, needing to think through everything he had to do to make a good home for his wife.

He was honest enough to admit he was entirely enchanted and intrigued by his wife, but being a husband entailed a whole lot more that he hadn't planned on. He needed time to warm up to the idea of being a husband.

He had little to offer Nancy, barely enough for her to purchase provisions for their pantry. He'd cashed in her return ticket to Buffalo, but that money wouldn't feed the both of them for long. If he didn't get more pieces out to Edwards and find a way to squeeze more production and hours out of his day at the mill, both of his businesses were destined to fail.

And so he set to work, sawing and sanding and joining pieces of a kitchen cabinet, working until his back and neck ached and his eyes burned from fatigue. At four o'clock in the morning, he stumbled into the house and collapsed on the sofa.

It seemed he'd just fallen asleep when the delicious scent of eggs frying in bacon grease woke him before dawn. His stomach twisted with hunger, and he reconsidered that having a wife would bring some advantages.

Then he remembered that Nancy had no domestic skills.

Groaning, he sat up and dropped his head into his hands. What a mess. He missed his brother with every fiber of his being, but at the moment he wanted to throttle John Radford.

"Are you all right, Mr. Grayson?"

He wasn't. Not by any stretch. But he said, "I'm fine." His voice sounded gruff and irritable, but he was only half sorry to greet Nancy in such an ornery mood.

"All right then. I made breakfast for you without smoking us out of the house," she said, a tremulous smile touching her lips.

Surprised, he cocked his head and eyed her. "I thought you couldn't cook."

"I can cook eggs. Please come to the kitchen, and I'll prepare your plate."

He watched her duck back into the kitchen. He used to cook breakfast for himself and John Radford, and every meal was wretched. And every memory of his brother was agony. And every look into Nancy's dazzling brown eyes made his thoughts spin.

The scent of fresh coffee wafting through the parlor helped Hal settle down. John was gone. Nancy was his wife. This was his life, like it or not. Drawing in a deep breath to clear his head, Hal got to his feet and crossed the parlor. From the doorway he surveyed the kitchen. "I'd meant to ask how you managed the enormous feat of cleaning the kitchen in one short day, but there were more important matters to discuss when I arrived home that particular evening."

Nancy stood in the middle of the spotless kitchen in a blue frock, her hair swept back in a tidy chignon, her dark gaze on him. She lifted one shoulder in a small shrug. "I wanted to make myself useful."

Useful? The mountain of dirty dishes he and John had piled up in the sink and on the surface of a rickety old sideboard was gone. The grease-spattered cookstove had been scrubbed clean and a pot of steaming coffee now sat atop the hot plate alongside a huge pot of steaming water. Three eggs sizzled in a large frying pan. Nancy stood watch over them, a spatula in one dainty hand and a singed potholder in the other.

He inspected her from chignon to boot heels. She'd been wearing a hat when he met her at the station, but yesterday in the orchard she'd only worn a ribbon in her rich copper hair. When her parasol was angled just so and sunlight splashed across her head, all he could think about was sliding his hands into the dazzling mass of shimmering copper strands.

"Are you quite all right, Mr. Grayson?" she asked, snapping him back to their awkward situation.

"I'm fine, Miss—" He sighed and shook his head. "I'm afraid it will take some time for me to get used to addressing you as my wife."

"Likewise," she replied. "Would you like the egg yolks cooked through or just lightly done?" she asked, a slight smile tilting her lips. "This is only thing I can cook, and I'd like to do an admirable job of it. So please state your preference before they cook through."

"Anything in between will do." He gestured to the sparkling kitchen. "It looks even cleaner than when John and I moved in." He nodded toward the canning jar with lilac blossoms that she'd placed on the scarred planks of the oak table, giving the kitchen a homey look that it had lacked. "You've been busy."

"You left me to my own devices quite early last night, so I picked a few of the remaining lilacs from out front." She slid the eggs from the frying pan onto a clean plate, and then added two thick slices of bread. After she slathered them with the last of the butter, she put the plate on the table and gestured for him to sit in one of their slat-backed chairs.

He waited for her to be seated first.

She sat and rested her hands in her lap. In place of an apron, she wore a scrap of linen tied around the waist of her blue day gown. She wore no jewelry that he could see, and yet she seemed out of place and too beautiful for his humble home. The lady, with her grand expectations of having a staff to manage, was obviously from a wealthy family. Had she thought John had money? If so, she must be sorely disappointed.

"I cooked the last of the eggs this morning," she said. "I'll have nothing to serve you for supper if I can't purchase a few items today."

"I'll leave you funds. I apologize for the oversight last night." Hal filled his mouth with a forkful of eggs. The semi-soft yolk melted like warm butter on his tongue, perfectly cooked, lightly salted and generously peppered. "Are you certain you don't know how to cook? These are delicious."

Although his praise made her smile a little, she nodded. "I'm afraid this is the extent of my cooking abilities. I only learned to cook eggs because they were Daddy's favorite—" She clipped off her words as if she'd bitten her tongue. "I thought I might ask Mary and Martha for some instruction in preparing meals."

Hal nodded as if he hadn't noticed her slip. "It would be a nice way for you ladies to deepen your friendship."

"I'd like that." Nancy was silent for a moment as if something troubled her. "You know, I'm not without skills, Mr. Gray—Hal. I can stitch and dance and play the pianoforte quite well. I can manage a household staff and host tea for several guests. I also have a good head for numbers and business, much to my father's consternation. Unfortunately, not one of those skills seems remotely relevant now."

For a moment he simply studied her. "You seem far wiser than your sixteen years."

"Almost seventeen," she said. "In *seven* weeks."

"Yes, you've mentioned that, I believe," he said, tongue in cheek.

"I just want you to understand that I'm not a naive child."

Her declaration made him grin. She had a bossy sort of manner about her, a bit of starch in her spine that he admired. She wasn't a child. The woman in her made that clear, and yet there seemed to be a girlish side of her that sought his approval. The mix intrigued him.

Perhaps she would learn her wifely duties well. It would certainly be nice to come home to a hot meal and a clean house at the end of a long, back-breaking day. John's idea hadn't been without merit. Still, to take on a wife and that heavy responsibility just to get a hot meal and a clean kitchen was more than he could afford now.

"Might you spare a bit extra for my initial trip to town?" she asked. "I'll need a couple of personal items in addition to our provisions."

"Of course," he said, but he had no extra. He turned his mind to finishing his breakfast. His mouth watered, and his stomach growled with pleasure as he filled his belly.

After he finished, Hal moved his plate aside and placed some coins on the table. "Will that suffice?" he asked, hoping that it would and that he had retained enough to support them for a few more weeks. Out of necessity, he and John had spent judiciously, buying only the absolute essentials. Hal had no desire to know what items a woman might need, and so he placed a bit more than he could spare on the table.

"It's plenty," Nancy said, and she scooped the entire pile of money into her palm and tucked it into her skirt pocket. "What kind of furniture do you build for Edwards?"

Just like that she took his money and then asked how he was going to make more. If this was what having a wife was like, his life had just gone from bad to worse.

"I make cabinets and stands and other furniture for Addison Edwards when I'm not at the mill." He gestured with his fork in the opposite direction of the village. "The mill is just a five-minute walk down the road, and there's a mountain of work waiting for me there. I need to be off and quit wasting daylight."

Concern marred her expression. "This must be a very difficult time for you. I'm terribly sorry about your brother and that you have to manage so much on your own."

He didn't wish to be rude, but he had no desire to talk about the many ways he would miss having his brother in his life. "Thank you. Breakfast was delicious."

"Perhaps I can help at the mill?" she asked. "I'm good with

numbers and getting things organized. I know nothing about your business, of course, so those skills might be of little help." A slight self-effacing grin tilted her mouth, and he found it ridiculously endearing, much to his irritation. "But if you need another pair of hands, I'm willing to offer mine."

The sincerity in her eyes made him feel about an inch tall. He should have given her a gentler greeting at the train station and helped her see that returning to Buffalo was in her best interest. He hadn't meant to be unkind. He just hadn't been able to think a clear thought from the minute he looked into her eyes.

Deflated, she sank back in her chair. "I know what you're thinking. A mill is no place for a woman. I suppose it was silly of me to offer assistance."

Tenderness toward the woman welled up again and unsettled him. Grossly uncomfortable with his urge to comfort her, he slid his chair away from the table. "I'll manage all right on my own, Miss Mitch—ah, Nancy. You'll be busy tending house and learning your other duties." He stepped away from the table wanting to escape the kitchen and any more revelations about his new wife. "I'm sorry the house isn't in better order for you."

A crooked smile tipped her lips, and she got to her feet. The top of her head barely reached his shoulder. "I'm glad to have tasks to keep me occupied. It was awfully quiet sitting here alone last night. I thought you might spend the entire night in the barn. I considered smoking up the house again just to get you to come inside." Without cracking a smile, she pointed to a small bundle wrapped in a kitchen linen lying on the table. "There are two apples and a slice of bread for your lunch. Be sure to take it with you."

With that dismissal, she picked up his breakfast plate and carried it to the sink.

He stared at her narrow back, oddly pleased by her spunk.

Hal left the house thinking about the challenge he'd seen in his wife's eyes. It intrigued him to no end. Thoughts of her plagued him all morning. He regretted his moments of unkindness and wondered at the tender admiration he'd felt while watching expressions shift across her delicate face.

He'd been enthralled. He was man enough to admit the truth. Seeing her lips tilt in an array of tentative smiles and frowns had thoroughly captivated him. John Radford would have been immensely pleased and would have enjoyed taunting Hal about his good fortune had John lived long enough to marry Nancy.

Still, whatever Nancy's reason for answering John's advertisement, Hal couldn't help feeling it wouldn't bode well for him.

CHAPTER SEVEN

After cleaning up breakfast dishes and setting her new kitchen in order, Nancy wiped her brow and opened the firebox, making sure she saw bright orange coals and flickering flames before depositing the chunk of wood.

She then gathered up the pile of dirty clothes she'd found in one of the small rooms off the parlor. Tending to chores in her new home made her heartache. If only she'd come here as the bride of a man who loved her, her stomach would be filled with a happy lightness rather than a constant swirl of nerves. What if her new husband couldn't come to care for her? What then? Would she be relegated to life as his servant and little else?

Squelching the heartbreaking thought, Nancy turned her attention back to the chores at hand. She carried an armload of sour smelling clothing out the back door and shook the sawdust off each shirt and each pair of trousers. Then she took the bundle of dirty clothes inside to the kitchen. She made another trip outside to the well where she pumped two buckets full of cold water and then carried the heavy pails inside. She placed one aside and poured the other into a deep copper bathing tub stored in the corner of the kitchen. Then she added the full pot of water that had been steaming on the stove.

Piece by piece, she submerged her husband's, and likely John Radford's, soiled clothing in the copper tub and scrubbed the items with lye soap. With the remaining bucket of water, she rinsed the garments then dropped them into the large kettle that had previously contained hot water. She would give them a final rinse near the well where it was easier to fetch fresh water. Finally finished, she dried her aching hands and then hefted the kettle full of wet clothing.

She gasped at the backbreaking weight of the deep pot full of wet garments.

For a moment she considered transferring some of the clothes back to the tub, but it was filled with dirty water. She didn't have time to pile wet items in the sink or split up the laundry and waste time making more trips through the house. The chores, all of them, must be finished before Mr. Gray—her *husband* returned home. She had to make her best impression today and show him she could be of value to him, that she wasn't useless, that having a wife would be of benefit to him and perhaps even a pleasure in his life.

Spending time together was the only way for them to build a relationship... and the only way to keep her homesickness at bay. But her husband had to *want* to spend time with her, or she had to find something that would allow her to spend time with him. But what?

Straining, she carried the pot to the kitchen door and lowered it to the floor with a heavy thud. She blocked the door open with a kitchen chair. Gritting her teeth, she gripped the handle on either side of the pot and lifted it to thigh level. She managed to wrestle the beastly caldron outside and carry it down three steps and out to the well in a side-to-side sort of duck walk that made her gasp and laugh at herself. If only Elizabeth could see her now. The thought was bittersweet, and Nancy chased it away before it could make her sad.

There were no pins on the clothesline, nor could she find any inside, so she rinsed the clothes and draped the sopping garments over the sagging line. After she finished she went inside to freshen up.

Thirty minutes later, after stretching her tired back, Nancy tied on her hat and headed out the front door. She needed supplies for the pantry, and there was still much to be done before Hal returned home for the evening.

NANCY PULLED the door closed behind her and stopped in the driveway to survey her new home. The small white house sat on a lovely piece of property. In one corner of the front yard stood a large lilac bush that was dropping its fragrant purple blossoms. At the corner of the house, a clematis vine filled with pink blossoms climbed a wooden trellis. A long driveway ended at a large red barn where Hal spent his time in the late evenings. A rectangular field, lush with green grass and dotted with purple and white wildflowers, enveloped the barn. The apple orchard sat between their home and the Tucker's house, the gnarled tree branches dropping their pretty pink blossoms to make way for growing juicy red apples. Her new home was quite beautiful, and a place Nancy was eager to explore.

But other duties called her, so she tugged on her gloves and headed for town. She must stop by the Tuckers to thank them for giving her a lovely wedding day and to see if she might be able to purchase some of their apples at harvest time. Nancy could already imagine the many tasty dishes and delicious cider she would learn to make from the fruit, that is, if Mary was willing to teach her.

As Nancy approached the far edge of the orchard, she spied Mary tending a garden beside the livery. A massive sprawling oak stood in the yard, partially shading a driveway and their pretty two-story home. William was working in the paddock on the opposite side of the barn. When he spied Nancy coming up their drive, he gave her a jaunty wave and called out to Mary that she had a visitor. With a final wave, he returned his attention to a spindly-legged gray foal who was galloping playfully around the paddock.

Hoe in hand, Mary lifted her head and greeted Nancy with a wide smile. "If you have a minute, come see how well my plants are doing."

Glad for the invitation and grateful for the warm welcome, Nancy crossed the yard and surveyed Mary's expansive garden. "Gracious, this is larger than our garden back home," Nancy said, her eyes taking in the vast patch of tiny green shoots that were poking up from the rich soil. It gave her hope that she, too, could grow and flourish here. "I wish Mr. Gray—my husband—and his brother would have thought to put in a garden."

"You still have time for planting, especially if you aren't starting from seed." Mary stretched her back and scanned the sprouting plants. "I started these plants in our spare bedroom two months ago. I'd be happy to help you transplant some of my onion, squash, and turnip plants to your garden if you like. I can also spare some rhubarb, cabbage, and spinach. There's a bit of corn seed left, if you want it. If you plant it soon, you'll have sweet corn by mid-September."

Surprised, Nancy said, "I'd love the plants, Mary, but not if it will short you at canning time."

"You'll be doing me a favor to take some of these plants," Mary said. "Truly, I'm afraid I won't be able to keep up with preparing and storing all these vegetables, and I'd hate to see anything left to wither on the vine. Prepare your garden bed, and I'll help you fill it with as many vegetables as you can tend."

Nancy released a breathy laugh and her eyes met Mary's. "I'll certainly do that. I wish I had something to give in return for your generosity."

"You do," Mary said, slipping off her gloves. "Your friendship. Now come along and have tea with me." She linked arms with Nancy and led her across the yard. Her dark beauty made Nancy wish she'd taken more time with her toilette. Mary wore a day gown of spring green with tiny white rosettes embroidered on the bodice and a plain straw gardening hat topped her head, but she was enviably pretty in her simple attire.

"It's a lovely morning for a stroll," Mary said, her cheeks slightly rosy from tending her garden. "Where are you headed?"

Nancy drew in a breath, enjoying the fresh air and warm sunshine on her aching shoulders. "I'm going into town to purchase a few provisions. I wanted to stop by and again express my gratitude for all you and Martha did yesterday."

Mary flapped her hand dismissing Nancy's comment. "We enjoyed every minute of it. Do sit while I fetch our tea. I'm glad for an excuse to rest my back a spell."

So was Nancy, but she had chores awaiting her, and it was imperative that the house be in order when Hal returned home. Still, in the face of Mary Tucker's warmth, Nancy gratefully agreed to a short visit.

For nearly an hour, they sat on the porch in thick cushioned chairs, sipping tea while Nancy prevailed upon Mary to teach her how to cook. "I have no one else to instruct me."

Mary's smile faltered. "I'm happy to teach you, Nancy, but I confess I'm baffled by the fact you've not yet learned."

"I was taught other less practical skills, I'm afraid."

Mary arched a shapely black eyebrow. "I admit I'm intrigued. May I ask what skills?"

Nancy paused, wondering how much she dared to reveal. Finally, she said, "A girl from a wealthy home learns to manage a staff and to host tea and dinner parties. They don't learn to cook or tend laundry. It shames me deeply that I have nothing to offer Mr. Grayson," Nancy said, deflated and yet feeling oddly relieved to be sharing her concerns with someone.

"May I ask if you left that wealthy home without your parents' consent?" Mary asked concerned.

"I did." Nancy's cheeks warmed, but she forced herself to meet Mary's sympathetic gaze. "I hope you'll understand that I can't share more than that just now. I will someday, though, I promise. For now, however, I'm throwing myself on your mercy and asking you to teach me the skills I need to become a suitable wife. I don't even know what provisions I'll need to prepare meals for my husband."

"Of course I'll help you," Mary said. "I'm certain you're already a good wife. I understand and will honor your request for privacy. I'm looking forward to the two of us spending time in the kitchen and garden together. As for provisions..." Mary shrugged. "To start stocking your pantry you might purchase pork, bacon, salt beef or fresh beef, flour, beans, rice, coffee, tea, sugar, vinegar, yeast, corn meal, and eggs and butter, of course."

Nancy felt her stomach plummet. Not only could she not remember the lengthy list of items, she certainly couldn't afford all of them. "Perhaps I could purchase what I might need for two or three meals?" she suggested.

Mary laughed. "Of course. I hadn't meant to be overzealous, but a full pantry makes preparing meals much easier. I have plenty of flour, sugar, eggs, and butter as well as some corn meal that I'll pack up for you. If you can purchase a nice cut of pork and some rice and beans, we can prepare three easy meals for you and Hal. Will that suit?"

"Perfectly," Nancy said, releasing a nervous laugh. "I was beginning to feel apoplectic."

Mary grinned. "You'll do fine, Nancy. In fact, if you'll allow me, I'll turn you into a fabulous cook."

Nancy's eyes welled up. "You can't know how much your friendship means to me. I'm just so deeply grateful—" Nancy clipped her sentence off and swung her attention to William who was climbing the porch steps.

"Ho there," he said, his gaze bouncing from Nancy to Mary. "Who are these beautiful woman lounging on my porch?"

Giving her husband a warm, inviting smile, Mary reached out and laced fingers with him. "Join us for tea."

"I was hoping for an invitation." William planted a loud kiss on Mary's neck, causing her to laugh and shoo him into the house for a glass.

Their love and passion were so palpable it made Nancy uncomfortable... and desperately lonely.

"I'm sorry to rush off, Mary, but I really must get to the mercantile now." Nancy set her glass on the wooden tray beside the pitcher of tea and stood up. "Thank you for such a lovely visit and for... everything."

"Stop back on your way home, Nancy. I have fresh cornbread and mutton stew on the stove. I have plenty, and it'll make a fine meal for your supper this evening. You can store your fresh meat in my spring-house, and tomorrow I'll show you how to prepare it," Mary said.

"Thank you, Mary. Someday I'll find a way to repay you for your generosity," Nancy said. As she descended the porch steps, the falling apple blossoms in the orchard caught her eye and she turned back. "Would you allow me to purchase a few bushels of apples when they ripen?" she asked.

"You're welcome to help yourself to as many as you like. Our crop produces far more than we need."

With a nod of thanks to her new friend, Nancy continued her walk to town, wondering how she would ever repay Mary for her kindness. She had nothing to give now, but someday, somehow, she would show Mary that she'd chosen to befriend the right woman.

Leafy maple and oak trees provided spotty shade as Nancy strolled into the village of Fredonia—her new home. Coburn's gristmill, a three-story gambrel-roofed board-and-batten building with a towering brick smokestack, sat at the edge of Canadaway Creek. At the back of the building was a small stone addition and a large waterwheel. The large building reminded her of the stables at home where she'd spent so much time with her beloved mare.

Nancy had known that leaving her loving home in Buffalo would be difficult, but she'd had no idea how lonely she would feel or how deeply she would miss her family.

Straightening her shoulders, she entered Squire White & Son on the opposite side of the street and took her first step toward building a new life. She would make Hal Grayson see that he needed her—even if he didn't want her—because there was no going back for either of them. Somewhere in his hard head, he knew that, but he just wasn't ready to accept the truth.

CHAPTER EIGHT

At eight-fifteen, after a long backbreaking day, Hal entered his small house no closer to a solution than he was when he'd left that morning. How was he going to manage the mill and build furniture for Addison Edwards? There simply weren't enough hours in a day.

Those thoughts plagued him as he entered the foyer, but two steps inside his jaw dropped. The parlor had been transformed from a disheveled sparsely furnished room to a place that beckoned his exhausted body to sit and relax. Miss Mitchell... Nancy... his *wife*... had moved the sofa and worn wingback chairs into a small grouping around the fireplace. She'd placed a small carpet in the center and placed a low white oak table, his favorite piece of furniture, atop a worn rug. A flickering candle and a cup of steaming tea sat atop the table. The floor that he and John had covered in mud from their dirty boots had been scrubbed until the hardwood gleamed.

The delicious scent of roasting meat drew his gaze to the kitchen. Nancy stood in the doorway, her expression warm but a bit apprehensive.

"I'd hoped you might be home earlier," she said, her hands clasped in front of her blue skirt. A brown and white checkered apron hung askew around her slender waist, one of her purchases today he presumed, and a curling tendril of red hair dangled at her neck. "I kept your supper hot for you."

This morning he'd thought a little fresh air and hard work would clear his mind enough that he could find a suitable solution to their awkward arrangement. He wanted to find a way to make her feel more comfortable in his home, and with him. She certainly seemed committed to her duties as his wife.

Problem was, he wasn't comfortable with *her*, and that reinforced the awkwardness between them. What a mess.

"How did you manage all of this?" He gestured to the inviting parlor to distract his mind from going down that dangerous path. "Did you sit down for a single minute today?"

"No, and I suspect you didn't either." Her cheeks flushed, and she stood in the doorway as if making a stand of some sort. "I don't mean to be... presumptuous, but I thought you might like to bathe before supper. I prepared a bath for myself earlier and just now freshened the water for you. You'll find clean clothes and linens on the table. You can place your soiled clothing in the crate near the kitchen door. I'll enjoy my cup of tea in the parlor while you bathe. Your supper will be ready when you finish."

Hal stared in stunned surprise. That she had worked so hard to clean his home, *their* home, and even prepare a bath for him was beyond kind. That she was letting him know he *needed* a bath, which he was most certainly aware of, made his face burn. His disreputable state wasn't because he disliked bathing but simply a lack of energy and time at day's end to fetch and heat water for a bath. Until coming to Fredonia, he'd been a gentleman with gentlemanly habits. But at some point in the last few months, he'd lost that civilized side of himself. And after John died, he simply hadn't cared.

Nancy had just made it painfully clear that *she* cared. Her forthright manner both shocked and pleased him. However inconvenient it was having a wife, he admired Nancy's starch and deeply appreciated the many comforts she was providing.

With eager anticipation, he headed to the kitchen to soak his weary bones.

Lantern light created a warm lustrous glow on the pine wainscoting and floorboards that had been scrubbed free of dust and neglect. A pile of fresh linens had been stacked on the sideboard ready for his use. Pressed trousers and a freshly laundered shirt lay across the back of a chair. Intrigued, Hal picked up a pair of his stockings, inspected the toe and slowly shook his head. She'd even laundered his underclothing and darned his stockings.

She'd been doing all of this, cleaning his home, and clothing and preparing his supper, tasks requiring hard work, while he'd been whining to himself about his own burdens.

Shame welled up within him, and he sat on the chair with a weary sigh. He didn't want to take her for granted or be inconsiderate, but he simply couldn't spare a moment of time to help her with chores. He wanted to spare her the backbreaking labor of carting water for laundry and bathing, but he couldn't be here to tend those chores for her. He wished he could afford to fill their pantry and provide more comforts in their home, but he hadn't yet established himself. He hadn't been ready for the financial responsibility of taking a wife, nor had he been emotionally prepared for such a prospect, especially with a woman he didn't even know. John had merely wanted a homemaker. But Hal wanted to marry for love and passion, neither of which he had time for now.

But what did Nancy want?

Why had she been so eager to marry the first man who crossed her path? She was intelligent and beautiful and had so much to offer. It didn't make sense why she'd thrown herself on Hal's mercy knowing full well the course they had set together. She was partially responsible for landing herself in this mess. Still, Hal felt awful about it.

Stripping off his soiled clothing, he dipped his aching hand into the bath water. The liquid heat soothed his scraped knuckles. He stepped into the deep copper tub parked in the corner of the kitchen and let the hot water embrace his weary, aching bones. In that instant he felt intense appreciation for his wife. It must have taken her an hour to prepare such a grand bath. And he'd also seen clean clothes hanging on the line, but his bath water appeared clean and fresh. She must have carted multiple buckets of water inside for washing laundry, then hauled out the soiled water, cleaned the tub, and then carried in that many more buckets to fill the tub for him. Plus, she'd had to heat several pails worth of water to warm his bath, which reached his armpits when he reclined. If he'd had to fetch and heat his own water tonight, he'd have bathed in the creek.

His tension and worry dissolved into the steamy water. How long had it been since he'd felt pleasure or comfort of any kind? Since before he'd left Buffalo, for certain. Perhaps this was why John had sought a wife. Perhaps he wanted to reclaim a few simple pleasures in exchange for providing a home for a woman. From the moment John and Hal had arrived in Fredonia, their lives had consisted of work. Not once had they taken a day, or just an evening, to relax. Hal had believed their situation was temporary and would settle down after they were productive enough to hire help. John disagreed and thought they should hire a man at the mill immediately. He thought they should be taking time to meet folks in town and begin building relationships and making Fredonia a real home.

They had taken time to meet their closest neighbors and business associates, but Hal felt that socializing would take their time and focus away from their business. Now he was beginning to believe John was right on all counts—especially in taking a wife.

And perhaps that was simply Hal's exhausted, aching body talking.

Fatigued and tired of his own circular thoughts, Hal washed his hair and scrubbed his face and neck until he felt as polished as the gentleman he'd left behind in Buffalo. At the least, Nancy deserved better than his worst. She deserved to be treated as a kind and gentle lady, not as an inconvenient servant.

When Hal entered the parlor, Nancy's heart skipped a beat and left her breathless. Clean shaven with his dark, wet hair combed back off his forehead, he seemed lighter and more relaxed. His eyes held a new warmth in them she hadn't yet seen.

She steered him straight back to the kitchen and bade him to sit at the table across from her, which he did. "I'll get your supper now."

"Thank you for the bath, Nancy. It was a rare treat after a long day of work." He smoothed his hands over his laundered shirt and said, "I didn't think we had an iron."

Stomach aflutter, Nancy laced her fingers in front of her. "I purchased the iron along with a few other necessary items. I hope you don't disapprove."

He leaned back in his chair. "I can hardly disapprove of coming home to clean clothes, a hot bath, and a delicious supper."

"You can't know if supper is delicious. You haven't tasted it yet."

A light chuckle rumbled in his chest, the sound falling pleasantly on her ears. "My nose already knows what my mouth will soon tell me."

She smiled because she felt her first real sense of hope. Maybe Hal would see that they could make the best of their situation and create a perfectly amicable marriage between them. "Let's see if your nose and mouth agree then. I'll get your supper now." She started for the stove, but he caught her hand. Startled by his touch, she glanced down at his strong, tanned fingers gently holding hers.

Their eyes met, and he released her. "Thank you," he said, his voice quiet and sincere. "I am in awe of all you've done here, and I deeply appreciate your hard work. I haven't meant to appear ungrateful."

The sincerity in his golden-brown eyes melted her. As if she'd swallowed a pot of hot coffee, heat filled her belly and blossomed outward until her cheeks burned.

His lips quirked up on one side, and lo... how easily this man could charm her with just a smile.

Never had Nancy experienced such a reaction. Her father had only just pronounced her of an age to court, and he'd arranged that courtship and marriage between herself and Stuart Newmaine, one of the young men who worked at her father's bank. Mr. Newmaine had visited on many occasions when her father had him to the house to discuss business. The man was always polite and attentive when Nancy spoke, but his attentions and his affections had been for her sister, Elizabeth. Never had Nancy experienced such admiration as that which she saw in Hal Grayson's eyes.

"What smells so good?" he asked, his voice warmer... friendlier.

"Mutton stew," she said, her own voice trembling. "Another gift from Mary Tucker." Turning to the stove, she said, "I hope you like it."

"I do, although I feel so refreshed by the bath that I'd be happy with anything you feed me."

Gracious, this couldn't be the same man who chastised her for lying about her age just the evening before.

"You've been here four days, and I feel as if I'm living in a new home," he said. "I wish I had a man even half as industrious as you to help at the mill."

She angled her back to him to hide her pleased smile as she filled their bowls. "I suspect I would be much less valuable at the mill. Are you looking to hire a man?" she asked, placing their plates on the table.

"I can't afford one just now. John and I spent our savings to secure the house and sawmill. I'm making monthly payments to Tom Fiske to pay off the balance. John and I were struggling, but we were making progress. Things had just begun to look up when John...when he died, and I've fallen behind. I need to get ahead again before I can hire help."

He dipped into the stew and filled his mouth. Two seconds into chewing he closed his eyes. "Delicious," he said, his mouth pursed.

"Mary's an excellent cook. She's going to teach me how to make meals like this." Nancy tasted the stew for herself. It was indeed delicious. In that moment, while she sat at the table sharing a meal with Hal Grayson, all her hard work and aching muscles felt worthwhile. A few days ago she couldn't have imagined this possibility. Mr. Grayson had been cool and unwelcoming when he greeted her at the depot. But this evening, after a warm bath and a good meal, he was very pleasant company indeed. The thought made her smile.

"Something delights you?" he asked.

For an instant she considered pretending her thoughts were still on the food, but she decided to see if her husband had a sense of humor. "I find it interesting that a hot bath and good meal can alter your disposition to such a great degree."

He grinned. "I suppose I am a bit more amicable this evening. The bath and tasty meal are having a positive effect on my manners. Is that what you had hoped for?"

"That was my plan, yes."

His laugh seemed to surprise both of them.

She smiled, liking the momentary connection she felt with him.

"May I be so bold as to ask why you and John weren't married?" she asked. "Many gentlemen of your age are betrothed or married, many of them with children already."

He sat without speaking for a moment and then placed his spoon in his bowl. For a moment Nancy thought she had gone too far. She wanted to know more about her husband and his family, but perhaps it was too soon for her to ask such personal questions, especially when they involved his brother.

"Perhaps I shouldn't have asked," she said, quietly. "I hadn't meant to be intrusive or insensitive."

"You have a right to ask questions, Nancy." Hal leaned his forearms on the table beside his plate. "I wanted to offer my bride more than a life of hardship and a heart full of grief. I wanted to give her a proper courtship and a wedding day we would both anticipate."

Their eyes held, and they studied each other. Her heart ached, and it made speaking difficult. "Sometimes one doesn't have a choice in the matter."

He sat back in his chair, silent, inspecting her. "Since we're being frank with each other, what compelled you to marry my brother, a complete stranger?"

Her mouth fell open. She hadn't considered that he would ask his own bold questions—questions she didn't want to answer. Still, he'd answered her probing question and therefore deserved an answer. "I preferred to marry a stranger who might possibly learn to love me one day rather than marry a man who is in love with my sister."

Hal's eyebrows raised, and he released a low whistle. "Did your sister return this man's affection?"

"Intensely," Nancy said. "Could you have knowingly married the woman John Radford wanted to marry?" she asked.

He released a long sigh and said, "I reckon I just did."

CHAPTER NINE

For three days, excluding time out for Sunday service, Hal spent from dawn to dusk at the mill, falling further behind on his furniture order. At day's end he dragged his weary self home, achingly grateful for the bath and warm supper Nancy had prepared for him. With Mary Tucker's help, Nancy was learning to cook and provide tasty dishes. He thanked his wife, of course, and he was cordial to his new bride, but he tended to keep their conversation businesslike during their meals because he didn't know what to do with Nancy.

She was supposed to have been his brother's bride—now she was *his* bride.

The complications and intricacies of marriage exhausted Hal.

But he would be lying if he said he hadn't realized he was compromising Nancy by bringing her to his home. He'd been captivated by her the minute her brown eyes looked into his. He was drawn to the possibility of discovering the mystery of such a beauty. While debating with her on the platform, he was entranced by the worry in her eyes and her soft, convincing voice that revealed her desperation. For those few moments, Hal's mind was preoccupied with something other than the searing pain of his brother's death. That brief distraction was such a welcome relief from his constant heartache that Hal had forgotten himself and the time and why he was at the station.

Not until the train pulled out had he realized it was too late.

Nancy had unwittingly thrown him a lifeline. For better or worse, he'd grabbed hold with both hands.

"Are you too tired this evening for a bit of conversation?" Nancy asked, breaking into his thoughts.

He looked up from the book he'd been trying, and failing, to read. Nancy stood in the kitchen doorway with a damp dishtowel clutched in her hands.

"Something on your mind?" he asked.

"Mary Tucker stopped by today. She is going to give us some vegetable plants she doesn't have room for. I'd like to plant them out back if it's all right to use the plot behind the house."

"Of course. However, I'm not sure how soon I'll be able to till up the garden for you."

"Perhaps I can manage it myself."

"I'll till if for you, Nancy. I just need a few days. I'm glad you've made a friend," he said, meaning it. He wanted her to have friends. "The Tuckers are nice folks."

"They are indeed." Sincerity filled Nancy's voice and her eyes with warmth. "Did William Tucker stop by your mill today? Mary told me he planned to do so."

"He did." Hal placed the book in his lap, far more interested in his bride than the almanac he'd been reading. "William invited us over after Sunday service. Did Mary mention the gathering?"

"She did. Shall we go?" Nancy asked, her eyes lit with interest. "Mary said the Fiskes will attend. They're planning lunch on the porch and a croquette match. It sounds like a delightful way to spend the day."

The hopeful note in her voice made Hal realize how inconsiderate he'd been. He hadn't spent more than a few minutes a day with her since she'd arrived because he'd been working around the clock... and because he had felt so guilty for dragging her into this predicament that he didn't want to think about Nancy, much less talk with her. But now that she was his bride, and there was no longer a question of what he was going to do with her, he needed to be more attentive. She was living in a new town with a husband who was mostly absent. How could she be anything but lonely?

"Would *you* like to go to the Tucker's on Sunday?" he asked, suspecting he already knew her answer but wanting to give her the opportunity to answer for herself.

A bright smile broke across her face. "I would very much enjoy visiting with everyone again. Did you accept William's invitation?"

A slight smile tugged at his lip because she looked so sweet and hopeful. Her innocence twisted him up inside. "I told him we'd be honored to attend, providing you desired an outing."

"Heavens, *yes!*" she said.

Her outburst made him grin because she was so passionate in her delivery. "All right then. I'll need to work in the woodshop awhile that evening, but it appears we'll spend some time getting to know our neighbors better after Sunday service."

"I can hardly wait." Her eyes lit with excitement, only to dim in the next instant. "Oh, dear, I don't know what to take. We don't have much... that is, I'm not certain what ingredients I have to..." She lowered her hands, the dishtowel dangling at her side. "I'm sure I'll find something to take along."

The tiny frown lines between her dark eyebrows was his undoing. "Don't fret, Nancy. I have a few coins left. I'll leave money on the parlor table, and you can get whatever you need."

"Thank you," she said, crossing the parlor to sit across from him. "I know our situation is... difficult at present. Is there anything I can do to help?"

"You're doing more than your share already." He shook his head, exhausted. "You can help by understanding why I need to spend my evenings working."

"I do," she said, softly. "I thought you would head to the barn right after supper this evening. I was surprised to find you still in the parlor."

"I needed to rest my back before hunching over a table to sand chair spindles. I'll head back out shortly."

She seemed to contemplate the dishtowel in her hands for a few seconds and then shifted her attention to the book he was reading. "Did you like to read as a boy?"

He shook his head. "I preferred to spend my time outside in the woods or fishing our pond and sometimes even spending a Sunday afternoon swimming and fishing at the lake."

Her eyes lit up. "Oh, that must have been marvelous fun."

"It was. We'd spend the day watching fishing boats and steamers coming in and out of the harbor."

"Did you ever see a ship?" she asked, her enthusiasm keeping her on the edge of her chair.

"A couple of times, but when I lived in Crane Landing, I actually watched a ship launch. Twice."

Nancy's brows furrowed. "Where is Crane Landing?"

"In southern Maine. My grandad has a mill there, and he saws planks and keel beams and other materials for Crane Shipbuilding. I lived there until I was nine, and then my father brought us all to Buffalo. But while I lived in Crane Landing, I saw the Cranes launch two ships, and it was spectacular. It's something I'll never forget." The memory of that paramount event still had the power to fill Hal with excitement and a wild sense of adventure. "Watching those huge sails swell with wind and lift the massive hull several inches higher in the water was incredible. That's the first time I understood how powerful wind and water can be."

Nancy laced her fingers and tucked them between her knees, creating a dip in the pretty blue fabric of her skirt. Her eyes filled with wonder as if she were standing in the midst of a busy shipyard or watching a launch from the shore. "I can only imagine how exciting it must have been to build those magnificent vessels and see them sail off across the ocean. Why on earth would your father leave all of that, and a beautiful ocean, to come to this small village?"

"Steamers. My father moved us to Buffalo, not Fredonia, where he built a sawmill and cut timbers and planks for the steamer trade. The Buffalo shipyards are building steamboats at a mad pace and they need lumber. My father saw an opportunity and decided it was time to build his own sawmill business. So he set up shop in Buffalo and captured some of that business. Or at least he had until recently."

"Do they not have other sawmills in Buffalo?"

"Sure, but my father has been sawing keel beams and deck planks and other materials since he was a boy. That experience gave the fellas building steamships a bit more comfort in buying materials from him."

"I'm surprised you didn't remain in Buffalo with your father. Surely you were part of his business by now?"

Inwardly, Hal grimaced. "John and I both worked for my father, but things didn't go as planned. I moved here to do some furniture building for A. B. Edwards, and I talked John Radford into buying this house and the mill and going into business with me." A sick feeling settled in Hal's gut and he released a sigh. "It had seemed like a good and reasonable plan for two industrious young men. But it's becoming a nightmare for one."

"I'm very sorry," Nancy said, her voice filled with sympathy. "I can only imagine how stressful it is to shoulder all of this on your own and how terribly painful it is to lose a sibling. It shames me deeply that I've complicated your life at such a heartbreaking time."

Any complications in Hal's life were of his own making. He shouldn't have left his father's business at such a critical time. He shouldn't have involved John Radford in his own pursuits. He should have put Nancy back on that train to spare her days of backbreaking work.

"I'm glad to have you here," he said, and he meant it. "You're making our home quite comfortable, and I appreciate your effort to make the best of an unexpected and awkward situation. Regardless of our circumstance, I need to do the same."

Her lips parted; her expression uncertain as if she meant to reply and didn't know what to say. Her face, so beautiful in the glow of the lantern, thoroughly captivated him. This petite, intriguing woman was his bride.

His *wife*.

The woman he would spend the rest of his life with.

But the innocence in her eyes reminded him she was as much a girl as a woman.

His expression must have reflected his thoughts because her uncertainty turned to unease, as if she knew he was admiring her and thinking about the children they would one day have together. They were new to each other and they needed time to get to know each other better, but at some point, they *would* make this a real marriage.

And that was a train of thought he couldn't afford now.

"I'd best get back to those spindles," he said, pushing to his feet and crossing the parlor. In the foyer he stopped and glanced back at her. "I'll be a while. Goodnight, Nancy."

Disappointment filled her eyes, but she didn't protest. She sat on the sofa and began working on a shirt she'd been stitching for him. Each evening after supper, she darned socks and repaired tears and added buttons to his clothing. It seemed everything she did was for him or to please him.

He'd done nothing for her. Not one thing. And that needed to change.

CHAPTER TEN

L ate Sunday morning, Nancy whacked the ball through the
wickets set up in the Tucker's side yard. Her ball sailed through
with ease causing groans of distress from the Tuckers and a chuckle
from Hal. Croquette was one thing she was good at. She'd spent many
hours enjoying the game on the back lawn with her sister Elizabeth and
oftentimes with her parents and family friends.

"Nancy, you'll be *my* partner next time," Mary said, laughing. She
turned to her husband and caressed his cheek. "William, darling, let's
give them stiffer competition."

"I'll try, my love, but I'm worried that Hal is catching on and will
make this more difficult yet."

Nancy laughed with her new friends and with Hal, who seemed
surprisingly attentive today. Was her tall, handsome husband actually
enjoying being her partner in their neighborly games? She hoped so
because she wanted the kind of love that Mary and William Tucker
shared. She wanted to laugh with Hal and exchange private glances
with him as Mary and William had been doing all day. Tom and
Martha Fiske were sharing that same silent, intimate conversation as
Tom lovingly tended Martha and the baby she was carrying.

Again, Nancy's eyes cut to her husband, wondering what might be occupying his thoughts as he played a lawn game with her on a sunny Sunday morning. For all she knew he was thinking about the mill or his latest project for Addison Edwards. But then their eyes met, and Hal's were filled with curiosity... and something warmer... as if he wanted to draw her into his arms for a private conversation.

Mary tapped Hal on the shoulder. "Mr. Grayson, if you can take your eyes off your bride for a moment, it's your play."

The others laughed, but a flood of heat rushed up Nancy's neck and face. Knowing her husband wasn't oblivious to her was encouraging, but his public display surprised and flustered her.

Hal simply grinned and shrugged. "Forgive my lapse. I find my wife far more interesting than a wooden ball and a cluster of wickets." To Nancy's utter shock, Hal gave her a flirtatious wink and then casually turned to make his play.

Stunned, Nancy stood with her mouth slack as Mary and Martha exchanged smiles. Perhaps they felt somewhat responsible for pairing Nancy with Hal and were pleased with their work. Whatever was at play between the ladies remained a mystery, much like her husband's surprising actions, as they finished their match.

Afterward, they lunched on the porch, Hal talking business with the men, and Nancy learning all she could about preparing meals and gardening from her new friends. Though Nancy did her best to follow along and learn, her thoughts continued to stray to her husband as often as his gaze seemed to stray to her face.

As the afternoon grew late, Nancy told Mary that she'd finally finished preparing the garden and was ready for planting. Much to Hal's surprise and displeasure, Nancy had tilled the garden herself. Her back ached, and despite wearing gloves, her palms were blistered from working the hoe. But she was immensely proud of managing the task herself and sparing her husband another chore he didn't have time to tend.

After a warm farewell, Nancy and Hal headed across the orchard. "They are such lovely people," Nancy said, keeping her hand tucked lightly in the crook of her husband's arm. "I thoroughly enjoyed myself today."

"They are indeed," he said, glancing down. "I gather this wasn't your first time playing croquette." His eyes sparkled, and a slight grin tipped his mouth.

Was he actually teasing her? "My sister and I spent many hours trying to best each other."

"And where did this take place?" he asked, his charming smile still in place.

"On our back lawn, of course."

"And that was in Buffalo?"

"It was, yes. I do wish, however, that I'd spent less time playing croquette and had taken time to learn more about gardening. I'll feel positively terrible if I take Mary's plants and they die."

He didn't comment. He simply gazed into her eyes as if he could see her innermost thoughts. "I confess, Nancy, that your ability to change the subject is an admirable skill, but I had hoped you would be more forthcoming about your past now that we're married."

A flood of heat burned through her body. She had just been congratulating herself for redirecting the topic without him noticing, but apparently Hal Grayson noticed everything... about her at least.

He stopped and faced her, his expression serious. "I've a right to ask questions, do I not? I'd like to know my wife before we... that is... I know next to nothing about you."

His unfinished sentence hung between them. Before what? Before they consummated their vows?

"Are you in danger?" he asked. "Is that why you ran off and agreed to marry a stranger?"

"I'm not in danger. I can assure you of that at least." As she looked up at him, streaks of pink and orange filled the evening sky. His face was shadowed, making it hard for her to read his emotions, but it didn't matter. "I told you why I left my home," she said, unwilling to share more until their marriage was consummated and Hal had as much to lose as she did. "I couldn't marry the man my sister loved. It's that simple."

He opened his mouth as if to press her, but then he gave a sharp nod and said, "All right then. I'll leave this for now because if I don't finish sanding those spindles and get those chairs finished tonight, I might have to shoot myself."

His declaration made her grin. "Please don't. I don't want to be left a widow, nor do I want to be responsible for finishing those spindles."

A surprised laugh burst from him, and he stared in amazement. "Nancy, did you just make a joke?" he asked.

She playfully arched her brow. "You doubt my ability to jest? Or to sand wood?"

"I'm not questioning your sense of humor. But after your first effort at building a fire, I'm certain I prefer that you leave the sanding to me."

A wave of embarrassment rolled over Nancy, but she enjoyed Hal's teasing. "I paid dearly for that mistake. I haven't smoked us out of the house since, have I?"

"Thank you for that."

"Thank *you* for this lovely day," she said, gazing up into his eyes. She loved the strength of his slightly squared jaw, the way his black brows and eyelashes made every look from his eyes seem private and heated. "This is a very pleasant side of you."

His eyelashes lowered as his gaze dipped to her mouth. For a moment they were still, as if the slightest movement would shatter the moment. She felt his hand come up and cup her cheek gently for just a moment. Then a slow sigh slipped between Hal's lips. He lowered his hand and met her eyes. "It's been a good day, but I'm afraid it's time for me to head to the barn. Shall I walk you back to the house?"

Like rain beating down a new blossom, the hope in her stomach grew heavy. "I think I'll stay and listen to the creek for a few minutes," she said, because she couldn't hold her husband's arm and not hope for more.

"All right then, I'll be off." And he was. Without a kiss or tender word, he turned and walked away, his long legs eating up the distance to the barn. He left the door open, but no light penetrated beyond the gaping maw of the entrance.

She couldn't see into the barn any more clearly than she could see into her husband's thoughts.

Had he enjoyed their banter and playful moment as much as she had? His laugh seemed to indicate as much. His eyes seemed pleased by what they saw. Still, the minute she got too close, Hal pulled back and kept her at a distance.

CHAPTER ELEVEN

Midday sun lit up the orchard and soothed Hal's aching shoulders as he crossed the driveway toward the barn. The thought of stretching out beneath one of the apple trees for a long nap was so tempting his step faltered, as if his body knew what it needed even if his brain insisted otherwise. But it was the middle of his workday, and he had hours of work ahead of him.

And so he placed one booted foot in front of the other. The luxury of napping was something he couldn't indulge for a good long time. He had a sawmill sitting idle because of a broken chain. He needed to retrieve some tools from the barn and get back to the mill. With any luck he'd get the wheel operating again and finish sawing the oak order that should have shipped a week ago.

Sighing, Hal surveyed his home and the mounting chores waiting for him. To his surprise, he spied Nancy behind the house, digging in the dirt.

She knelt in the middle of her small garden wearing some type of smock over her dress. Her blue skirt spread around her like a lake in the dark soil. A gray tiger cat, the same one that had been hunting in Hal's barn since he moved in, arched his back and rubbed against her leg.

Flabbergasted, Hal stopped at the edge of the garden bed. "How did you manage to get your hands on that little terror?" he asked in amazement. Hal had tried to approach the tomcat on numerous occasions, but it wouldn't allow him within five feet of him.

Nancy glanced up in surprise, a wide smile breaking across her face. "I didn't realize you were home!"

The tomcat eyed him, but it was used to Hal popping in and out of the barn and knew he wouldn't be chased off. And Hal was still safely outside the cat's declared territory.

"Is this your cat?" Nancy asked. Her eyes were as brown as the soil but filled with light and tenderness.

"No. He's a little rascal I tolerate because he rids the barn of mice."

Crestfallen, she turned back to the cat and stroked its head. "Hey there, little fella, where do you live?"

"I suspect he lives wherever he can find a meal," Hal said, moving closer but making sure he didn't step into the cat's territory.

Nancy looked up at him, a hopeful expression on her beautiful face. "If he doesn't have a home, may we give him one?"

"He's welcome to hunt the barn and field all he likes."

"But what happens when winter comes? Surely you won't leave him outside?"

"He can shelter in the barn. I suspect that's where he's been sleeping."

Nancy wrinkled her nose at him and then whispered to the cat, "I'll sneak you in the kitchen door, Captain, and we'll snuggle together next to the stove. Just don't tell Mr. Grayson."

"Captain, is it?" Hal laughed because her conversation was so silly and endearing.

"Yes. Captain tells me he's a great explorer," she said, stroking the cat's ears. "The name fits him."

It did, actually, and that made Hal shake his head. He not only had a wife now but had apparently just acquired a cat as well.

"I didn't realize you'd be stopping home for lunch," she said, standing to brush the cat fur and garden soil off her dress.

But Hal was too surprised by what she was wearing to comment. He cocked his head and surveyed his bride. "Nancy, are you... are you wearing my shirt?"

"I hope you don't mind, but I wanted to protect my dress. I borrowed the oldest most worn one in your closet."

If not for Nancy, that shirt would have been dirty and lying on the floor or tossed over a chair. The shirt dwarfed her torso and hung nearly to her knees. The whole scene was so... unexpected, and yet so endearing that Hal felt a flood of warmth fill his chest. "You're welcome to whatever you need, Nancy. I hadn't meant to interrupt your day. I just stopped home to fetch a tool for the mill."

"Come to the house on your way out, and I'll prepare lunch for you."

"I won't have time—"

"An apple is not a proper lunch," she insisted, cutting off his protest. "You're as stubborn as you are skinny, Hal Grayson. Give me a minute to scrub my hands, and I'll fix something for you to eat." With that she hiked her skirt and picked her way through the garden, planting her small booted feet between rows of spiky green shoots and leaves that she'd been tending like a mother hen since she'd planted them a week ago.

"Nancy, if you can wait a day or two, I'll give you a hand with the garden."

She stopped and looked at him as if he was being ridiculous. "I'll not have you out here weeding and tilling soil at midnight, Hal. Because that's the only time you could possibly do it. I might not be as strong or adept as you, but I'm quite capable of tending our garden."

Without another word, she walked to the house, leaving Hal watching in surprise and admiration. His wife was becoming adept at many things, mainly at stopping his nonsense. For a petite gal, she possessed backbone and grit, and that was as attractive to Hal as her shapely backside and the sway of her skirt.

It took a full minute for him to realize she had talked him into keeping a stray cat he didn't want and eating a lunch he didn't have time for. The woman turned him around and distracted him to no end. She poked her way into his thoughts at every turn. Even when he needed to keep his mind on the work at hand, thoughts of her flitted through his mind and a longing for more whispered in his ear.

HAL RETURNED home that evening later than normal, delayed by the repairs to the mill and the extra time he'd taken to eat lunch at home. He just wanted to relax for a few moments and then spend a few solid hours in the woodshop.

As with most days since Nancy had come into his life, he was greeted by a clean house and the smell of supper on the stove. Nancy had been adding little touches here and there, and he found himself wanting to linger more and more each evening, both to enjoy his comfortable home and the pleasant company of his wife.

But when Hal stepped inside, he was immediately greeted by a cat that had clearly made himself at home. Captain lay on the old worn bench in the foyer licking his paw.

"What's this?" he asked, daring to scratch the cat behind the ears.

Captain stopped mid-lick, his eyes on Hal as if trying to determine if Hal would threaten his new comfortable perch.

"Don't worry, Captain, looks like you're here to stay, you little rascal." Hal left the cat to his bathing and crossed the parlor, heading to the kitchen at the back of the house. "I see that Captain has supplanted me as master of the house," he said to Nancy as he entered the kitchen.

Nancy smiled, her eyes lit with affection for the cat. "Seems he's claimed the bench in the foyer for his bed."

"Well, he'll have to share it with me when I come and go. I can't put my boots on while standing."

"I'm sure he'll give you the bench when needed," she said with a laugh. "Dinner is ready. You can wash up and then we'll eat."

They had a pleasant meal together, talking about the plants in the garden and how the vegetables were growing. After they were done eating, Hal retired to the parlor to rest for a few moments before heading out to the barn.

When Nancy finished the dishes, she walked into the parlor, her hands clasped behind her back and a little smile playing about her mouth. "I have something for you."

Surprised but also suspicious at the same time, he asked, "What is it?"

She brought her hands from behind her, presenting him with the most brightly colored and possibly the ugliest knit slippers he'd ever seen. He literally had no words.

"They're slippers," she said.

"I see that." Hal bit his lower lip to keep from laughing out loud at the mishmash of red, green, and beige yarn haphazardly knit together.

"I found some scraps of yarn in the attic and I thought I'd try my hand at knitting. They're not pretty, but they should keep your feet warm."

Hal was struggling to restrain himself, not wanting to insult his wife. But attempting to find the most complimentary response to her well-intended gift was no easy task. "Well, I, ah, they look right cozy. Thank you, Nancy."

The corner of Nancy's mouth turned up into a smirk, and suddenly she burst into laughter. "They're hideous!"

Hal joined her laughter when he realized that she shared his opinion of her gift.

"I couldn't resist testing your reaction," Nancy said. "I'm still learning how to knit. I knew how to stitch before I came here, but I didn't know how to knit more than basic stitches. I wanted to make you slippers for purely selfish reasons."

"And what were these purely selfish reasons, if I might ask?" Hal inquired. He was intrigued with Nancy's laughter and her playful jesting.

"Well, if I wasn't always having to clean the floors from all the wood chips and mud you track in, I'd have more time for other projects.

Now that you have these slippers, there will be no more boots in the house, Mr. Grayson."

Hal grinned, impressed with his wife's ability to lead him directly where she wanted him to go without him realizing until it was too late. He pulled off his boots and slipped the knit slippers onto his feet, lifting them proudly onto the parlor table so he and Nancy could admire her work.

"I appreciate the slippers, Nancy. And I'm sorry I haven't been more aware of my messy habits. I'll correct that one immediately. And I will wear the slippers proudly."

"That would please me immensely," she said, her voice soft, her smile warm.

Hal looked upon his wife with growing fondness, and to his surprise he was able to look at his new slippers with the same affection. Nancy had made them for him, and they had shared a good laugh over the them.

Knowing he needed to get started in the woodshop, but wanting to spend a few more moments with his wife, he said, "Would you play the piano for me? I've really enjoyed listening to you play, despite the fact the piano is sorely out of tune."

"If it pleases you. Would you care to join me?"

"I don't play."

"I can teach you."

"I wouldn't subject you to the torture of listening to me attempting to peck out notes."

"At least sit with me while I play," Nancy said, her persuasive smile both too playful and beautiful to resist.

"That I can do." Hal took his place beside her on the bench. His thigh brushed against hers, and the jolt of attraction was not only becoming familiar but welcome. He hadn't asked for this marriage, but he was coming to find that he was enjoying getting to know his wife.

Hal listened as Nancy played a flowing hymn, her clear, beautiful voice filling the parlor. Before long, he found himself humming along with the notes, feeling connected to her through the music she was playing. When she reached the chorus, he sang along with her.

As soon as Nancy finished the song, she turned a brilliant smile on him. "You have a wonderful singing voice, Hal! You've been keeping secrets."

He winked and placed a finger over her soft lips. "Shhhh... I don't want word to spread for fear our good minister will have me leading hymns each Sunday."

Nancy arched a shapely brow. "And would that be so bad?"

He reared back in mock horror. "Why, yes! I'd have to attend service every Sunday in that case!"

Nancy laughed. "You'll attend every Sunday anyhow."

He grinned, enjoying their spontaneous and surprising play acting. "Of course I will, but I'd prefer to sit in a pew with you rather than in the choir." He stood and gave her a playful bow. "Thank you for that beautiful song, Nancy. Your talent humbles me."

Color rose on her cheeks. "I... well, thank you. You quite surprised me this evening as well."

"Well... I should hate to be too predictable." He lifted her hand to his lips and kissed it. "I need to head out to the woodshop now. Goodnight, Nancy, and thank you for the um... colorful slippers and the beautiful music."

With that, he turned on his heel, grabbed his boots and headed to the foyer to pull them on. Heaving a great sigh of annoyance, Captain gave up a sliver of the bench to Hal. But Hal didn't care because he just wanted to pull on his boots and get out of the house before he did something stupid like kiss Nancy's beautiful mouth.

CHAPTER TWELVE

Nancy sat on the piano bench utterly flummoxed by her husband's spontaneous play. She'd seen glimpses of Hal's sense of humor. He could turn on the charm when he desired, but she'd had no idea he could sing or be so romantic. Had he been playing at romance, too? Or had that warm look in his eyes been real?

The thought encouraged her. Perhaps she was truly making headway with her husband. Perhaps those ridiculous slippers she'd knit for him had set the mood for their joking and playing. He'd certainly received them in the spirit in which she'd given them, as a playful attempt to try her hand at knitting and to encourage him to stop soiling her floors. She'd only hoped they would result in fewer days of mopping the hardwood floors of the parlor and kitchen. She couldn't have anticipated the affect they would have on her husband.

She placed her hand over her fluttering heart. Hearing Hal's rich baritone filling the parlor as she played the melodic notes of one of her favorite hymns was a moment she'd never forget. She had barely heard him sing when they attended Sunday service. But when that warm, rich sound come from her handsome husband, it nearly made her swoon, especially when he gazed into her eyes and kissed her hand.

Had she caught a glimpse of the man Hal Grayson was before hardship and grief had overtaken his life?

If so, how could she get that man back?

If not, then she was pleased to have given him a few moments respite from his burdens. The poor man was running himself ragged, attempting to do the work of three men. Yet he continued to insist that he tend to chores and projects she was plenty capable of completing herself.

Hal was a decent hardworking man, but he was fooling himself if he thought he could continue at this pace for much longer. And so she was determined to find a way to help lighten his burden and prove herself in her home, in her marriage, and to create a rich life of community and friendship in Fredonia.

She found her first opportunity to make new friends the next morning.

"I'm delivering a small piece to Edwards furniture store this morning," Hal told her over breakfast. "If you don't mind a walk into town, I thought you might like to come along."

Nancy paused in the act of wiping her mouth, her eyes locking with his. Was he really asking her to spend time with him on a workday?

He arched an eyebrow. "You don't have to go along if you have other pressing chores."

She lowered her handkerchief that she'd been using as a napkin. "I'd love to go. I'll just put these dishes in the sink first, if that's all right?"

"Of course. I have to get the item from the woodshop. I'll be back in a few minutes and we'll go into town."

The prospect of walking to town with Hal, of spending time with him during a work day, felt as if they were sneaking away from their duties together without permission. And to get a small glimpse into what kept him in the barn night after night was just as intriguing and exciting.

Nancy placed the dishes in a dishpan filled with water. She would wash them when she returned. Then she hurried to the foyer, tied on her bonnet, pulled on gloves, and stepped onto the stoop to await her husband.

He appeared a moment later with a small wooden box tucked beneath his arm. Upon closer inspection, Nancy could see that it was a recipe box with a carved top. A trailing vine and tiny rosettes created a circle around the initials *DE*. The box had been stained coffee brown and varnished to a rich luster that fairly glowed in the morning sun.

Nancy glanced up at her husband in amazement. "I'm impressed beyond words, Hal." She gestured to the box. "This is absolutely beautiful."

He turned and offered his free arm to her, putting himself between her and the box as if uncomfortable with her praise. "Thank you."

She linked arms with him. "Truly, Hal, it's simply gorgeous and the work is exquisite. I didn't know you possessed such talent."

"I appreciate your praise, Nancy, but it's a simple recipe box with a design that I could have carved during my first year of learning the craft," he said, escorting her down the drive.

"Then I cannot even imagine what some of your finest pieces look like."

"At the moment, my finest resembles a pile of doors and drawers that need sanding and staining." He smiled down at her as they headed up Liberty Street toward the village. "I'm building a baker's cabinet."

"How did you come to work for Mr. Edwards?" Nancy asked, wanting to learn more about her husband. Talking with him about something he loved seemed a good place to start.

But he seemed to hesitate as if he didn't want to talk about it, which she found curious.

"Am I being intrusive?"

"Not at all. It's just... well, I preferred making furniture over sawing timber, much to my father's dismay, so I sent a sample of my work to Addison Edwards about a year ago. A friend of my father's had recently traveled through Fredonia and heard that Edwards was looking for an apprentice at the time."

"I suspect your father wasn't pleased with his friend, or with you?"

Hal shrugged. "He was disappointed that I didn't want to stay in the family mill business. He fears I'll starve trying to make a living from building furniture."

"If sawmilling is all he has done, it's probably difficult for him to believe a vocation as a furniture builder is viable," she said, shifting her gaze between his thoughtful face and the leafy maple trees lining the road. The sky overhead was a cloudless blue filled with sunshine that warmed her shoulders and chased off the chill of the morning. What a fine day for a stroll with her husband, and she decided she enjoyed this side of marriage very much.

"My father knows a great deal about the vocation. He taught me everything I know about woodworking. He is a master craftsman himself, but rarely finds time for his craft due to his obligations at the mill."

"A situation not wholly unlike the one you find yourself in now, I presume?"

"Indeed. And my father's fear isn't far from being realized, Nancy. As you're well aware, we're not in the best financial shape at the moment."

"We're getting by, Hal. So finish your tale. You disappointed your father by coming here?" she asked as Liberty Street merged with Water Street and they were coming into the village.

"That I did. After Addison Edwards saw the cigar box I carved, he was interested in bringing me on as his apprentice. The timing and the arrangements were amenable, so I relocated to Fredonia about six months ago. Before John moved to Fredonia, I lived alone in a small room above the furniture store working days in Addison's woodshop. It was only recently that John and I purchased the house and mill and that I set up my woodshop in the barn. You pretty much know the rest. We worked around the clock and created a terrible mess in the house."

Nancy smiled at him, remembering quite clearly her shock when she'd seen the mess. The sudden realization of how far she'd come in creating a cozy home for them filled her with a sense of pride and contentment. She found herself walking just a little taller and with a bit more spring in her step.

They traveled two blocks down Water Street in companionable silence, both of them seeming to enjoy the morning air and birdsong. They turned left onto Main Street in the village and headed to A.B. Edwards furniture store. It sat just past the watchmaker's shop, the place where Mary had suggested Hal could purchase a wedding ring for Nancy. But Nancy had known Hal couldn't afford a ring and so she'd quickly suggested using the ring her mother had given her. She'd convinced Hal that the ring, a family heirloom passed down from her grandmother to her mother and then to Nancy, would bring her great comfort on her wedding day. Although Hal had accepted her suggestion, and even seemed relieved to be spared the burden of an expense he couldn't afford, he seemed grossly discomfited with the whole subject. So as they passed the watchmaker's shop, Nancy refrained from peering in the window for fear Hal might think she desired something he couldn't afford. She couldn't bear the thought of making her husband feel even more uncomfortable with their current financial situation.

As Hal opened the front door of the furniture store, the jangle of bells announced their arrival. He guided Nancy across the threshold in front of him. She was immediately assaulted with the deep, rich smell of fresh cut wood and the slightly pungent odor of oil. The shop was larger than it appeared from the outside and was filled with all manner of wooden furniture and crafts, many of which were likely carved by the talented man at her side. Three large headboards, beautifully carved with spindles much like she imagined Hal sanding in his wood-shop, were leaning up against the side wall. In the middle of the floor sat smaller pieces similar to the low parlor table she had in her own parlor. There were even stools, coat racks, and other items hanging from iron hooks in the ceiling. Every bit of open space was occupied with beautiful artistic woodwork. A beautiful rosewood chest of drawers sat in a corner and Nancy imagined how lovely it would look in her bedroom—in *their* bedroom. It would be a long time before Hal had the money or time to add such a piece to their home, but she firmly believed it possible someday.

She smiled up at her husband. "I suspect many of these items were made by you?"

He gave a nod, but rather than seeing pride in his eyes she saw deep appreciation for the work, for the craft, and for the money his skill earned them. "I'm afraid we can't linger," he said. "I need to meet with Addison now, and I'd like to introduce you to his wife before I head back." As he placed his hand on Nancy's lower back, she felt a warm rush circle her waist.

Nancy's heartbeat stuttered, and she felt a lightness in her belly, something she'd been experiencing since they first met and that was increasing in intensity by the day.

As they approached the counter at the far side of the room, a woman about twenty years Nancy's senior walked out from the back room, a pleased smile breaking across her face when her eyes lit on Hal.

"What a pleasure to see you, Mr. Grayson," she said, but somehow the greeting seemed laced with a tad of sarcasm.

"I'm sure," Hal said with a laugh. "Mrs. Edwards, I've brought your recipe box so now you can stop chastising me each time I stop in. I've also brought along my bride whom I'd like to introduce. Mrs. Edwards, this is my wife, Nancy." He turned to Nancy and winked. "This lovely lady is Desmona Edwards, who is quite put out with me for delivering her recipe box two weeks late."

"That I am, young man," Mrs. Edwards said, but her tone was forgiving. She greeted Nancy with a warm smile. "I must confess I've been most eager to meet the young lady who has captured this young pup. I'd thought to pair him with my daughter, but he would have none of it."

Nancy nodded, a bit taken aback at the unconventional greeting, but Mrs. Edwards' warm smile eased her concern. "I'm pleased to make your acquaintance," Nancy said.

Mrs. Edwards arched a black eyebrow at Hal. "I'd hoped you'd come to tell me you're tired of running that sawmill."

"Sorry to disappoint you, Mrs. Edwards."

"Foolish boy." She flapped a hand at him. "You're as hardheaded as Addison. If you were my son, I'd order you back to our shop and I'd work that fool notion of running a sawmill right out of your head." She looked at Nancy, a spark in her eyes. "I don't know why all men insist on ignoring facts that are right beneath their nose. This young man is too talented to waste his time sawing timber. Just look around and you'll see all the reasons I keep pestering him to return."

Nancy smiled at Mrs. Edwards' obvious teasing. She could clearly see that the lady genuinely cared for Hal as if he were her own son.

Hal merely laughed. "When I lived above the shop, Mrs. Edwards, you called me a rascal and claimed you could hardly tolerate my bad behavior. I should think you would be glad I'm no longer around to pester you all day."

"Stuff and nonsense, young man. You brought a much-needed dose of playful repartee to my days and I find I miss that." A tender expression crossed her face. "But despite all my protesting and badgering, I'm truly glad to see you well and married to such a lovely young lady. I wish you both only the best, of course." With that, Mrs. Edwards took up a bell from the store counter and gave it a sharp ring. "Run along now, Mr. Grayson. I've let Addison know you're here. Your wife and I will use your absence to get to know one another better."

Hal turned to Nancy. "I should warn you that Mrs. Edwards will launch a full assault for you to persuade me to shut down the mill and return to her woodshop full time."

"It sounds like a reasonable idea to me," Nancy said, casting a sideways glance at Mrs. Edwards.

"Oh ho!" Hal said with a laugh. "Already the women are set against me. Well, then, I know when to beat a hasty exit. I'll return shortly." He tipped his head toward Nancy and Mrs. Edwards and then disappeared down a hallway.

Nancy listened to his boot heels thump down the wooden floored corridor. The instant he was out of earshot, she and Mrs. Edwards exchanged a wide smile, establishing their friendship.

Mrs. Edwards tilted her head, gave Nancy a thorough looking over, and ended with a decisive nod. "I'll admit I was disappointed that Hal showed no interest in my daughter, but I'm entirely convinced that you are exactly what that young man needs."

Nancy felt her cheeks color at the bold statement by the older woman.

"The look on your faces assures me you're both pleased with the arrangement. Hal is like a son to me and Addison, and we are honored to have the opportunity to work with such a talented craftsman."

"He speaks very highly of you and Mr. Edwards as well. Which of these pieces did Hal make?" Nancy asked, gesturing to the room full of beautifully carved furniture.

"He made this headboard," Desmona said, laying her hand on one of the more ornate pieces leaning against the wall. "It's made of white pine, and just look at how beautiful these birch posts are carved with such intricate designs and yet they're strong and sturdy. I imagine Mr. Grayson will be filling your home with exquisite pieces such as this soon."

Nancy smiled at the thought of having some of Hal's pieces decorating their home. She could envision sitting on the bench seat of a beautifully carved coat tree to put on her boots and then peer in the tall mirror to tie her bonnet before heading out in the snow. She could just picture the decorative iron hooks of the coat rack and how the piece would look in the foyer near the front door. She couldn't wait until they were both settled in and could talk about some of those additions to their home.

And so went the duration of Nancy's visit with Mrs. Edwards. The lady was forthright but friendly and kind. It was only Hal that Mrs. Edwards seemed to taunt, and when he returned, Hal responded to her needling as if she were his well-meaning mother.

Nancy watched their byplay with interest. Gone for the moment was the haunted look and ragged exhaustion in Hal's face, replaced by a playfulness that she'd only recently glimpsed. He was clearly comfortable here among his masterpieces and with these people. Were they substitute parents of a sort while he was living away from home? The idea intrigued Nancy.

While she was occupied by her observations about her husband, another man with wild brown hair and intense blue eyes entered the room from the back hall. He was quite handsome and approximately the age of Mrs. Edwards.

"I hear you've been harassing my apprentice and bending his wife's ear," he said to Desmona as if exasperated with her, but his eyes were sparkling with what appeared to be humor.

Desmona simply lifted her chin defiantly. "I have indeed, Mr. Edwards, and I shall continue to do so until that boy regains his good sense. Now mind yourself and let me introduce you to Hal's lovely wife Nancy."

"I see that Hal's artistic eye is not only for selecting wood and creating art. I must say he also has most excellent taste in selecting a bride."

Nancy's face flamed, but Hal wrapped his arm loosely around her waist and drew her to his side. "Thank you for a memorable morning, Mr. and Mrs. Edwards, but we must be off now."

Desmona glanced up at her husband. "I suspect he's in a hurry to get back to his sawmill."

Addison made a face as if in great pain. "Yes, I'm afraid you're right, Desmona, but sometimes you just have to let the young'uns go out in the world and learn their own hard lessons." They both gave him a mock scowl as if he'd been roundly chastised.

Hal's laughter filled the room, so rich and hearty it thoroughly captivated Nancy. She'd never heard him laugh with that abandon. He tipped his hat to the Edwards who were beaming benevolent smiles at Hal as he guided Nancy out of the store.

Tucking Nancy's hand in the crook of his arm, he escorted her up Main Street. "Are you in need of anything while we're in the village?" he asked.

"Yes, an explanation for what I just witnessed. I've never seen you like that. I want to know where you've been keeping that happy, light-hearted man I saw talking with Mr. and Mrs. Edwards. I like him."

Hal's smile faltered, and he shrugged. "The Edwards seem to view me as their prodigal son, and I supposed I can't help acting the part when they're badgering me."

"Well, I'd like to take their prodigal son home with me then. It's a very pleasant side of you, Hal."

"I'm pleased that you were finally able to meet Desmona and Addison. They're good friends and I'm sorry I haven't been able to bring you by sooner. Desmona reminds me of my mother, actually. Although it's highly unusual for a woman to help run a business, Desmona spends a good bit of her time at the store assisting folks needing pieces to furnish their home."

"I enjoyed meeting them and seeing this side of you," Nancy said as she accompanied her husband out Liberty Street toward their home. She promised herself she'd find a way to bring out that side of her husband each day. If they could just find a few moments to be that happy and playful each day, they could build a joyful and loving marriage.

CHAPTER THIRTEEN

The next morning brought a dark sky with angry clouds and hard rain. It was the first day since arriving in Fredonia that Nancy was confined to the house. She stared out the window, hoping that the violent storm wasn't affecting Hal's work at the mill. It was certainly complicating her day. She'd hoped to visit Mary and see if she might borrow a couple of eggs for their evening meal, but the rain was coming down in sheets and Nancy couldn't even see the orchard on the other side of her driveway.

So she scoured the pantry trying to figure out how to make a meal with a cup of flour, one egg, and a small tin of bacon grease.

Her last trip to town had emptied Hal's purse, and she'd only been able to bring home a small sack of flour, six eggs, a slab of bacon and a small chicken. She had made chicken and flour dumplings and had stretched the leftovers for two days. She'd reserved half a jar of leftovers and stored it in the well to keep it from spoiling. So that's what she had to work with.

And this meal, however paltry, would empty the pantry.

Dread filled her stomach like a deluge of icy water. She'd never experienced such lack. The idea of not having a meal on the table had never entered her mind. The knowledge that many people struggled to put food on their tables made her heartache. Hal worked nearly all his waking hours and still hadn't the means to buy even the most necessary items. Until this moment, she had taken her good fortune for granted. She hadn't known any better.

But now she knew firsthand what that struggle was like—and it was terrifying.

Her father could help financially, but even if she could contact him, she knew that Hal Grayson would never accept the assistance. And so that left Nancy in a dire quandary.

Gathering her sparse provisions, she carried them to the stove. She scooped the bacon fat into a pot, cracked the egg on top and then poured in the flour. She fetched the jar of leftovers from the well and added the contents and two cups of water. Surely, she could make something that would pass as stew. While it cooked, she straightened the kitchen and began making a shopping list in her head.

She was standing at the stove stirring the thick liquid in the pot when a clap of thunder nearly startled her out of her boots. Her heart raced, and she peered out the window, frightened by the violence of the storm. The branches of the maple and oak trees in the backyard were being whipped by a hard gust and rain. The grass in the field was swept sideways as if combed by the wind. Nancy had always feared storms and had often sought the comforting arms of her father during those events. But she couldn't run to him now. Not for money, not for comfort. She was a grown woman and a wife, and she needed to act like it. So she returned to the stove and stirred the pot of mush.

A huge flash of lightning followed by another startling clap of thunder rattled the windows and shook the house. She yelped in alarm and dropped the ladle in the pot just as a huge snap sounded outside. Heart thundering, she peered out the window and was aghast at what she saw. That loud sound hadn't been a clap of thunder but rather the splintering of a large branch breaking off of what appeared to be the oldest tree in their yard—and it had fallen directly on the barn roof.

Captain was in the barn!

And Hal's woodshop and all his beautiful carvings were right beneath the part of the roof the branch was lying on.

Panicked, Nancy grabbed her cloak and hustled out the kitchen door. Holding her cloak over her head, she rushed toward the barn.

Wind whipped around her, the strong gusts nudging her this way and that as she leapt over puddles and darted around clumps of mud in the yard. Finally, she reached the barn and wedged open the large door far enough to slip inside and out of the out of the storm.

"Captain!" she called, trying desperately to peer through the darkened interior. "Where are you, little one?"

No yowling met her ears, but perhaps Captain's greeting was drowned out by the storm.

Afraid for his safety, she called out again, "Come on out, honey. I'll take you inside."

No movement. No sound. No Captain.

Tears welled in her eyes as she stood for several long moments, no cat in sight. What if he was outside with no shelter?

She lit a lantern and searched, calling his name again and again with no answer. Finally, she crouched down on her knees and peered under the lower shelf of Hal's workbench. The glow of two eyes peering back at her filled her with relief. "Oh, thank goodness. Come on out, sweetheart."

Setting the lantern aside, she gently drew Captain from beneath the bench. The poor little tiger was trembling and immediately sought refuge in her arms.

She held him close and rocked him, cooing, and rubbing her chin against the top of his head until his trembling subsided and was replaced with a low rumbling purr.

"I know, sweetie. It sounds terrifying outside. I'll bet that branch breaking through the roof scared you sideways. Poor baby. You're all right now. I'll take care of you."

As she held Captain close to her breast, Nancy looked around, seeking any damage to the barn. The branch had broken clear through the roof and was poking inside a foot or more. The damage appeared to be far enough from Hal's woodworking that nothing had suffered water damage. Not yet anyhow.

She placed Captain out of the way and then hurried to move a few pieces that might become damaged with the continued rain. Deciding there was nothing else she could do to protect Hal's work, she retrieved Captain, tucked her cloak around him, and headed to the door.

Sheltering Captain, she forced open the door enough to slip outside and then rushed back across the muddy, rain-soaked yard and into the house.

Nancy dumped her cloak at the door and settled Captain in the kitchen in a crate of scrap fabric she'd found in the attic the previous evening. She dried off, plucked a piece of chicken from the stew, and set it on the stove to cool. She gave Captain a dish of water and the piece of chicken. She would gladly give him her share. While Captain devoured his meal, Nancy went about finishing her chores, hoping Hal would return home soon. The barn roof needed his attention—and she needed his comforting arms.

HAL TRUDGED up the muddy street, exhausted and frustrated. The storm had made soup of the mill yard and slowed his work to a crawl all day, and so he'd shut down the mill in the late afternoon. The pressure to finish up an order that was already a week late was mounting and tying his gut in knots. He walked with his head down and the collar of his coat turned up against the rain. Thankfully the raging storm that had pounded the mill all day had abated to a fine mist as he walked up the drive to his home. Still, when Hal lifted his head, he came to a dead stop, shocked to see a large branch from their maple tree lying on the barn roof.

He rushed down the drive, afraid of the damage the branch had caused to the roof and possibly to his woodshop and the many projects staged there. He couldn't afford to lose even one of his pieces, nor could he afford any further delays with the projects he was working on.

Addison had been extremely understanding of Hal's circumstances, but Addison was a businessman and would be forced to find himself another apprentice if Hal couldn't deliver pieces on time.

Miraculously, the barn door had remained closed against the storm. A hard gust would often wrench the door open while he was working. Fixing the door was another job he'd been neglecting.

Hal ducked inside and quickly surveyed the barn. The branch was indeed lodged in the roof, but upon examination, Hal realized he could saw the branch into pieces and pull the remaining piece back through the hole it had created. The roof, however, would need to be patched straightaway.

As he looked around the woodshop for something with which to patch the roof, he was relieved to see that none of the pieces were damaged. Some pieces, however, had been relocated.

Was it possible that Nancy come out and moved some of the pieces out of the path of the rain?

Upon further inspection, he decided that she must have seen the branch on the roof and had come out at the height of the storm to rescue his work. Even he had taken refuge beneath the mill lean-to during that wild twenty-minute frenzy of whipping wind and slashing rain. Hal shook his head, filled with admiration and affection for his daring and beautiful wife.

After climbing onto the roof and seeing that very little of the rain had dripped inside, Hal decided to wait for the drizzle to abate before removing the limb. The sky was clearing, and a hint of late day sun was trying to peek through the gray sky.

He slogged into the house, determined to eat some supper before he tackled the barn. Yet another unexpected delay that would prevent him from finishing his current project this evening. He opened the door, wiped his boots, and crossed the parlor to the kitchen. Nancy was at the stove, peering skeptically into a pot of what appeared to be stew. The look on her face suggested she didn't like what she saw, but Hal knew better than to ask if anything was amiss.

The instant she caught sight of him her head came up and her eyes filled with pleasure. "You're home!" She rushed to him and circled his waist with her arms, pressing her head against his chest. "I was terribly worried about you."

Stunned, Hal stood stock still for a minute. "I... ah, I was worried about you, too. The storm did more damage here than at the mill." He clasped her shoulders and eased her away enough to see her face. "Are you all right?"

She nodded, but he could see the stress the storm had caused her. She'd been alone during the howling and thundering storm and had likely heard the branch crash onto the barn. Of course she was shaken. A feeling of intense tenderness washed through him, and he pulled her back to his chest, cradling her in his arms as he thanked her for rescuing his work in the barn.

"How bad is it?" she asked, seeming in no hurry to remove herself from his embrace.

Truth was he was in no hurry either. Holding her in his arms was surprisingly fulfilling. He lowered his head and inhaled the floral scent of her hair. He wanted to press his lips to the silken strands and bury his face in her hair. For one wild moment he considered doing so, but Nancy was seeking his comfort, not romance. And so he eased her away and said, "Actually, it's not too bad. I'll need to saw the branch in pieces to get it off the roof and I'll have to patch the hole where it broke through, but that can wait until after supper. What's in the pot that smells so good?" he asked, hoping to turn her thoughts away from the storm that had upset her enough to throw herself into his arms.

As if she suddenly became aware of her actions, she whirled away and focused her attention on the bubbling pot. Keeping her face turned from him, she said, "Sit down and I'll fill a bowl for you. After supper, I'll help you repair the barn."

"That won't be necessary," he said, taking his usual seat at the head of the table.

"I didn't ask if it was necessary," she said, placing a bowl in front of him.

Hal was beginning to learn that arguing with Nancy about

anything was a losing battle, so he bit his tongue and prepared to savor his meal.

Nancy sat opposite him. After giving thanks for their meal, they dug in.

The stew was a good bit thicker than he expected, but he scooped a heaping portion with his spoon and brought it to his mouth. The scent of bacon filled his nose and made his mouth water. He was starving. He blew once on the hot spoon and shoved it into his mouth—and froze.

Argh! How could something that smelled so good taste so bad?

He clamped his mouth shut, smiling as he forced himself to swallow the unappetizing glob of whatever she'd prepared. He honestly had no idea what he was eating. It tasted like flour and grease.

"It's delicious, Nancy," he forced out of his lips as he spooned another bite. She smiled at him and dipped her spoon in as well, taking a bite as he forced another into his mouth.

Her eyes rounded, and she clapped a hand over her mouth. She glanced from him to the kitchen door and back to him again before bolting from the table. She flung open the door and spat out the gooey mess. "Argh. This is *terrible!*" Nancy wiped her mouth on her apron, her eyes tearing. "I'm so sorry, Hal. I thought I might be able to make a meal from what we had in the pantry, but I've created an unappetizing mess. I'm sorry, but I simply could not swallow that disgusting stuff."

Hal had taken advantage of her rush to the back door to spit his mouthful back into his bowl. But it was seeing his petite, beautiful wife spitting a glob of mush out the door made him laugh until his stomach hurt.

"It's not at all funny, Hal." She sniffed and glared at the gummy mess in her bowl. "I have no supper for you."

"It's alright, Nancy."

"It's not alright. What are we going to eat?"

"We have apples left, do we not?"

"Two."

"Then that shall be our supper."

"But that's not enough."

"It will be plenty for me. But if you need more, perhaps you can borrow a couple of eggs from Mary. I'll find a way to return them to her tomorrow."

Nancy's upset seemed fade and she shook her head. "There's no need for that, Hal. After tasting that vile stuff, I'm not at all hungry. I'm sure an apple will taste lovely later, though. If you like, I'll help you with the roof now."

He couldn't leave her in the kitchen with the potful of mush feeling she'd failed him, and so he said, "I'll be glad to have a helping hand. If we go now, we can enjoy a bit of sunshine before it sets for the day." With that he hooked his arm around Nancy and guided her out the door.

When they reached the barn, Hal adjusted the ladder and climbed back onto the roof. While he sawed the limb into smaller pieces, Nancy milled about below, clearing smaller branches that had come down and chucking aside the scraps from the limb.

"What else can I do to help?" she asked.

"Nothing." Hal looked down and saw her looking up at him, her pretty white throat exposed to the waning sunlight, tempting him to place a kiss in the hollow above her collarbone. "I can manage this now. Go back inside and I'll be in when I'm done."

He saw frustration and determination cross her face as she planted her fists firmly on her waist. "As long as you're up on that roof risking your neck, I intend to stay right here."

Hal grinned. He loved her spunk. And he knew she was still dwelling on the inedible meal she'd prepared, so he thought he would set her mind on another track. "If you keep up this obstinate streak, I'll cart you into the house and lock you in the bedroom."

Nancy's eyes rounded. Then she laughed, which is exactly what he'd hoped for. "I don't believe for one minute, Hal Grayson, that you would do that since you refuse to set foot in our bedroom!"

She had turned the tables on him so swiftly and with such impact that Hal felt his face heat. It wasn't that he didn't want to set foot in the bedroom. He wanted to, but Nancy deserved to be courted first, and so he'd been tamping down his growing desire for his beautiful wife to allow them time to become better acquainted—and to explore the obvious attraction they felt for one another.

Bantering and playing with each other was simply another way of deepening their relationship, but sometimes Nancy's witty repartee hit too close to home.

"What are you going to patch the hole with?" she asked, gazing up at him with her hand shading her eyes. The sun was at his back giving him a view of her face and her white smile. She was enjoying their play, and he was enjoying the fact that he'd put that gorgeous smile on her face.

"I don't know," he said. "Look in the barn and see if you can find a board about a foot wide and maybe eighteen inches long."

"At your service, milord." She executed a deep, ridiculously beautiful curtsey that made him laugh. Flipping her skirt aside, she spun on her heel and ducked into the barn.

Hal finished sawing the limb into pieces and extracted the last of the debris from the hole.

Just as he was about to climb down, Nancy returned with an old piece of barn siding that had been leaning against a stall in the back of the barn. "Will this work?" she asked, stepping onto the bottom rung of the ladder to hand the wood up to him.

He inspected the board and then the hole and determined it would be sufficient to create a temporary covering.

"I think this will work nicely. But I need to figure out how to seal the board to keep the water out," he said, more to himself than to her.

"Do you have patching compound I can fetch?" Nancy asked, standing at the bottom of the ladder.

"No, and that's got me perplexed. I need some pine tar or something that will create a seal the rain won't wash away."

"Well, perhaps you can use the stew I made for supper," she said. "I still can't get the grease out of my mouth."

Hal gave a shout of laughter and immediately clamped his mouth shut. The last thing he wanted was to hurt her feelings, but her comment about the thick, greasy goo was so appropriate he couldn't stop laughing. He held his mirth inside, but his shoulders shook from the effort.

"I know you're laughing, Mr. Grayson. I can see the smirk on your face and your shoulders are shaking."

Her twitching mouth and the laughter in her voice was his undoing. Hal laid the board on the roof and let loose with a belly laugh.

Her own light laughter filled his ears and the air around them.

Hal leaned over the edge of the barn, gasping. "You won't hold this against me, will you?"

"Not if you won't hold my supper disaster against me. It was awful stuff, wasn't it?" She wiped away tears of laughter.

Suddenly, the fact that they had a hole in their barn roof and no supper to eat didn't seem so bad. They still had the ability to laugh in the face of dire circumstances. They had each other.

"Perhaps you should fetch your mush, and I'll see how well it holds a seal."

Nancy shook her fist at him. "Keep this up and I'll serve it to you for breakfast in the morning."

"Oh, that won't be necessary. I'm saving my apple for breakfast. But you're welcome to have the stew for your breakfast," he said in jest. He watched as she continued to smile and again thought to himself how beautiful she was—and how he wanted to make her laugh every day.

Together they completed a temporary repair to the roof. Hal ran to Tuckers and borrowed a bit of pine tar from William and a couple of eggs from Mary. Then they secured Hal's tools and closed up the barn. Hal accompanied his wife back into the house, determined to spend a few minutes with her before heading to his woodshop. He'd rather spend the evening with her, but they were in desperate need of funds. He needed to finish one of his projects tonight, so they could eat tomorrow. But the possibility of that seemed frighteningly slim.

And so he thanked Nancy for her help and the laughter and returned to his shop, his thoughts still on his wife. The more time he spent with her, the more intrigued and enchanted he became. She invaded his thoughts and his dreams. Even at times when he needed to focus, his thoughts strayed to his wife: her smile, her stubbornness, her industriousness, and her gentle beauty. He was thoroughly enchanted with her and was going to court his wife.

CHAPTER FOURTEEN

The next evening, Hal entered his house with his stomach touching his backbone. He was exhausted and hungry. But what carved a trench of pain through his gut was the thought that his wife was hungry too.

He'd worked all night to finish carving a walnut parlor lamp table and had then carried the small table into town at first light. He delivered it to Addison's home and said he'd be grateful if Addison could pay him on delivery in this case.

Addison Edwards pulled him inside, paid Hal, and offered him breakfast. But Hal couldn't eat knowing his wife was going without. So he thanked Addison and headed directly to the mill where he'd worked all day. He quit early, though, so he could walk back to the village and purchase a few items for their supper.

And so with utter exhaustion and a small measure of relief, he carried the small sack of staples into the parlor. A gentle breeze blew through the house, and he paused a moment to enjoy the refreshing coolness from the heat of the day. The sweet scent of honeysuckle growing alongside the house mixed with the scent of baking chicken. Both the parlor windows and kitchen windows were open. The evening sun shone through clean windows, casting dancing shadows on the hardwood floors. The sight of the gleaming floors reminded Hal to shuck his boots, so he stepped back into the foyer and used the boot jack. He placed his boots in the corner and pulled on the hideous looking slippers Nancy had made for him. As he headed to the kitchen, he nearly tripped over a sleepy Captain who was dozing on the floor, basking in a warm swath of sunlight coming in through the open window.

"You little rascal, you nearly got squashed," Hal said as he picked up the sleepy cat and tucked him in his arm. "I see you've moved in lock, stock, and barrel."

Captain settled himself in Hal's arms. A rush of affection for the cat took Hal by surprise. What was happening to him? He was becoming a happily married man. With a cat!

Stunned, he surveyed his home. Clean curtains flapped in the breeze. Bright white and stiff with starch, the curtains had been recently laundered and bore no resemblance to the dingy linens that had hung at the windows when John and Hal lived here alone. Looking around, he noticed all the little things about his house that Nancy had added. An old jar filled with sprigs of honeysuckle blossoms sat on the table atop an embroidered linen, a treasure she'd found in the attic with an old sack of rags that she proudly displayed on the low parlor table. Nancy was a resourceful woman and it was clear she'd gone out of her way to make his house a home—for them.

The aromatic scents of supper reached his nose.

And then it hit him. The pantry had been empty last evening. So why was he smelling a chicken roasting? He returned Captain to the floor and his warm swath of sunshine.

Hal headed to the kitchen, surprised to find it empty. He opened the stove to see a whole chicken roasting. Beside the roasting pan was a pie tin filled with fresh spring vegetables and a fluffy loaf of cornbread in another pan. He drew in a deep breath, savoring the scents of supper —of home.

He had worked all night to get funds so that he could provide a meal for them today. And yet he was staring at a whole chicken roasting in his oven. How could that be?

"Nancy?" He called out to his wife, wanting to see her, needing, and dreading her explanation for how she'd come by the meal that was making his mouth water and his stomach howl with hunger.

Hal closed the stove door and turned to see Nancy coming in the kitchen door with a large basket heaped full of clothes in her arms. So she'd been out back taking clothes off the line when he arrived. That explained her absence, but it didn't explain the delicious smelling meal.

When she saw him her face lit up with a beautiful, beaming smile that made his knees weak.

"I didn't realize you were home," she said. "You're a bit early, aren't you?"

"I am."

"It's certainly a nice surprise, but I hope nothing is amiss," she said, lowering the basket to the floor.

"I quit early so I could go to town to pick up staples for our supper," he said, lifting a small burlap sack in his hand, "but it appears you've taken care of that task yourself."

The way her eyes shied from his made his stomach knot.

"Let me take care of this, and I'll explain over supper." She carried the basket through the parlor and into her bedchamber.

Hal let her go, but he intended to get an answer when she returned. He walked over to the sideboard and dipped his hands into a large pail of water, scrubbing with the soap until he'd removed all remnants of his day at the mill. He was drying his hands as Nancy returned to the kitchen.

"Please tell me you didn't borrow food from our neighbors for our supper?"

"Of course I didn't," she said, appearing offended by his question.

"Then how were you able to secure the items baking in the stove?"

"It's not important —"

"It *is* important, and I'd like to know. I didn't think we had any staples in the pantry," Hal said.

"We didn't," Nancy said cryptically and then went about putting supper on the table.

"You must have gone to Mary or Martha then. How else could you have come by them? Nancy, I don't want our friends thinking I can't provide for my own wife."

"I did not ask our neighbors for charity, Hal Grayson! I visited the watchmaker's shop and sold a piece of my jewelry today."

"What?" Hal felt his breath sail out as if she'd planted her small boot smack in the middle of his gut. "Why would you do such a thing?"

"Because we need to eat."

"It's my job to provide for us, Nancy." He jiggled the sack in his hand. "I've brought provisions for our supper."

"Wonderful," she said. "We can have them for our supper tomorrow night."

He felt the heat rising in his face as his embarrassment grew—what kind of man couldn't provide for his wife? Hal plopped the sack on the table, attempting to slow his pounding heartbeat. He looked at Nancy, but she stood with her chin cocked at a defiant angle. For as hard as he had been working at the mill and in his woodshop, he still couldn't adequately provide for them.

"Please don't look so shocked, Hal. Mr. Bosworth is a very nice gentleman, and he gave me a good price for my brooch."

That she had to sell her jewelry to eat struck Hal in the heart.

"I was able to get the chicken and some other staples that we need-ed," Nancy continued. "I'll get several meals from the chicken and the other items I purchased. Why, I even negotiated a good price with Squire White, so it didn't take too much of what Mr. Bosworth paid me. I still have a few coins to help keep our pantry stocked. Or for whatever you might need." Nancy pulled a few coins out of her apron pocket and placed them on the kitchen table in front of Hal's chair.

Hal barely heard her explanation through the roaring in his ears. His blood rushed through his veins, coursing hard, his head filled with anger and embarrassment. He sought to control the crash of shame sloshing in his stomach. "Never do that again, Nancy. I'll not have our neighbors and local business owners thinking that I can't provide for my own wife."

"Hal, I'm sure other women purchase and sell their jewels, and not simply because their pantries are empty. Mr. Bosworth didn't require a reason for my wanting to sell the brooch, nor did I offer one. We needed staples for the house much more than I needed that brooch."

Hal felt humiliation burn through his chest. "Well, I need to be able to hold my head up in this town, and more importantly in my own home. I'll not have you selling your jewelry, do you hear me? I'll not have the town folk gossiping about poor Hal Grayson not being able to take care of his own wife."

Rather than wilting beneath his admonishment, Nancy lifted her chin and placed her hands on her hips. "It was a discreet sale, Hal. We're in this marriage together, and I'll do whatever necessary to ensure we have food to eat. And frankly, selling my brooch is my business. It was mine to do with as I saw fit—and I saw fit for us to eat, so I sold it."

Hal's mouth fell open. In all his years he'd never seen a woman stand up to a man in such a manner. His first thought was to issue a stern reprimand and show his wife who ran the roost, but she had a right to find a way to put food in her belly. She hadn't known he would bring home staples for supper. She had sacrificed for both of them, had prepared a delicious meal for them, and all he'd done was think of himself and his own wounded pride.

"Come here," he said, drawing her into his arms. "I'm sorry I was harsh with you. I know you meant well, and supper smells so good my mouth won't stop watering, but please trust me to provide for us."

He felt her nod against his chest. "I'd never meant to hurt your pride, Hal, and I'm truly sorry that I did. But it's my job to feed us, and if my pantry is empty, I'll do whatever it takes to put together a meal. Even if that means serving something you can shingle the roof with." She leaned back, met his eyes, and gave him a soft smile. "Now please sit down and let me dish up supper before it burns."

THE FACT that her husband was working himself to a frazzle didn't sit well with Nancy. Hal was so tired at night he could barely stand, and yet he pushed himself to the point of being too tired to eat. And so she began taking lunch to her husband each day.

Hal would tell her she didn't need to interrupt her day to carry a meal to the mill for him. But she was through listening to his ridiculous protests. He was a grown man who needed to eat to keep up with the many demands on his time and body. The man needed to eat more than an apple for lunch and to take better care of himself.

Each day Hal would thank her and say he couldn't stop to eat just now. She wouldn't press him, knowing he would return home that evening with an empty lunch sack. His work was hard and demanding, but her visits seemed to lighten his burden and bring them a little closer. Spending time, however brief, with her husband provided glimpses into his mind and character.

After two weeks of delivering his lunch and being promptly chased from the mill, Nancy decided that her stubborn husband was in need of an education. A wife needed more than a roof over her head. She needed companionship.

When Nancy arrived at the mill, Hal was deeply engrossed with the waterwheel that powered the mill, and he didn't look happy.

He nodded when he saw her arrive. A quizzical look crossed his face when he saw the large basket she was carrying. Drawing a soiled handkerchief across his wet forehead, he crossed the yard to meet her. "Looks as if you brought enough for two," he said.

"I did. I thought it would be enjoyable to share a midday meal together."

"Thank you, Nancy, but I can't take the time. I've got a jam in the waterwheel that I need to fix."

"How long will that take?"

He shrugged and huffed out a breath. "I don't know. I've been at it since first thing this morning, and I can't loosen the jam."

"Perhaps I can help?"

He shook his head. "I have a snarl of timber jammed in the waterwheel, and it caused the saw blade to bind in another piece of timber."

"I'm quite adept at problem solving," she said, smiling up at him. "I unravel thread all the time."

"This isn't thread, Nancy." He shoved his fingers into his hair and sighed. "This isn't woman's work."

"Then you need to focus on something else and let your mind rest. After a good lunch, you'll be refreshed and see everything in a new light."

"I can't—"

"Hal Grayson!" The crack of her voice commanded his full attention. "You need to sit down, eat lunch, and rest your back for a few minutes. I'll not accept any excuses today. That oak timber poking above the other logs is your problem and it's as plain as the nose on your face, but you can't see it because you're tired and hungry." She thrust the basket into his dirty hands. "That spot of shade beneath the maple will make a lovely picnic area. Surely you can give your wife fifteen minutes of your day?"

For a minute she thought she'd gone too far, but in the face of his scowl she merely raised her chin. Her husband was ready to drop from fatigue, and someone needed to drive some sense into his hard head.

"Do I smell roast pork in here?" he asked, nodding at the basket in his hands.

Her mouth fell open in surprise. She'd expected him to express his displeasure or perhaps even reprimand her, but his empty stomach must have taken the reins and directed his thoughts straight to the source of the food. "I... yes, I brought leftovers from our supper last evening."

"Since you went to the trouble to carry this heavy basket all the way here, I'll take time to eat."

Nancy bit her lip to ward off a smile. She hadn't meant to be demanding or to bribe him with food, but now that she knew where her leverage lay, she tucked the information away in the event her husband insisted on being difficult again.

Hal spread the threadbare tablecloth on the grass, and she sat the basket between them. As Nancy unpacked a small dish laden with moist pork roast and added thick slices of bread to their plates, Hal studied the mill. The longer he looked the deeper his scowl grew.

Finally, she shook her head and sighed. "You're like a dog with a bone, Hal Grayson. Sometimes the best thing you can do is step away from a perplexing problem so that when you return you can see it in a different light."

"Perhaps," he said, but his gaze and his thoughts remained on the mill.

"Did I mention that I once raced my father's thoroughbred?" she asked, casually taking a sip of cold water from the jar she'd brought along.

That statement got Hal's full attention. A sheepish look crossed his face and he said, "I'm sorry, Nancy, I was preoccupied and fear I wasn't listening. I believe you said something about your father buying you a horse?"

"No, Hal. I said I raced one of his thoroughbreds."

He laughed. "You've made your point, Nancy. I'm properly chastised for not listening. You don't have to shock me to get my attention. "

"I'm utterly serious," she said, delighting in his surprise.

His eyebrow quirked, a habit of his that she was growing fond of. "*You* raced a horse?"

"I was fourteen and frustrated with my father continually telling me this is a man's world. No matter what I wanted to do he would tell me it wasn't proper for a woman. Daddy and I crossed words every day. I would say *I want,* and he would say *you can't.*" Those tiresome memories agitated her and straightened her spine. "One day I decided to show him that he was wrong about a woman's place. I borrowed clothes from my cousin Joseph and hoodwinked my father—and the man who was interested in buying a pair of my father's best thoroughbreds—into believing me a boy."

Plate forgotten in his lap, Hal seemed completely captivated by her story. A breeze ruffled the tree leaves and tossed a lock of his hair across his forehead, but he didn't seem to notice.

Delighted by his full attention, Nancy continued her story. "I spent time in our stables every day. I knew everything about our horses. I rode like a proper lady within sight of the house, but the moment I was out of sight I rode like a boy chasing the wind." She sighed and leaned back on her hands. "I loved riding, but I was forbidden to ride Maverick and Renegade. So I forced Joseph to loan me some clothes and let me ride Maverick that day." The memory made her smile. "It was a moment I'll not forget."

"I'm dying from suspense," Hal said, a mix of dread and eager anticipation on his face. "Do tell."

His reaction made Nancy laugh. She faced him and leaned in as if sharing a secret, loving their unexpected moment of connection. "Joseph was supposed to show each horse individually; to race him from the stable to the creek at the far edge of the meadow and back through a series of jumps. But we took the horses out together and oh my..." A fit of girlish giggles overtook her for a moment, and she covered her mouth to stop them. "Maverick and Renegade seldom got the chance to test their skill against each other, but Joseph and I had ridden together many times. We were thick as mud and had many adventures out of eyesight of the stables. I wasn't riding my gentle mare, though, and I felt the difference in Maverick's powerful stride. Joseph and I were as eager as the horses, and so we abandoned all good sense and raced like the wind across the meadow." She clasped her hands in front of her heart, now beating hard from the memory. "I'll never know how I kept Joseph's cap on my head because we fairly flew over the jumps. We arrived in a flurry of flashing hooves and wild laughter. When my father realized it was me sitting astride his favorite horse, he was nearly apoplectic."

Disbelief filled Hal's eyes. "You're going to tell me this is a tall tale intended to distract me, right?"

Grinning and thrilled with her husband's attention, Nancy shook her head. "At the risk of horrifying you, I must admit it's true. Mr. Hewitt was so taken with the horses and our race that he never noticed he was addressing a girl. My father was livid, but he didn't expose me. Hewitt spent several minutes inspecting the horses and asking us how they handled and other questions that Joseph and I readily answered. In all that time, the poor man never caught on to my deception, but Daddy was seething."

Hal stared at her in stunned fascination. "I don't know you at all, Nancy."

"You know all you need to know."

"Not true," he said, smiling. "I need to know what happened when your father got you home."

Nancy laughed. "He took me to the library and roundly chastised me for pulling such a dangerous prank."

"I'll bet he did. What did your mother think of your exploit?"

The heavy weight of sadness filled Nancy's chest and her smile faltered. "He didn't tell her. Daddy always protected me even when I deserved to be punished."

"So you didn't get disciplined for your daring stunt?"

She smiled and shook her head. "No. Daddy thanked me for selling his horses."

Rich laughter burst from Hal. "Is this tomfoolery what I'm in for with you?"

"Not if you don't challenge me."

Hal laughed again and shook his head as if he didn't know whether to admire or fear her.

They lounged beneath the tree and ate their lunch. Hal finished off the pork and two slices of bread. When Nancy retrieved a piece of mince pie from the basket, he raised his eyebrows.

"While you eat this, tell me about your family," she said. "Do you have any sisters?"

"Yes," he said around a mouthful of pie.

"Older or younger?"

"Both." After swallowing, he told her he had six siblings including

John Radford. A cloud seemed to darken his eyes, and he stared off toward the mill. Nancy waited, knowing he needed a moment, but hoping he would share something of himself today. She'd seen the haunted look in his eyes each time John's name was mentioned, and she knew Hal was deeply wounded by his brother's death.

But instead sharing his heartache, Hal sat upright, eyes squinted and fixed on the oak timber. "That's it!" He glanced at Nancy. "I've figured out how to remove the log jam. You were right about the oak timber."

"I don't want to say I told you so, but..." She shrugged one shoulder to help keep the mood light.

"But you did." He leaned over and pressed his warm lips to her cheek. "Thank you for an utterly intriguing afternoon."

His kiss surprised her. She'd only been kissed once, on her wedding day, by Hal. She had never shared a picnic blanket with a man. She had no experience in romance, but she knew she loved the feel of her husband's lips and the new closeness she felt with him.

That feeling of warmth, the prickle of his whiskers and his lips against her cheek, stayed with her for days... and haunted her for many lonely nights.

CHAPTER FIFTEEN

Each evening, immediately before or after supper, Hal sat at the kitchen table and retrieved a dirty scrap of paper from his pocket. He would spend several minutes, and sometimes much longer, transferring numbers to a worn ledger he kept on a shelf in the kitchen.

Nancy finished cleaning up supper dishes and then sat across from him, seeming to be waiting for him to finish. But he had several entries to make, so he looked up to let her know he would be a while.

"What is it that's making you frown so?" she asked, concern in her dark eyes.

"I'm trying to recall how long it took me to sand those spindles, and I'm also recording the number of board feet of oak, pine, cherry and other woods that I sawed today," he'd answered, but his mind was still preoccupied with trying to determine if recording the information was of any value, or if it was just one more burden on his time.

Nancy sighed. "I'd hoped for a few minutes of conversation before you head to the barn."

"What would you like to talk about?" he asked, feeling impatient to get back to his ledger. The crackling sound of the stove cooling seemed to keep time with the tapping of his pencil upon the wooden tabletop.

"You must have sawed an awful lot of trees today because you've been working on your ledger for nearly an hour now."

"I have?" He glanced at his pocket watch and frowned. He released a hard sigh. "I thought that noting the time and process involved for building the furniture I'm making for A. B. Edwards would help me determine which items yield the most profit, but it seems I'm wasting more time on my notes than the effort is worth."

"Not if I help you," Nancy said. "Keeping books is something for which I'm most qualified."

"I've no doubt you are," he said, "but you can't record what's only in my mind."

"I can if you tell me what to put down."

"Then I might as well record it myself." He tossed the pencil onto the table and leaned back in his chair, his eyes burning with fatigue.

"What if I joined you in the barn tonight? If you dictate to me while you're working, you can accomplish two things at once. And I won't be spending another evening alone."

For a minute Hal thought to immediately reject her offer, but to his surprise her idea had merit. He passed the dirty scrap of paper to her. "If you're certain you want to keep my ledger, then you'll need to know what my abbreviations mean." With the tip of his pencil he tapped the first line that read O–84–#1C. "That means I sawed eighty-four board feet of oak with a grade number of One Common." He moved the pencil tip to the second line that read WP–128–SM. "This means I sawed one-hundred-twenty-eight board feet of white pine graded as Select Merchantable."

Nancy groaned and wrinkled her nose, a reaction so adorable Hal nearly kissed her.

She said, "I think I can manage your abbreviations for the type of wood and the number of board feet you sawed, but I'll need to make a list of your abbreviations for these grading equivalents."

"All right," he said, but the whole while his eyes were drinking her in, absorbing every detail of her creamy skin, her flushed cheeks, the fringe of dark lashes around her eyes. "I'm afraid that will have to wait until tomorrow night, though," he said, getting to his feet. "I need to get out to the shop and work on that cabinet, or it'll take me another week to finish it."

Nancy scooped up the paper, ledger, and pencil and said, "I'll come with you. You can share your abbreviations and other information with me, and I'll record it all while you work."

He arched an eyebrow at her. "Isn't it getting a bit late for you? I thought you'd prefer to relax in the parlor for a while before turning in."

"I'd rather spend the time with you." Her forthright statement surprised him.

"Are you certain, Nancy?"

"Yes." Her wide eyes seemed to beseech him. "I enjoy spending time with you and I'm more than capable of tending your ledger, so I'd like to come along if you don't mind the company."

A half-smile tilted his lips. "I don't mind at all," he said, and gestured for her to precede him from the kitchen.

And so they went together to the barn where Nancy set up a makeshift desk using one end of Hal's workbench and a wooden staved milk churn for a seat. Hal playfully scoffed at her ingenuity, and she countered that she could be quite creative when necessary.

"I see that," he said, giving her a tired smile. "You never cease to surprise me, Nancy." And it was true. She was such a fascinating mix of grit and tenderness, of demanding and giving, that she'd kept him in a spin since her arrival.

For a moment their eyes held, hers filled with curiosity and warmth.

"I hope I always surprise you," she said, her voice quiet.

Captured by the dark depths of her gaze, Hal forgot himself and slid his palms up her forearms, drawing her close.

NANCY HELD her breath in anticipation. She wanted her husband to kiss her. She wanted to shock him awake and please him and make him laugh and forget that he hadn't chosen her... that he hadn't fallen in love with her... that everything, including love, was possible between them.

But instead of kissing her, he sighed and stepped away. "You also distract me to no end," he said, his own voice quiet. "I suspect I'll get far less done with you here."

"But you'll also get your ledger updated." She offered a half-smile to disguise her disappointment.

"That is one benefit," he agreed with a laugh.

"I would hope that spending time together would be another benefit," she said, her face heating at her boldness.

One dark eyebrow arched above his golden gaze, but he seemed amused rather than shocked. "Any time with you is a benefit, Nancy." A look of amusement crossed his face, and he gestured to her makeshift desk. "You have apparently chosen to use Captain's bed for a desk."

Confused, Nancy glanced behind her and saw Captain sprawled across the worktable sniffing at the leather ledger. "Hello, sweetheart," she said, reaching out to stroke Captain's furry head. "Were you trying to sneak up on me?"

The cat ignored her, making them laugh.

"Typical," Nancy said.

"You're getting more of a welcome than I've received," he said. "At least Captain's fascination with the ledger explains why I'm finding cat hair on my tools."

"Perhaps he wants to help."

"If that's the case, he can help by staying off my workbench." Hal leaned in, reached past her shoulder, and retrieved a cloth from the workbench. "If I don't work, we don't eat. And Captain has made it clear we have another mouth to feed."

He was jesting about feeding the cat, of course, because they had both fallen in love with the furry little rascal who was picking his way across Hal's tools. But the thought of having another mouth to feed—a *baby's* mouth—sent a warm rush through Nancy's chest. They would make a fine family indeed.

"What are all these things?" she asked, gesturing to numerous tools hanging from pegs on a rough wood wall above Hal's bench.

"It's everything I need for building furniture." He lifted a chisel and told her it was a socket chisel.

And then he gave Nancy his abbreviations for grading lumber, and she made a reference list in his journal. As he worked, Nancy took notes, documenting his process, time and expense related to each piece of furniture he had recently built for Edwards. With each new tool Hal used, he gave Nancy a quick education. She learned about joining tools like a smoothing plane and a Tenon saw. Hal had other furniture-making tools, too: a compass saw and a keyhole saw and pinchers and awls and augers and gimlets and gouges, and a multitude of chisels she couldn't remember the names of, as well as levels and mallets and an axe-like tool he called an adze either hanging on the wall or stored in drawers and crates.

Her poor mind was awhirl, but her heart was soaring. Hal was working hard, but he seemed to be enjoying their time together as much as she was. He was playful with his instruction and had even pretended to use one of his gouges on her side, tickling her and making squirm away in a fit of laughter. It was as if here in the cozy wood-scented workroom, he could shut out the world and allow his grieving heart a moment of lightness.

Even Captain seemed to sense a difference in Hal because the little rascal kept swatting playfully at Hal's hand each time he reached for a tool. Hal's amused chuckle warmed Nancy's heart. He threatened to banish Captain from the barn, but she knew he wouldn't.

In the face of Hal's threat, Captain just yawned and stretched his lithe body across Hal's chisels.

Hal turned to her, shaking his head in amazement. "Are you giving him lessons on how to distract me?"

She laughed. "Although I'm in awe and rightly proud of Captain, I can't claim any credit for his behavior."

The evening flew by with Hal working and Nancy taking notes and the two of them talking about safe subjects like his work and her garden and the aloof and disdainful Captain.

The evening grew late, and Hal stretched his back for a final time. He laid his tools on the bench and turned and cupped his palms beneath Nancy's elbows, bringing her to her feet—and the two of them face to face.

Nancy's breath caught, and she barely moved. Would he kiss her after all?

He smiled a tired smile and gazed down at her, a new warm and tender look in his eyes. "Thank you for all your help and for making an evening of work feel like an evening of play." He lowered his head then... and Nancy held her breath in anticipation.

His lips pressed to her cheek, warm and tender. His hair tickled her nose and smelled of fresh air and wood shavings. "Goodnight, Nancy. I'll be in shortly," he said, stepping away.

For a moment she stared in stunned disappointment. She ached to feel the comforting warmth of his arms and the tender connection she'd felt blooming between them.

But she walked through the chilly evening alone.

She entered her new home alone.

She went to bed...alone.

CHAPTER SIXTEEN

J uly sunshine warmed Nancy's shoulders, but she felt chilled and
heavy-hearted as she and Hal walked home after Sunday morning
service. The Tuckers had invited them to stop in for tea, but
Nancy pleaded a headache because... well, she felt lonely and miserably homesick.

It had been well over a month since she'd last seen or confided in
her sister or felt her mother's warm hug or heard her father's amused
chuckle during one of their lively debates. Her father had delighted in
her spirit... and she had delighted in his adoration. Leaving her family
had cut deep into her heart, and the bleeding was growing more
profuse and more painful by the day.

"Shall we walk a bit farther?" Hal asked, giving her arm a light pat
as if to draw her thoughts back to the present. "I need to retrieve my
tally sheet from the mill. Won't take but a minute."

She struggled to dredge up a smile. "You go on without me. I need
to change. It's getting warm, and I don't want to soil my dress."

"All right then, I'll return shortly," he said, leaving her at the end of
their driveway.

She watched him continue out Liberty Street, his long legs quickly eating the distance. Would he return shortly as promised? Or would he get caught up in some project or another and leave her home alone?

Sighing, she went inside. After slaking her thirst with a small glass of water, she wandered into her bedroom to change. Unmindful of the open door, she stood in her corset, chemise, and drawers, looking around the barren room, feeling wretchedly alone. Although Hal had been more attentive and kind of late, she still spent the majority of her days and nights alone.

Nancy tossed her dress onto the bed. If only her sister were here, they would share lively conversations and would laugh until their cheeks and stomachs hurt. But this coming Saturday, for the first time in their lives, she and Elizabeth would celebrate their seventeenth birthday without each other. That day had always been met with joy and celebration by their parents, and by them. Memories of the many girlish talks and youthful dreams she and Elizabeth had shared brought a smile to Nancy's lips.

And then they made her cry.

With her face in hands, Nancy wept, recalling her last glimpse of home. She had left to spare her sister a lifetime of heartache and herself an unbearable marriage, but her own heart bled, and she longed for a pair of comforting arms to hold her.

Hal's concerned voice came from the open doorway. "Nancy? Are you all right?"

She spun to face him, shocked to find him home, embarrassed to be caught with tears soaking her face. Unable to speak, she turned her back to him and bit down on her lip.

"Are you in pain? Shall I fetch a doctor?"

"I'm fine," she said, but her voice wobbled, and she wasn't at all fine.

Ignoring her state of undress, he strode into the room as if they were a real married couple. He pulled her into his arms and held her tight. "You're terrifying me, Nancy. Are you ailing?"

The arms she'd longed for were her husband's, and they felt strong and capable and exactly right as he held her against him. His firm chest was wonderfully warm against her cheek. Fresh air and soap scented his neck and collar. For a moment, she simply held onto to him, needing his tenderness and supportive embrace, needing to know she wasn't alone and unwanted.

"You're trembling," he said, his breath warm against her ear. "What troubles you, darling?"

For an instant, she thought to say something inane or to blame her upset on a headache, but doing so would push him away. And she desperately needed the moment of intimacy, and so she told him the truth. "I'm homesick," she whispered, loathing herself for her momentary weakness. "And I'm angry with my father. I know I'm being ridiculous, but I can't seem to get hold of my emotions today. I'm sorry."

"No, Nancy, *I'm* sorry," he said, and she could hear regret in his apology. "I've been so wrapped up in my own troubles I haven't given a thought to how difficult all of this must be for you. Of course you miss your family. I miss mine, too, and I should have been more considerate of your feelings."

She leaned back in his arms and met his eyes. "Of course you understand because... Oh, Hal, I'm so sorry. I'd never met John Radford so he's not often at the forefront of my mind, but I know his absence weighs heavily on your heart. I feel positively selfish indulging in my own small discomforts while you're soldiering on so bravely."

Hal's jaw clamped, his eyes dark pools of grief. "That doesn't mean you're not entitled to your feelings as well, Nancy."

"I'm being childish," she whispered. She suddenly realized her state of undress and the inappropriateness of conversing in her undergarments. Face burning, she stepped away. "I'm acting like a foolish girl and being wholly inappropriate." She crossed her arms over her chest. "I need to dress."

"Being homesick doesn't mean you're being childish." Instead of leaving the room, he pulled a quilt off the bed and draped it around her shoulders. "Could any of those tears in your eyes be for Stuart Newmaine?" he asked, shocking her with his question and the change of subject. "Do you miss him?"

"What? No," she said with certainty. "I had no feelings for him whatsoever."

He cocked his head and studied her. "Then you're not crying over another man?"

She opened her mouth to assure him that, no, she wasn't weeping for another man, but as the truth dawned, a new surge of emotion flooded her eyes with tears. Her father had betrayed her trust, and that betrayal lay at the root of everything. Horrified by another flood of tears, she clapped her hand over her mouth.

For the second time, Hal drew her into his comforting embrace. This time, however, he simply held her and let her pour out her heartache. She told him how she and her father would debate every-thing from how to best set up an account ledger to what a woman's proper place was in the world. She challenged him at every turn, raising his blood pressure one minute and reducing him to belly laughter the next. He spoiled her and indulged her every request—until the day she asked to be released from her arranged courtship and ulti-mate marriage to Stuart Newmaine.

"He wouldn't hear of it," Nancy said, wiping her eyes. "I couldn't tell him that Stuart and Elizabeth had been stealing time alone each Tuesday afternoon when Stuart met with my father. He would have forbidden Stuart to call again, and it would have broken Elizabeth's heart. So I told him I didn't love Stuart and debated with him about the logic of the arrangement and pleaded and pushed my father to acqui-esce. But all I succeeded at was pushing him to the limits of his patience. He grew so vexed with me he forbade me to speak to him again until I could mind my tongue."

"I'm sure that hurt you deeply," Hal said.

The painful memory left her shaking her head in confusion. "It doesn't make sense why he would be so protective and indulgent all my life and then refuse me the thing I wanted most. I know that sounds childish, but it wasn't the fact that he wouldn't give in to my demands that upset me. It's that he couldn't see that he was breaking my heart by pushing me into a relationship I didn't want. Even Mother intervened on my behalf, but he claimed I was young and dramatic and would soon see that Mr. Newmaine was the perfect man for me. That's when I realized Daddy couldn't be moved off his position on the subject, and I was honestly stunned. It was the first time my father had refused me anything. I know it's selfish of me, but I felt betrayed that day. His refusal to end what could only become a disaster on all fronts forced me to leave a home and family I love." She bit her lip. "That's why I feel betrayed and angry and... homesick."

"I've been a selfish fool," Hal said, drawing his hands down her forearms to clasp her hands in his. "I've been so wrapped up in my own troubles I've been blind to your struggle. I'm sorry, Nancy." He drew her against him and gave her a gentle hug. "Truly, I apologize. I'm usually a better man than I've been."

She wanted to stay in Hal's arms forever, but she heard his stomach growl... and she had already said too much. Hal had his own troubles and didn't need to be burdened with hers. And she didn't need him to start asking questions she couldn't answer. Lifting her chin, she stepped away and clutched the quilt around her shoulders. "Let's forget about apologies and tears for the day, and I'll get dressed and prepare our lunch."

"I have a better suggestion. Put on a walking dress. I have something I want to show you." In two strides he was at the door. "I'll fetch some of the cold chicken and biscuits we had for supper, and we can take our lunch with us. I know the perfect spot to eat." With that, he was gone.

CHAPTER SEVENTEEN

As Hal guided Nancy across a worn path through the grassy field behind their house, his mind was in turmoil. He was worried about her and the secrets she was keeping. He knew there was something she wasn't sharing with him, but was she keeping it to herself because she wasn't yet comfortable with him? Or because it was something too terrible to share?

That thought bothered him more than he wanted to admit.

But Nancy's heartache wasn't the only issue burdening Hal's mind on what was otherwise a beautiful summer day. He couldn't afford to sacrifice desperately needed work hours to take a walk, no matter how blue the sky or how refreshing the breeze. It was Sunday and he knew shouldn't be working today, but the hard truth was if he didn't work every day, he couldn't put food on the table. That thought made him think about his recent conversation with Thomas Drake, who was pressing Hal to lease his sawmill out for a year.

Leasing the mill to Drake would be an intelligent solution to the overwhelming load of work that burdened Hal's mind and body nearly every minute of every day. Drake was willing to pay a healthy fee to lease the mill for twelve months. Hal wasn't even making that much running the mill, mostly because he was doing it alone.

Hal had never wanted to own or run a sawmill—that was John Radford's dream. And yet Hal found himself doing just that, and all the while his dream of building furniture was getting buried beneath the burden of the mill. He finally understood his father's struggle as the desire to work on his craft continued to be supplanted by the needs of the mill and providing for his family. Leasing the mill to Drake would provide enough monthly income to allow Hal to focus on building furniture and a life with his wife. It would be a wise decision.

But the thought of turning the mill over to anyone twisted Hal's gut. He'd promised John Radford they would build a successful mill together. For Hal to consider abandoning that dream, for even a brief time, was like abandoning his brother and killing the memory of their shared dream.

He couldn't do it.

"You're awfully deep in thought," Nancy remarked, startling him out of the basement of his mind where he'd been rooting around for answers that just weren't there.

Her puffy, red eyes tugged at his heart, and he felt ashamed that his thoughts had drifted to other matters when he needed to be attentive to his wife.

Her hand still trembled slightly in the crook of his arm and told him he needed to be here physically and mentally with her. She'd done so much for him, supported him all these many weeks. And today she needed him. So he would lay aside all else and give her a day to remember. She deserved that much.

Adjusting the picnic basket on his arm, he said, "You can blame this path for carrying my thoughts away. Seems every time I walk this field, I end up on the other side wondering how I got there."

Her smile pleased him and made him feel as if he'd done something good for her. "It's easy to understand how one can get lost in thought here. It's so peaceful," she said.

It was peaceful, and they both seemed to enjoy listening to the twitter and chirping of the birds, the buzzing of bumble bees dipping into clusters of beebalm and wild chives that grew in the field.

Hal drew in a deep breath and exhaled slowly, feeling his tight shoulders unlock. The deep, vibrant green grasses of the pasture behind his home gave way to the shaded deep greens and browns of the woods. They walked a wooded path that led along the steep bank of Canadaway Creek. Birdsong mingled with the burbling sounds of the creek. Periodic yelping of a distant fox interrupted from time to time. A rustling in the underbrush along the creek betrayed the presence of a wayward raccoon or some other creature trying to remain hidden.

Hal and Nancy continued their walk in companionable silence. He couldn't help but smile at that thought—they were companions. His life had certainly been upended by Nancy's arrival.

The bright blue sky was now muted by tree branches heavily covered with their full summer leaves. Splotches of sunlight danced on the hard dirt beneath their feet.

"Step carefully, Nancy," he cautioned, gesturing toward the jutting tree roots growing across the path.

She lifted her skirt a little higher and gracefully stepped over them.

At times, he would reach out and place a supportive hand on Nancy's elbow or a guiding hand on the small of her back. He found himself relishing the opportunity to touch his wife, even in these little ways. Despite her starch and backbone, she was a gentle and compassionate woman, and to see her in tears had torn at his heart. He understood her homesickness and wished he could take away her heartache. He was sorry for her pain, but he was secretly relieved to know that her tears hadn't been for a love she'd left back home.

"Gracious, how I've missed walking through grassy fields and pine-scented woods," she said. "I haven't taken such a walk in months."

Despite her earlier tears, however, Nancy's heart seemed lighter. Her steps beside him were lively as if the walk was rejuvenating her spirits as it always did his. Perhaps the setting calmed her as much as it did him. She seemed content not to talk much as they walked, a quality he appreciated today while his mind was burdened with problems. He wasn't an overly talkative man himself and appreciated that Nancy recognized it was simply his way and that it bore no reflection on her company.

"This is such a treat today. It's just so lovely here," he heard Nancy say, her voice barely above a whisper.

Hal smiled down at her. He had thought the walk would sooth her heartache and was pleased that she was taking as much comfort from the jaunt as he was. "In the months I've lived here, I've walked all over this town, and this is one of my favorite places."

"I can understand why. I hope you don't mind sharing it with me."

He looked down and was rewarded with her smile. "I'm honored, Nancy."

They walked a few moments longer, each enjoying the setting and the leisure to drift in their own thoughts a while.

"The path from here on is a bit more treacherous, I'm afraid," Hal said, "but I assure you that it's worth the trip down the bank."

"It's not the first time I've climbed a bank or played in a creek, Mr. Grayson."

The playful taunt in her voice made him laugh. He was glad to see his wife coming back to her more vivacious self. "I'm sure you're quite adept, Nancy, but I suspect you'll appreciate my assistance in a spot or two nonetheless." He stepped forward and extended his hand to her. "This is one of those particular places." The path was narrow with a hill on one side and a drop into the gorge on the other. Tree roots jutted up like knuckles with their fingertips sticking out of the bank and hanging over the creek.

"Well, you were accurate on this count," she said, placing her hand in his. "I'll gladly accept your assistance."

Her hand, so small and warm, made his heart do a crazy somersault in his chest. How could her small hands carry so much? How could this petite lady create such disruption in his life—and more importantly in his heart?

The thought circled his mind as they traversed another twenty feet or so of the narrow path that took them deeper into the gorge. The path leveled out again, but only when they reached an outcropping of rocks that created a natural shelf above the babbling creek did he release her hand.

"I'm going to start down this shelf of rocks, and then I'll help you down." Hal stepped quickly down three of the natural steps formed by the rock formation. Loose shale and stones spattered the small beach at the edge of the creek. As soon as he got his footing on the lowest rock, he placed the picnic basket aside and then turned to assist Nancy. Nancy gripped his hand and tried to navigate the steps, but as he watched her do so in her flowing skirts and heeled boots, his heart leap in his chest. He and John had both lost their footing and slid down the rocks on more than one occasion before they'd successfully learned how to navigate them.

Nancy made the same mistake he and John had made. She moved too slowly, which allowed the rocks to slide and carry her straight toward the edge.

Knowing she was about to fall, Hal grasped her waist and lifted her off the cliff. The added weight made the shale debris beneath his feet shift. Loose rocks and shale gave way and he slid backward down the bank. He pulled Nancy against him, back-peddling with both feet, trying to keep them upright. Instead, he found himself stepping backward into thin air and then landing hard on his feet in the creek.

Momentum kept him moving backward, but keeping his footing on the rocky creek bed was impossible.

Nancy's shriek startled the birds as they both went tumbling into Canadaway Creek.

He wrapped his arms around her and twisted his body so that he landed on his back, buffering most of her fall with his body. Water splashed up like a geyser on both sides, thoroughly drenching them. He felt a shock of pain as his elbow struck the shallow creek bed.

Nancy gasped in shock.

Hal pushed himself up on his injured elbow and steadied Nancy with his free arm, attempting to keep her from rolling off and falling deeper into the water. His backside and throbbing elbow rested on the rocky creek bed, and his knees jutted up out of the water on either side of Nancy's hips.

"Are you all right?" he asked, mortified that he failed to get her safely down the bank, and worse, that he hauled her into the creek.

Water dripped down her face. Her chignon hung sideways with sections of wet curls that had sprung loose from the fall. Small droplets clung to her dark eyelashes, framing large brown eyes filled with surprise and... intense awareness.

Hal's heart pounded from the unexpected fall and from being face to face, body to body with his beautiful bride. Crystal clear water flowed over them. Birdsong filled the gorge. Blue sky and sunshine created a beautiful canopy above them, but Hal's eyes were filled with Nancy. With her beautiful face. With her pink lips parted in surprise. With the fact that he simply could not resist her.

He slid his free hand up to cup her head, and he kissed her.

He tasted creek water on her lips and smelled flowers in her hair and he forgot where they were and the circumstances that brought them to this moment. They were simply a man and a woman experiencing their first kiss with each other.

The rushing water nudged them as if it wanted to tumble them downstream like fallen timber. It saturated Nancy's skirts and tugged her away, breaking the kiss and ending the moment. But his eyes locked with hers, and he saw warmth and love in his wife's eyes—and he wanted to see that look again. Now. Forever.

But the creek had other ideas, and it fought to separate them.

Sitting up, Hal gently lifted her off him and helped his wife to her feet. The water swirled Nancy's wet skirts around her knees, rocking her off balance. He leaned down and lifted her, cradling her in his arms as he carried her out of the creek. "Are you all right?" he asked, setting her on her feet on the loamy shore of the creek.

She smiled. "Yes, but I must confess that this is not what I expected when you suggested a walk."

"I'm terribly sorry, Nancy."

"I'm not." She released a warm laugh. "Truly, I haven't been this surprised or experienced such an adventure in far too long. And despite being thoroughly soaked, I must confess that the cool water on this warm day felt divine." As if the absurdity of their fall into the creek was dawning fully in her mind, her shoulders began to shake, and then tears of laughter began to wet her cheeks. "Gracious, Hal! I can't believe we actually fell in the creek!"

Hal laughed, too. He felt a fool for losing his footing and hauling them into the creek, but the accident brought an unexpected moment of romance to their marriage and tears of joy to his wife. That was worth the damage to his pride. "Are you sure you're all right?" he asked again.

"I do believe I banged my knee, but I'm otherwise unbroken. But look at you, you've torn your shirt and your elbow is bleeding." Her expression shifted to one of concern as she leaned down to inspect his elbow.

Hal bent his forearm and angled his elbow, trying to see the damage. The sharp pain he'd felt when he hit bottom had been quickly forgotten in his concern for Nancy, and then he'd forgotten everything during their kiss. But it appeared he did indeed have a rip in his shirt sleeve and a spot of blood staining the fabric.

"Let me look," Nancy said, pushing up his sleeve. She had to work it over his elbow to expose a long scrape across his forearm. "Well, you've got a nice sized scrape here, but the good news is that you'll survive the trip home."

Hal hadn't expected anything more than a scraped forearm, but he knew Nancy would need to appease her curiosity, and so he let her inspect the damage. "I guess we're both a little worse for wear. I hope you'll forgive me for pulling you into the creek with me." He surveyed Nancy's dress, soaked with water, the skirt covered with particles of sand and smudges of dirt. "I hope I haven't ruined your dress."

"Falling in the creek was completely my doing," Nancy said, as she twisted at the waist, moving her skirt back and forth to access the damage. By the time she'd finished, she'd turned a full circle.

Hal laughed. "You look like Captain chasing his tail."

"Very funny, Mr. Grayson. Frankly I find it quite adorable when he does that."

She was adorable.

Hal resisted the temptation to pull them both back into the creek, if only to see her laugh again. He loved the sound of her laugh, the flash of her pretty white teeth, the spark that lit her eyes—and he liked that he was able to make her laugh, even unintentionally.

"Shall I take you home to change?" he asked.

She glanced at him as if he'd just said the most foolish thing. "I'm perfectly content, unless you wish to return home to change *your* clothes."

"Not at all. I was simply thinking of your comfort."

"I haven't felt this refreshed all day. I might just take to wetting my gowns on hot days."

Hal laughed. "Not a bad idea on the whole. All right then, if you're sure you wish to continue, there's a nice spot to picnic just up ahead."

"Wonderful, but I do hope there are no more banks to traverse."

"Just a flat beach and a few stepping-stones to cross."

"That I can manage," she said, hiking her sopping skirt and squeezing the water out of it.

Hal got an unexpected glimpse of her lovely legs that nearly stopped his heart. His first thought was that he should turn away to afford her privacy. Hard on the heels of that thought, his brain presented him a simple and most treasured fact—Nancy was his *wife*. He didn't need to turn away.

But he did so anyhow because she did deserve his respect and consideration.

Still, as he stood there listening to water splatter the stones around Nancy's feet, the image of her shapely legs imprinted itself in his mind.

"Shall we go then?" she asked. "I'll fix my hair once we're settled."

Hal retrieved the basket he'd thankfully set aside before they had tumbled into the creek. Arm in arm, they picked their way along the narrow rocky shore of the creek until the beach ended. "We can picnic here or use those stones to cross to the other side and get closer to the falls."

"Oh, let's go to the falls." Nancy hiked her skirt and started to step with her left foot.

Hal caught her arm and held her back. "If you start with your right foot, you'll be able to cross over without as much trouble."

Instead of questioning him, Nancy eyed the stones for herself. After a couple of seconds, she said, "You're right. I can see how they're laid out. Did you put these huge rocks here?"

"It would take a team of horses to move one of those stones. I've just crossed them often enough to know the best method."

She smiled up at him, her eyes sparkling with happiness. "I do like the way your mind works, Mr. Grayson."

Hal grinned at her preference for calling him *Mr. Grayson* during their playful banter with each other. She was such an intriguing mix of sweet and sassy that he couldn't take his eyes off her.

"Here I go then." She stepped out onto the first large rock, the easiest of all of them to navigate. "If I fall in, please fish me out before the creek carries me too far downstream."

"I shall do my best, darling."

"Are you distracting me on purpose?" she called over her shoulder, laughing as she fought for balance. What was an easy step for his long legs was a step-and-a-half for Nancy. She had to leap to cover the distance to the next rock and nearly missed it altogether.

"Nancy, watch your step."

"Then save your endearments until my feet are firmly on the ground, Mr. Grayson. You distract me too easily already."

He did? She was distracted by *him*? Why? Did she like being called his *darling*?

Hal's heartbeat thundered in his chest as he stared in wonder at his beautiful wife picking her way across the stepping-stones. *He* distracted her?

The thought was preposterous and... utterly fascinating.

Nancy leapt onto the opposite shore and turned toward Hal,

shading her eyes. "Are you joining me, or was this your plan so you wouldn't have to share the lunch in your basket?"

He laughed, enjoying her sense of humor. Hal pretended to dig in the basket as if he was indeed going to devour the meal himself.

Nancy's light laughter echoed through the gorge. The sound filled his ears and warmed his heart and fed a place in his soul that had been begging for sustenance. Hal just hadn't known what it needed until meeting Miss Nancy Mitchell. He needed *her*.

And more importantly, he *wanted* her in his life.

The realization fueled his desire to be the kind of man she wanted in return. He had little to give financially, but he could please her and make her laugh and bring her joy. He could court her properly and give their marriage his best effort. Perhaps that would be enough to win Nancy's heart.

With that in mind, Hal made quick work crossing the stepping-stones. "The falls are just around the bend," he said, offering his arm.

"Good," she said, glancing down at her feet. "My boots are squishing in a most uncomfortable manner. I should like to dispense with them, but I don't want to shock you."

He glanced down to see the teasing glint in her eyes. "I'm afraid the shock would be to your delicate feet. These stones can be sharp."

When they reached the falls, Hal spread their blanket on the shore beside a large pool of water at the base of the falls.

Nancy stood gazing at large slabs of rock from the gorge walls that had fallen into the creek and created the small but beautiful waterfalls. "Nature creates such magnificent art," she said, quietly.

Hal looked at his wife, magnificent in her own right, and said, "I agree." He placed the basket on the blanket. "Come and sit. You should take your shoes off so that they can dry a little while we're here. I do believe I've still got half of Canadaway Creek in mine."

"With the size of your boots, I might believe it."

"I suppose I deserve that for hauling you into the creek," he said, and helped his sassy wife sit on the blanket. As they exchanged grins, he sat beside her, unlaced his boots, and pulled them off, placing them beside the blanket where the warm sun could dry them. "I think I could use those pretty slippers you made for me right about now."

She laughed, and her cheeks turned pink. "They are rather shocking in their appearance. You don't have to wear them if they are too colorful for you."

"Not at all. I find that the red and green yarn makes them hard to misplace."

"Well, that's something to recommend them, I suppose." She shook her head and gazed up at him, a soft smile tilting her lips. "Would you mind terribly helping me shuck these boots. They feel positively dreadful."

"Of course," he said, moving to assist her. He sat on his knees and placed one of her small boots on his lap. He had no button hook, but he did have a kitchen knife in the basket, which he had Nancy ferret out. With a bit of maneuvering, he was able to slip the loops over the hooks and open her boots.

When he removed the first boot, Nancy sighed and said, "Thank you! It felt as if I had my feet encased in mud. I do hope my boots will dry some before we head home."

"Well, the longer we linger, the longer they'll have to dry."

She leaned back on her hands and lifted her face to the sun. "I like the way you think, Mr. Grayson."

He liked the way she looked, relaxed, serene, and stunning with the sun on her face. He wished he could give her more days like this where she could simply lounge on a blanket beneath a blue sky instead of toiling in the garden or kitchen.

She sat up and reached beneath her skirt but stopped and looked at him. "Would you find it unforgivably crude if I were to remove these wet stockings?"

"Nancy, it's just the two of us here, and… please do whatever makes you comfortable," he said. But he simply could not sit and watch her strip off her stockings. "I'll set out our lunch while you make yourself comfortable." With that, he turned his back and rooted in the basket, taking a good long time to set out and arrange a plate of chicken and linen full of biscuits.

"You can turn around now, Hal. I'm appropriately covered." Nancy's laughter turned him around to face her. "If my mother could see me now, barefoot and soaked to my unmentionables, she would disown me."

"I suppose this would seem a bit unconventional to her."

Nancy shook her head. "No, she fully expects this behavior from me, she just doesn't wish to tolerate it. As I said earlier, this isn't the first time I've doused my skirts in the creek. I used to ride my mare through the creek and soak the hem of my dress. It vexed Mother greatly that I was unable to retain some sense of decorum as a lady. I got in trouble a number of times for coming home with my skirts wet and my boots full of mud."

As he listened to his wife talk about her childhood, Hal hooked an elbow over one bent knee and leaned on his opposite hand. He was pleased she was sharing a pleasant memory of home, especially after her heartbreaking homesickness earlier. It made him think of happier times he'd shared with his own family... with John.

"All parents should just understand that their children are going to wade in water and play in the mud," she said. "We should make a note of this lest we forget when we have our own children. Don't you agree?"

Hal couldn't respond because he was too caught up in the idea of Nancy bearing him children. Someday they were going to have children that called them mother and father.

"Would you mind dishing up lunch? I'd like to keep my skirt fanned out to help it dry."

"Of course," he said, turning his attention to their lunch. He filled a plate and passed it to her.

"Did you and your siblings tax your parents' patience overmuch?" she asked.

The question made him laugh. "We did indeed. Every day. In fact, this part of the creek is a lot like the fishing hole I went to back home.

John and I would walk down there with our birch poles and a bucket and toss in a line. The two of us would sit there for ten minutes and then leave our poles in search of other excitement. That usually involved getting soaked and getting dirty."

"My point is made," Nancy said with a laugh.

Hal laughed too. "Yes, I brought home more mud than fish. I can't count the number of times I promised to bring home supper and would come home empty-handed. I don't think my mother ever really expected me to bring home supper, which was just as well."

Nancy pulled a face. "At least you had big dreams and you tried. My mother never thought fishing was a proper pastime for a young lady. But when I could sneak off with my cousin Joseph, we'd go to a deep section of the creek and fish. Anything I caught I had to give him credit for, but I didn't mind. I just enjoyed the adventure."

"This cousin of yours seems to have risked a lot to help you in your exploits."

"He was more like a brother than a cousin. He worked in our stables as a groom, so he was always around. I snuck pastries and other treats to him each time I visited the stables."

Hal shook his head. "Your father must have had his hands full with you. And you say you have a sister... is she as willful as you are?"

"Gracious, no!" Nancy said with a laugh. "Elizabeth and I are twins, but that's where the similarity ends.

Hal pulled back in shock. "Twins! I can't imagine how your father dealt with two beautiful daughters."

"Fairly and with great love," she said, her smile fading. "Elizabeth and I have always been close. We could often be found together, and many couldn't tell us apart. We've always liked a lot of the same things, but at the same time we're truly very different. Elizabeth is calm, and in all ways proper, and I dare say far less stubborn than I am."

Hal could easily picture two red-haired girls dashing across the green lawn in front of a grand house in Buffalo. He was, however, having trouble picturing a quieter, calmer version of Nancy. He was coming to deeply appreciate this headstrong, bright, determined woman that he'd married.

And in that moment, he intended to woo her with everything he had. Because he wanted the playful and passionate woman who was rapidly stealing his heart.

Unaware of his silent realizations, Nancy continued talking about her sister and her life in Buffalo. "Elizabeth and I got along famously. We both liked what we liked, and sometimes it was the same and sometimes it wasn't. But there were never any concerns until it came to Stuart Newmaine. While my father intended the young man to become my husband, I could summon no feelings for him. But Elizabeth and Stuart were smitten with one another the moment they met. I can only hope that my leaving has opened my father's eyes to the situation and helped them find their happiness," Nancy said, sadness creeping back into her voice, and Hal understood firsthand just how painful it had been for her to leave her family.

"Why don't you write your sister and ask her? And you could tell her a little about your life here in Fredonia and that you've married a fine and dashing man of your own."

His comment garnered the smile he'd been hoping for.

"You certainly are a fine and dashing man," she said, "and I'll take great pleasure in sharing that detail with my sister someday."

"Why wait? Maybe if Elizabeth knows you are married, it will help smooth the way with your father."

Nancy's eyes cut away, but not before he saw the anguish in them. Why would writing home cause her tension? He pondered that thought for a moment and then tucked it away, not wanting to further distress her.

"I hadn't meant to be intrusive," Hal said quickly, not wanting to fracture the comfortable relationship they were forging this afternoon. He placed his hand gently over Nancy's, and after a slight hesitation, she turned her palm up to link fingers with him. That simple contact was comforting and somewhat incredible as he realized the two of them were holding onto each other.

"You haven't been intrusive," she replied, her gaze fixed on their clasped hands as if she found it incredible as well. "It's just that it's complicated. Elizabeth deserves a chance at happiness, and my leaving was the only way she'd get that chance. I need to give her time to make that happen."

Not once did Nancy meet his eyes, and Hal suspected there was more she wasn't sharing. She was skilled at evading his questions and changing the subject, but he would eventually get to the truth.

Nancy swung her knees to her side and tucked her feet under her skirt. Facing Hal, she said, "Tell me about your family, Hal. I'd really like to hear about your life."

He suspected she was sincere, but he also knew it was a perfect way for her to shift attention away from herself. Still, he'd brought her here to ease her heartache, and so he leaned back on his hands and said, "My sister Charlotte is two years older than I, and she's married with two rambunctious boys that call me Unca Hal."

Nancy laughed. "How darling!"

Hal couldn't help smiling as he thought about his nephews. Before his sister had kids, he was content being a bachelor. Even when John Radford had advertised for a wife, Hal was comfortable with his single life. But now that he was married and thinking about the future, he eagerly contemplated having a family with Nancy although he wanted to wait until he could more adequately provide for his family.

"You said you have two sisters," Nancy prodded, nudging him away from thoughts of children.

He wouldn't push Nancy into intimacy. They would build that path together. Part of that construction needed to begin with sharing their lives and their feelings. And so he opened up about his family. "My younger sister, Martha, and my three younger brothers, James, George, and Samuel all live at home."

Nancy raised her eyebrows. "Gracious, that must have been a houseful when you and John Radford lived at home too."

"It was utter bedlam. I looked forward to the day I'd be able to escape the clamor and have my own home. But honestly, I miss my

155

family and even the noise more than I'd ever anticipated. It just hadn't occurred to me that you'd be missing your family as well. I'm sorry I wasn't more aware of your feelings, Nancy."

"Thank you, Hal, but my homesickness is a result of my own actions, not anything you've done or not done. I'm the one who has been unmindful of your feelings." She placed her hand over his and rubbed her thumb across his knuckles. "I can only imagine how your heartaches over leaving your family and losing your brother. It makes my own heart bleed for you."

The familiar lump of grief lodged in Hal's throat and made it difficult to speak, but he pushed himself to share everything with Nancy. The success of their marriage depended on it. And so he dragged in a pained breath and began. "John and I had such grand plans here in Fredonia. We wanted to build a profitable business here and send money home to help our father get back on his feet. Instead, John died, and now I can barely keep food on our table much less send anything home to help my father." Hal shook his head, still unable to believe John was dead. "I still expect John to come slogging into the house at night, boot heels dragging and a big smile on his face because he loved what we were building. There are times it hurts so much I can't breathe."

"Oh Hal..." Nancy squeezed his hand, her eyes filled with tears. "I'm so sorry. I wish I could help ease this burden on your heart."

"You have," he said, and he meant it. This sweet, sassy, take-charge lady was teaching him to live around his grief, to wade right through the middle of the muck when necessary and then to haul himself out of that swamp and keep moving.

Drawing in a deep breath, Hal smelled fresh pine and fresh dirt and fresh air, scents that reminded him of John Radford. It felt good to think about John Radford with something other than overwhelming grief in his heart. Perhaps comforting Nancy through her heartache had soothed an ache in Hal's heart as well.

"During our walk here today, I smelled the pine trees and it reminded me of John," Hal said. "John said he liked the smell of fresh cut pine even better than Mother's baked bread." Hal laughed. "I like the smell of pine, too, but it simply can't compete with Mother's bread. John would tuck pine shavings in his pocket, and it would vex Mother terribly to find piles of sawdust on the floor under John's chair at the table."

Nancy laughed. "Keeping the floors clean with all those children must have taken the better part of her day. I'm glad, though, that the memory is a good one for you. It does make me curious why John would leave your father's mill to come to Fredonia. Did they not get along?"

Hal took a deep breath, pondering the best way to answer her question. Even now, he could feel his hands tightening into fists at the memory of his father looking broken and defeated as he watched his beloved mill being auctioned on the courthouse steps. Even after several months, Hal's anger toward the man responsible had not subsided and had in fact been heightened by John's death. His brother would still be at home and alive if not for Lloyd Tremont.

"If you'd rather not talk about it, I understand."

"No, it's not that," Hal said. "I'm just not sure where to begin."

Her lips quirked up on one side. "At the beginning would be a good place to start."

Her small jest turned him from his anger, and he sought the best words to describe the events that changed his life. "Well... my brothers and I helped my father run his sawmill at our home in Buffalo. It was a small, successful mill, but we had a hard time keeping up with the steamer orders. So Dad bought a second larger mill thinking that John and I would run it. I didn't want to run the mill. I wanted to build furniture, so I accepted an apprenticeship with A. B. Edwards. I left John and my father to run the family business." Hal's gut twisted saying those words. "I shouldn't have left them like that. It was selfish. When the steamer contract fell through my father couldn't afford the new mill. We didn't have enough orders to pay for the new mill, so the bank repossessed it."

"Oh, no, that's heartbreaking."

"It was maddening!" Hal declared, his attempt to control his anger a pitiful failure. "I tried to reason with Lloyd Tremont, but the wealthy banker wouldn't hear a word of protest."

Nancy gasped, and the blood seemed to drain from her face.

"I had a little savings set aside, and I offered every cent of it to Tremont if he would just give my father another couple of months to start making payments. I really thought Tremont would consider it. He and my father were friendly acquaintances. I had even been to the man's estate years earlier to help my father carve the family crest on Tremont's front door."

Her eyes locked with his. "*You* carved it?"

"Yes, with my father," he said. "And you'd think that would have meant something to Tremont. My father considered the man a friend, but apparently Tremont considered their transactions nothing more than business. It seemed he had no sympathy for my father's hardship, and he not only repossessed the mill but sold it to our biggest competitor at auction."

"Hal, I don't... I don't know what to say." Nancy clasped a palm to her stomach, a look of horror on her face.

Hal shoved his hand through his hair but resisted the urge to stand and pace as he spoke. "The man even had the gall to tell my father that he should have known better than to make such a risky investment. It broke my father's heart to watch his mill being sold to his competition on the courthouse steps. It was like a dagger in his heart, and mine, to watch his dream dashed in a single instant."

"I'm sure it was, but perhaps—" Nancy shook her head and looked down the creek. "I'm so sorry, Hal."

Taking a deep breath, Hal forced himself to calm down. His ranting about Tremont's treatment of his father had obviously upset Nancy and possibly ruined their day. "I'm sorry, too, Nancy. I've said too much—I hadn't meant to trouble you with my past and a problem neither of us can do anything to resolve."

And he hadn't even spoken of the crushing guilt he felt over the situation. If he had only listened to his father and stayed to help at the mill instead of chasing an apprenticeship with Edwards, maybe he could have helped save the mill before it was too late. And John Radford would still be alive.

"I'm glad you told me," she said, but her smile wobbled, and he wasn't at all convinced that she was glad to know the thoughts that burdened him.

"I'm afraid I've ruined our picnic," he said, disappointed in himself. "My intention was to fill your day with sunshine and laughter, not with my clouded past and hot anger."

"Well, I could cool you off by shoving you into the creek again."

He met her wry grin with one of his own. "I wouldn't blame you if you wanted too. I deserve another dousing for raining on our picnic."

"I rather enjoyed our plunge into the water."

The sweet sincerity in her eyes warmed him. He thought about the kiss and their play that followed. He'd enjoyed it all. And he wanted more of that wonderful feeling and to be the cause of his wife's laughter. "Shall we see if I can brighten this day again?"

Her answering smile gave him hope, but there was still a reserve in her eyes that hadn't been there earlier. "What do you have in mind?" she asked.

"Are you daring enough to walk to the falls in your bare feet?"

A surprised laugh escaped her. "Most certainly. But the real question is, are *you* daring enough to keep up with me?" With that, she leapt to her feet and danced away. Three steps later, she yelped and jerked her right foot off the rocky beach. "Gracious sakes! It's like walking on glass!"

Hal laughed and playfully taunted her for having feet too delicate to support her fierce nature. Then he surprised her, and himself, by sweeping her up and cradling her petite body in his arms. "Allow me to carry you the rest of the way," he said, turning them toward the falls and a new and wonderful romance.

CHAPTER EIGHTEEN

H al went to the mill the next day with a spring in his step and a renewed hope for the future. Despite losing several hours of work time, his heart felt a lot lighter after his afternoon with Nancy. Telling her about his father and their troubles had helped him more than he'd realized, and though he regretted casting a shadow over their day, his confession had seemed to bring them closer.

She'd shared a bit of her childhood with him as well, and he appreciated getting to know her better, although he still felt there was something she wasn't telling him.

After they'd returned from the gorge, they had spent a pleasant evening together, eating dinner in the kitchen and taking a short walk in the orchard as the sun was setting. Later Nancy played the woefully-out-of-tune pianoforte and joked that the badly tuned strings added new element to her songs. Hal found her music beautiful and the discordant notes a bit haunting. Still, he could easily see that Nancy enjoyed playing and that music had been a big part of her life. He wished he could get the pianoforte tuned for her, but it was an expense he could ill afford and a difficult task to find someone skilled enough to tune it.

And so went his thoughts as he wrangled an oak timber onto the saw table, slabbed and squared the long sawn planks. He carried the heavy lengths of lumber a piece at a time and loaded them into wagon. He would finish sawing this order for Burton's Tannery tomorrow and deliver it after he dropped off the kitchen cabinet, which he planned to finish tonight, at Addison's store.

The morning at the mill went quickly, and before Hal realized it, he was watching the clock, awaiting lunchtime when he knew Nancy would be arriving. His gaze kept darting to the road, and when he finally saw her cross into the mill yard, his heartbeat accelerated. With a light stride, she crossed the yard in her pretty green dress with a basket hooked over her arm and a stylish bonnet framing her beautiful face and wide smile. Hal shut off the mill and left the lean-to wiping his dirty hands on a soiled rag.

With feigned nonchalance, he leaned in and placed a quick kiss on Nancy's cheek as if he'd done so every day for several years.

But his act didn't fool Nancy. She laughed and said, "Are you angling for food, Mr. Grayson?"

"I'm willing to *beg* for whatever you've stashed in that basket. I'm famished." Hal lifted the edge of a lap quilt she'd used to cover their food and attempted to peek into the basket.

Nancy playfully tapped his knuckles. "Let me set out our lunch beneath the maple. It's dreadfully hot today and I need to sit in the shade."

Hal took the basket from her and escorted her to a grassy corner of the yard shaded by sprawling branches of a large, leafy maple. With each step, he felt her nearness, the weight of her small hand hooked over his arm, the floral scent of her hair, the length of her stride—and his heart was flooded with warmth.

She glanced up at him, the look in her eyes telling him she felt that same exciting awakening.

It amazed him to feel this way and to see the same connection in Nancy's eyes. He hadn't been looking for Nancy or marriage. His mind had been filled with too many plans and dreams. But his mother had always said that love would find him when he was least expecting it. Hal wasn't ready to give a name to his feelings just yet, but after yesterday, he knew his growing affection for his wife was real with roots that went very deep. Whatever the emotion, he knew he was defining his relationship with Nancy, not as John's brother, not as her "rescuer," but as a man who'd stumbled upon a treasure and couldn't stop admiring it or believing it was really his to hold.

Nancy smiled up at him. "I'd sure like to know what put that look of wonder on your face."

She had, but he couldn't bring himself to say such things to her just yet. "It's the delicious smell coming from the basket."

Laughing, Nancy lifted the quilt from atop the hamper. "Will you lay this out, please?"

He spread it across the grass and placed the basket in the center.

As Nancy sat, she said, "I brought leftover chicken, and I cooked up some of the squash that Mary Tucker brought over yesterday. Ours should be ready in a week or so."

"We're very fortunate to have them as neighbors."

"And more so to have them as friends," Nancy said as she pulled a plate of chicken and a bowl of sliced squash out of her basket. The fact that she quickly covered the basket again had Hal suspicious.

"What else did you put in here?" he asked, trying again to peek inside.

Nancy laughed and tucked the basket behind her back. "I brought a sweet, but you must eat your lunch first. I know you're always rushed, so if you don't have time to eat it today you can have it with your supper."

"Actually, I found that I'm more productive in the afternoons since I've been taking time for lunch. I think the break has enabled me to go back in the afternoon with a clear mind. And I have you to thank for that. I just wish I could increase the mill output enough that I wouldn't have to be here from dawn to dusk, but I suppose I'd still have to spend most of the evening hours in the barn."

"But I understand why you have to do it. You've had such a rough start here. It pleases me to do at least a little something for you, even if that's just bringing you a lunch. I wish I could do more to help." Her shoulders slumped, and she sighed. "If I were a man, I could be of far more help here."

"And you'd be far less desirable," he said, placing his hand over hers. "You're doing more than you likely realize. And even before you came, John and I would work all day at the mill and I'd work half the night in my woodshop. Until you came, my life was in shambles. You've brought great improvement to my days."

"I've also foisted another financial burden upon your shoulders." Nancy fidgeted with the edge of the quilt as she spoke.

He stilled her hand and gently caressed it with his rough thumb. "The only thing you've added to my life is joy. You've forced me to slow down and enjoy a few stolen moments in the midst of unending work. You've opened my eyes to the potential for happiness in Fredonia and given me hope that I can become a man worthy of your respect and perhaps someday your love."

Her lips parted as if her words were trapped in her mouth. He'd clearly made her uncomfortable, but he wanted to express his appreciation for everything she'd done to make his life better. And he'd wanted to present the idea of love, that perhaps they might develop that level of feeling for one another. But he hadn't wanted to make her uncomfortable or to push her.

"You should eat," she said, her voice nearly a whisper.

"I should," he said, "but I'd rather do this." He leaned toward her and pressed a tender kiss to her mouth. "Thank you for being a strong, stubborn, and remarkable woman."

Nancy released a breathless laugh and pulled back to look at him. "Was that meant to be a backhanded compliment?"

"No. Simply a statement of fact," he said, and promptly bit into a piece of baked chicken breast. It was still cool from being stored in the well overnight, which reminded him that he needed to build a spring-house for Nancy, but like so many other things, it would have to wait.

Her eyes sparkled with humor as she helped herself to a piece chicken. They spent the balance of their lunch laughing and joking. As Hal finished eating, he leaned back on the blanket, full from a good meal and enchanted with Nancy's company. "Are you going to tell me now what sweet you've got tucked in that basket?"

Nancy rooted in the basket and pulled out two small bowls. "I've brought custard. I'd thought something cool might be a treat today, but I'm afraid it's turning to soup in this heat."

"Well, at least it won't be as thick as that stew you tried to make with flour and bacon grease. That wouldn't have melted in a hot oven"

Nancy burst out laughing. "You are full of praise today, Mr. Grayson."

"Only because I'm scared to try the custard."

She laughed again and thrust a bowl into his hands. "I promise you, it's edible."

He took a bite and groaned.

"You're jesting, right?" Her smile fell away. "Is it not good?"

The worry in her eyes melted him, and he was sorry to have teased her. He reached out, cupped her beautiful face in his palm, and said, "It's delicious, Nancy. I can't thank you enough for being so thoughtful and for bringing sweets and laughter to my day."

With that, he moved in and stole a kiss.

To his surprise, she welcomed the spontaneous moment.

Then a shock of cold water hit his scalp and streamed down his neck. He gasped and reared back, unable to believe his sweet little wife had just poured water over his head.

Her laughter rang across the yard.

Hal stared in amazement. "You just doused my head!"

"I did indeed." Eyes sparkling, shoulders shaking with laughter, she set aside the half-full jar of water. "Let that be a lesson not to poke fun at my cooking abilities."

He couldn't hold back the laughter that had been building in his chest. Each moment with his wife was filled with surprise. She shocked him. She delighted him. She enchanted him.

Living with her expanded his life in a way he'd never anticipated or could have even dreamed.

They spent the last few minutes of his lunch break in playful repartee. Hal ate the custard and savored every delicious bite. "This is really good, Nancy." And it was. But he remembered how barren their pantry had looked last night and the worry he felt over how he would find the funds to stock it before next week. Suspicious, he asked, "What's in this? What ingredients are needed to make custard?" he asked casually.

"Eggs, cream, sugar and flour. Why would you ask? Do you not like the splash of vanilla I added?"

"The custard is delicious. I'm just wondering if we had the staples in the pantry or if you made another trip to town with your jewelry."

The smile dropped off her face, and she glanced down at her clasped her hands.

Hal's gut clenched, and he knew the answer. Still, he'd hoped Nancy would be honest with him. He thought they were arriving at a more intimate place in their relationship. "I don't recall having sugar in the pantry, or I'd have added a lump to my coffee. Did you borrow some from Mary?"

"No," she said, looking at him with a spark of defiance in her eyes. "I did not borrow the sugar. I went to town, sold a necklace I seldom wear, and then I bought some provisions."

Heat engulfed Hal's head, and he stalked away from the blanket, not wanting to say something he'd regret. But unable to hold his tongue, he turned back, rubbing his hand over his mouth, and breathing deeply as he sought words that wouldn't harm their marriage. He stared down at his wife sitting on the blanket. Her eyes met his and displayed a fire he was growing accustomed to. "I thought I'd made myself clear, Nancy, but apparently not. So let me repeat one final time that I'll not have you selling your jewelry to stock our pantry. That's my job, and I'll find the means to take care of it."

"I understood you the first time we discussed this, Hal." She stood then and faced him, her cheeks flushed bright pink. "You just admitted yourself that taking time for lunch has made you more productive at the mill. Without the extra funds from my jewelry, we would be getting one meal a day and I prefer to eat more often than that. You can't work effectively if you don't eat, so I'm making sure we both get those meals. Like you, I'm just doing my part to take care of us. I'm truly sorry if I've hurt your pride, Hal. You must know that's not my intention, and I'm extremely discreet in my dealings with the watchmaker. But if this is something I can do to make our lives a little less difficult, then that's what I'm going to do."

Embarrassment and a deep sense of shame welled up in Hal. The situation shredded his pride, but this wasn't just about him. He and John Radford might have been willing to live hand-to-mouth with nary enough to eat, but Nancy wasn't used to a life of scarcity, nor should she be subjected to such if there was a means—any means—to avoid it. And so he heaved a hard sigh and shoved his hands in his trouser pockets, knowing he had to swallow his pride for her sake. "It hadn't dawned on me that I was causing more hardship for you. I hadn't meant to be inconsiderate."

"Oh, Hal, you are one of the most considerate men I know. Please don't make more of this little transaction than it is. If I had sold my necklace to purchase a new dress, you wouldn't have said a word."

"Yes, Nancy, I would have said the same thing. I will purchase your dresses. Are you in need of one?"

She parked her hands on her hips and groaned. "No, and you are intentionally missing my point. I didn't care about the necklace. I care about being hungry and putting a good meal on the table for my husband, as well as for myself." With that, she returned to the blanket and packed up the remnants of their lunch. She snatched the blanket off the ground and shook off the crumbs and the dirt before throwing it over her arm. She walked back to Hal, pressed her palm to his heart and said, "You're a good, dependable, and kind man, Hal, and I'm proud to be your wife. Stop fretting over this, and get back to work. Dinner will be on the table when you get home this evening."

He watched her stride across the mill yard, the back of her skirt switching to and fro like an agitated cat's tail. Without a single glance back, she headed down the street. And he went back to work with a head full of uncomfortable thoughts.

NANCY STRODE HOME in a state of agitation. She'd known how Hal would react to her selling another piece of jewelry, but she'd done it anyway because it was necessary, because it was a logical thing to do. She'd scrimped and carefully spent the funds from her brooch and stretched their provisions as far as she could. Hal might be upset with her, but he had no idea how difficult it was to make a meal without proper staples, especially for one who was learning how to cook. She didn't know all the shortcuts that Mary and Martha knew. She'd only just learned that she could use starch instead of flour to thicken custard. She needed to follow Mary and Martha's recipes exactly or risk ruining a meal, and she couldn't do that if she didn't have those staples in her pantry. And she couldn't afford to make mistakes and waste a single bite of their meager provisions. So she'd sold her necklace. So what? This marriage wasn't just about Hal Grayson, and the sooner he learned that the better. Someday they would have children, and she would not let her husband's pride keep her from taking proper care of their babies.

It wasn't that she didn't understand Hal's complaint. She did, and it hurt her to think his pride was wounded because he couldn't provide for her in the manner he desired. Simply knowing he wanted more for them was enough for Nancy. She'd come from wealth and never once worried there wouldn't be a meal on the table. But having a full belly wasn't any more desirable than knowing her husband cared about her. She didn't need wealth. She needed to have food for their table and to make a loving home for her husband, and someday for their children.

What good was a trunk full of jewelry and fancy dresses if her stomach was burning with hunger? What good was she to her husband if she was simply a financial burden?

To see Hal work nearly every waking moment day after day and still struggle so desperately broke her heart. Hal hadn't asked for or wanted a wife. But he'd made the best of their situation, and she felt she had to do something to contribute. But what else could she offer other than selling her few items of value to put food on their table?

Her agitation dissipated as she walked into the yard. The small house and expansive yard was finally beginning to feel like home to her. She hoped that at least her contribution in making the house clean and cozy made it more inviting to Hal.

She stopped to remove her boots just inside the door to avoid tracking sawdust across her clean floors. She slipped her feet into her house slippers and headed into the kitchen where Captain was sleeping on a chair. He opened one eye, saw it was her, and promptly returned to his slumber.

He was so cute she wanted to scoop him up and nuzzle his furry little head, but she resisted and went to the back door. Staring outside, she placed her hands on her hips and surveyed her garden and the field of grass and wildflowers beyond. She'd accomplished a lot since coming to Fredonia, and she was proud of that, but she still felt there was more she could do. Selling her jewelry had brought in desperately needed funds, but it had wounded Hal's pride in the process. She needed to come up with a way to contribute to their family in a manner that would help rather than hurt her husband. But what?

CHAPTER NINETEEN

On Friday evening, Hal walked home from the mill feeling grateful that he'd had a productive week. However, even four days after the discussion he'd had with Nancy about selling her jewelry, he was still troubled about it. It had been a painful hit to his pride for certain, but he'd bitten his tongue because he couldn't bear the thought of Nancy going hungry. And how could he fault her for trying to help?

Because of her contribution she'd served tasty meals all week, and yet she hadn't mentioned the incident once.

And so Hal had done the same, although he hoped to one day save enough funds to replace her jewelry. The best he could do for now was to keep the pantry stocked and prevent her from selling more of her baubles.

His mother had sold pieces of her jewelry on a couple of occasions that Hal could remember. That was how his father and mother had gotten through tough times, and they'd certainly had plenty of them. But even during their most recent disaster with losing one of their sawmills, Hal couldn't recall either of his parents raising their voices. During rough patches they would sit at the kitchen table and take stock of all they had. If business was slow at the mill, Hal and his brothers would hunt with their father and sell or trade pelts and meat. They would gather up any unnecessary possessions, extra furniture, his father's tools, his mother's jewelry, and sell them. They all contributed. They didn't blame one another. And when times prospered, they would modestly improve the food for their table and the comfort of their home.

That's what Nancy had been trying to get through to Hal. This situation wasn't just about him. It involved both of them, and Nancy was simply doing what she could to help and contribute.

And he'd condemned her for it.

Hal felt a fool as he crossed his yard. Lantern light glowed from the windows and smoke wafted from the chimney telling him Nancy had supper cooking. She'd been starting her own fires in the stove for some time now, a skill she was immensely proud of. And though she'd had a couple of unfortunate meal disasters in the kitchen, on the whole the dishes she provided were quite tasty. She'd come here unskilled in every facet of housekeeping and expecting to have a staff to manage. And instead she'd taken his partially furnished dirty home with an empty pantry and turned it into a home filled with warmth and light and laughter. This was *their* home—and Nancy had made it that way.

Like a flower that blooms where it's planted, Nancy's petals were unfurling a bit more each day. She had completely and irrevocably transformed his house into a home. She'd turned a rocky swatch of soil into a garden of vegetables that was beginning to produce an admirable yield. She'd adopted animals of all sorts—from Captain, the barn cat who had taken up permanent residence in their house, to a mother doe and two fawns that foraged the back field and woods.

She helped him tend his books and organize his life. She was building good relationships with their neighbors and helping them both become better members of their community. She had a wonderful sense of humor and constantly surprised him with her candor and tomfoolery. Despite her tender heart and nurturing nature she possessed an inner strength that Hal admired. She wasn't afraid to challenge him when it was warranted and refused to let him make decisions based on his frustration and exhaustion. Despite their rough start and her own heartache, she was creating a home in Fredonia, making friends, and thoroughly charming him.

For all his protestations of not wanting to marry, Hal found himself unable to imagine life without Nancy—and that thought consumed him as he entered the house.

Life without her would be... colorless.

Cold.

Empty.

As those realizations sank in, he shucked his boots. The house was quiet. Too quiet.

He strolled to the kitchen, but it was empty as he'd suspected. He smelled something delicious cooking on the stove. Lifting the lid on a deep pot, he was greeted with the mouthwatering scent of ham and bean soup. With supper on the stove, he knew Nancy couldn't be far. After a quick search of the rest of the house, he realized she must be outside in the garden. So, he stuffed his aching feet back in his boots and slogged out back.

She wasn't in the garden either.

Perplexed, he looked around, wondering if perhaps she was out in the field talking to her little family of deer, Mama Daisy, and babies Raindrop and Honeydew, as she'd named them. The idea of naming deer still made Hal laugh. He'd never heard of such a thing.

After a moment of scanning the empty field, he looked across the yard and saw the barn door open. A minute later he entered his wood-shop and found Nancy seated on an overturned milk churn in front of his workbench. A dark ring of soil ran around the hem of her day dress telling him she'd been working in the garden at some point. Her flowing green skirt was covered with wood shavings and sawdust. So were her hands and arms. Nancy's chignon, usually so tidy, was hanging loose, and several stray hairs fell across her face and into her eyes.

Taking it all in with a mixture of surprise and horror, Hal watched as she swiped her arm over her forehead, sweeping hair out of her eyes and depositing a layer of sawdust along her brow. Her forehead was furrowed, and her dark brows framed determined eyes as she studied the wood piece before her.

"What are you doing?" Hal asked.

Nancy gasped and clutched the wooden piece to her chest as she spun to face him. "Gracious, Hal! You startled me."

"I'm sorry. What are you doing out here?"

"I'm sanding these panels for you."

Hal swiped his hand over his mouth to hide his grimace. "I planned to get to those tonight or tomorrow. Sanding affects the quality, Nancy. If you don't get it just right, the entire piece is ruined. I don't mean to sound ungrateful, but I'd just as soon that you don't help me out here. I can't afford to replace any of those pieces."

A look of dread crossed her face. "I thought I'd be helping, but now I'm terrified I've ruined your work." She stood up and handed the flat panel to him. "Please tell me I haven't damaged this panel. I've been out here so many nights watching what you've been doing that I thought I could manage this for you."

Her level of concern made him feel bad that he'd said anything. He should have waited for her to go inside to put supper on the table, and he could have looked them over without distressing her. But here they were, her eyes filled with worry as she handed the cabinet panel to him.

And so Hal took the rectangular piece of cherry to the workbench where he could view the piece in the bright light of the lantern. He angled the panel and ran his fingers gently along the edges. He lifted it and eyed the corners finding them smooth and straight. There were no noticeable gouges or scratches or divots from inexperienced sanding. He ran his palm and fingertips over the door panel, surprised and immensely impressed that it was smooth as satin. Astonished and deeply relieved, he looked at Nancy standing beside him wringing her hands. "This is an excellent job."

Skepticism lingered in her eyes.

"Truly, I couldn't have done finer work myself."

"Then I haven't jeopardized the piece?"

"On the contrary, you've just saved me a good bit of time. How many panels did you sand?"

She cringed. "All of them."

"Are they all like this?"

She nodded. "I believe so, but perhaps you should check to ensure I haven't compromised them."

"All right. I suspect they're fine, but I'll check them over when you head inside." Hal laid the panel on the workbench and then cupped Nancy's shoulders in his hands. "You are one amazing woman, Nancy Grayson."

A tremulous smile lifted her mouth. "I expected you to say I'm one intrusive and irritating woman."

He laughed. "Headstrong and sassy maybe, but not intrusive or irritating."

"Then you're not upset with me?"

"No. I'm touched and awed by all you do." He rubbed his thumbs across her slender arms and their eyes met. She looked back at him with the same depth of feeling he'd witnessed the day they had tumbled into the creek. He'd kissed her that day... and she'd kissed him back.

A gentle softness filled her eyes, and she said, "I missed you today, Hal. After I finished weeding the garden, I wandered in here and saw you'd left these panels on the workbench. I knew you'd planned to sand them tonight, so I thought perhaps I could do that job for you. I thought if I could relieve even just a little of your burden it might shorten your day. I had hoped by easing your workload you wouldn't have to be out here so late every night. It would please me if we could spend more time together in the evenings."

"That would please me as well," he said, and he meant it. He cupped her cheek and rubbed his thumb across the smudge of garden dirt and sawdust. "You are quite a sight, you know."

Nancy dipped her head. "I can well imagine. I'm covered in dirt and sawdust, and my hair is falling down everywhere. I'm a mess."

Hal pulled her into his arms and held her close. "You are positively stunning, and I find you irresistible."

She laughed and pushed him gently away. "You're just being kind because you're happy you don't have to sand those panels."

"You wound me, woman." He playfully wrestled her back into his arms. He'd been aching to hold her again, to connect with his beautiful wife. "I confess that I am happy I don't have to sand those panels, but I meant every word I said. You are amazing and simply irresistible." With that he tilted her chin up and placed a tender kiss upon her sweet lips. "And you're beautiful." Before she could react, he clasped her hand and spun her away as if they were dancing. "I have a surprise for you."

Gasping from the unexpected kiss and twirl around the workshop, she stared at him with wide eyes and a happy smile. "I hope you're not going to tell me you have more panels for me to sand."

Hal's hoot filled the room. "No, darling, but I'm not revealing my hand just yet. I shall arrive home early tomorrow evening at which time I'll clean up and put on my suit. You'll need to wear a dress and shoes you can dance in."

Her eyebrows lifted. "Is someone having a ball?"

"No, but we *will* be dancing. Please be ready at five o'clock."

A delighted smile graced her face, and she executed a deep curtsey. "I shall be waiting with great anticipation, sir."

Hal was riveted, mesmerized by her smile, lost in her sparkling eyes, and thoroughly taken with his beautiful wife. But as he reached to pull her back into his arms, she backed toward the door.

"I must see to our supper before it scorches." She continued walking backwards, a twinkle in her eyes. "I shall have supper on the table in twenty minutes." With that, she spun on her heel and hurried from the room.

A deep sense of gratification filled Hal's chest. It pleased him to know that Nancy was receptive to his romance and that she was excited about their plans for the following evening. It surprised him to realize how eager he was for a romantic evening with his wife.

CHAPTER TWENTY

The sun had not yet risen when Nancy abandoned any hope of further sleep. She had spent the night dreaming of her husband and anticipating an evening out with him. They had shared a very pleasurable hour together before going to bed the previous evening, but at bedtime he'd merely pecked her on the cheek and wished her a good night.

And so she was starting out yet another day of her untraditional marriage lying alone in her bed. And on her birthday to boot.

A wave of melancholy washed over her. She'd always spent her birthday with her sister and her family. To know that Elizabeth would also be celebrating alone made Nancy's heartache. She could only hope that her sister would be able to spend part of her day with Stuart. And hopefully one day Nancy and Elizabeth could again spend their shared birthday together.

For now, however, Nancy's life was in Fredonia with her husband, and she had much to be thankful for right here. She had tonight and Hal's surprise to look forward to.

Sitting up, she swung her legs over the edge of the bed and placed her bare feet on the worn floorboards. What a relief to get off the lumpy, hard-packed mattress. She simply couldn't face one more night on the wretched thing. It stank and offered no comfort whatsoever. This was one chore she could take care of herself.

As soon as she got Hal off to work she would open the tick, dump the soiled stuffing, and wash the dust and smell of perspiration out of the tick. While it was drying on the line she would gather scrap pieces of fabric from the attic to patch the worn areas. Then she would visit William Tucker to see if she could collect some fresh straw for stuffing. That would do for now. Later on, when Hal had extra funds, she would see about adding a soft feather- or horsehair-filled tick to lay on top of the straw mattress. At home she'd slept on a luxuriously thick feather mattress, and it was one comfort from her former way of living that she truly missed.

Determined to make herself a fresh bed for the night, Nancy took her blue, quilted housecoat from the hook on the closet door and slipped it on over her night dress. She hadn't been able to pack all of her possessions, but she was glad she brought some of her best clothes because it would be a long time before Hal would be able to afford more than necessities. She wrapped her housecoat tightly around her waist and secured the tie. Not wanting to take time to pull her hair up, she brushed it and drew it back with a ribbon. She'd always had soft, smooth hands because she'd not been required to do the type of physical, backbreaking, callous-causing work that she was currently doing. Despite the fact that her rough hands snagged her ribbons and clothing, she loved her new life. She was proud to have learned so much in the short time she'd been here, and she was growing more eager by the day to become a wife in every way to Hal Grayson.

When she crept into the parlor Hal was sprawled across the sofa, one long leg hooked over the back, the other sticking a good foot off the end, his arms slung above his head. His long, bare feet stuck out from beneath a worn blanket, and it appeared he wasn't any more comfortable in his bed than she was in hers.

This situation simply must change.

Hal might think he was being a gentleman to give her time to adjust to him and to what marriage entailed, but it just seemed silly and unnecessary to Nancy. They were married, and it was time the man accepted and fully acknowledge that fact by sleeping in his bed—with his wife.

It was not only time to cross that bridge—it was a bridge she *wanted* to cross.

Giving her husband a last admiring look, Nancy left him to his restless sleep and slipped into the kitchen.

She worked quietly to start breakfast, first filling the kettle with water and placing it atop the stove while she started a fire in the firebox. The simple act of building the daily fire never failed to bring a smile to her face as she remembered her first attempt and the ensuing mess she made. She'd come so far since her first days in Fredonia. The ache in her back and callouses on her hands were her badges of honor. Before coming here, she would have never thought that the simple act of making breakfast for her husband and tending their home would please her so deeply. It was such a change from her high expectations of directing a staff when she arrived that it made her laugh.

The fire blazed to life in the firebox, and she set to work pressing out the dough she'd left to rise the night before. Throwing a bit of flour onto the sideboard and generously covering her fingers, she pushed and pulled until the dough was just the right thickness. She floured the rim of a glass and used it to cut several round biscuits, and then placed them on a baking pan.

She had just finished putting the biscuits in the stove when she heard Hal stirring in the parlor. Eager to see him after their playful moments in the barn and in anticipation of the evening ahead, she quickly cleaned her hands on her apron.

"Good morning," he said, strolling into the kitchen buttoning his shirt. The man was a disheveled mess with his clothing hanging askew and his hair uncombed, and yet he took her breath away. She watched him stride confidently across the room and stop directly in front of her. He placed a quick kiss on her cheek. "Happy birthday."

Surprised by his familiar greeting and that he remembered her birthday, Nancy touched her cheek where the feel of Hal's lips lingered. "I... well, thank you."

He reached into his pocket and withdrew something. He extended his closed fist to her and then turned over his palm and opened his fingers. "This is for you."

A small flat piece of shaped wood rested on his palm. Intrigued, she picked it up and studied it more closely. "It's a hair pin!" she exclaimed in amazement.

"That it is," he said, a small grin tugging at his lips.

Nancy examined the two-pronged hair pin. A carving of three maple keys perched on top like birds in flight. Whirligigs, that's what she and Elizabeth used to call the maple keys that would flutter from the trees and cover their lawn. She ran her finger along the smooth edges. "This is simply exquisite. It's a work of art, Hal. Where did you find such a thing?"

"I made it."

"Truly?"

He nodded.

"When could you possibly have found time to carve something so beautiful?"

He tucked his hands into his pockets and shrugged. "I've been working on it since the day I met you, but the piece only recently revealed itself to me."

"It *revealed* itself?" she asked, puzzled.

"When I start carving a piece of wood, I don't know what's hiding inside. I just start carving away the excess wood until the piece reveals itself. I had started out thinking that this piece of white walnut was going to be a knife handle when all along it was a lady's hairpin. Imagine my surprise."

Nancy laughed and stared at her husband in amazement. "I've married an *artist*."

Hal laughed. "That sounds so much better than pauper."

"Oh, Hal..." Unable to help herself, Nancy slipped her arms around his waist. "I feel incredibly blessed to be your wife. You can't know how I see you because you've got your eyes filled with your own vision of yourself. When I look at you I see a tall, dashing man. I see an artist and a gentle and kind husband who is going to take me out dancing this evening."

"I think you have stars in your eyes, darling."

"Only when I look at you," she said, surprising herself with her boldness. But as she gazed up at her husband, he lowered his head and kissed her. It was just a soft, brief meeting of their lips, but the moment was filled with tenderness.

He cupped her face, his eyes filled with warmth. "You, my darling, are a work of *art*."

She smiled because he was so charming and sweet. "Well, you are like a piece of basswood hiding a treasure within."

Hal laughed. "Thank you, but I suspect I'm more like a piece of old driftwood." He tapped her nose with his finger. "I'm dying for a cup of coffee, and I need to get to the mill if I'm going to get back here in time to take you out for the evening."

"Well, then, you better stop trifling with me and let me fix your breakfast," Nancy said, shooing him from the kitchen.

Hal left to wash up, and he returned just as she was pulling the biscuits from the stove. "Those smell delicious. I'm famished, but I'm woefully late. I'll need to eat my breakfast during my walk to the mill."

"If you must," Nancy said, experiencing a momentary disappointment until she remembered she had a day full of chores ahead of her as well. "Let me butter a few of these biscuits for you." She placed the pan on the sideboard, then buttered four fluffy biscuits and wrapped them in a kitchen linen. She handed the bundle and an apple to Hal. "Where are we going this evening?"

"Out." With a playful wink, he hustled out the door with a laugh on his lips and a spring in his step before she could prod him for additional details about his surprise.

NANCY RUSHED through her daily chores before taking a long, luxurious bath, something she didn't have time for during the week. She rarely had time to do more than wash up before dressing for the day ahead, but she was done with her work for this day. Now she would finish her lovely bath and get ready to go dancing with her husband.

She washed her hair, a time-consuming task because it nearly reached her waist. When she finished her bath, she stepped out of the tub onto an old scrap of linen. She dried off and drew on her wrapper. Hal would want to bathe when he got home, so she kept a tall pot of water steaming on the stove, so she could heat his bath when he came home. She hurried to the bedroom where her freshly laundered and newly filled mattress awaited. She had also freshened the pillows and laundered the quilts. The quilts had still been a bit damp before her bath so that she would have to pull them off the line just before Hal came home.

After her hair had nearly dried, Nancy started to dress for the evening. She'd decided to wear the dress that she'd worn for their wedding. But when she reached for the gown, she was struck by a moment of melancholy. She traced her fingers along the beautiful lace that adorned the bodice and circled the puffed sleeves. Her father had originally commissioned the dress for her birthday ball, which would have been happening tonight. Was it still happening in her absence? Would her sister be attending, smiling at their guests with a gentleman at her side? If so, which gentleman? Robert, her intended? Or Stuart, the man she loved?

Nancy longed to know whether her departure had provided an opening for Elizabeth's happiness with Stuart, but she couldn't write to ask such a question. But she ached to communicate with her family, to apologize for worrying them, to tell them she was well and to assure herself that they, too, were well.

She pictured her mother, her smile forced as she hosted the ball without one of her girls. A stray tear ran down Nancy's cheek. Her mother didn't deserve this. She was a kind and loving mother, and Nancy missed her fiercely.

But there was nothing to be done today to remedy the situation, and so Nancy wiped her eyes and pulled the dress out of her closet. It appeared she'd be wearing the beautiful dress for her birthday after all.

Nancy slipped her corset on over her chemise and fumbled with the lacing at her back. She had rethreaded her corset ribbon so that it would tie at the bottom, instead of at the top, so she could dress herself. Giving the ribbon a firm tug, she tightened the corset around her waist. It was the best she could manage without a maid or a husband to assist her.

After pulling on two underskirts that allowed the dress to flow around her, she carefully pulled the dress over her head. It was a struggle to thread her arms into the sleeves and to tug the gown down over her shoulders without ripping the stitching. But she couldn't unlace the back of the gown because she would never be able to lace it up again without assistance. The best she'd been able to do was loosen the lacing as much as possible without slipping the ribbon from the loops. It was times like this that made her miss some of the luxuries she'd once taken for granted. Even on her wedding day, she'd had Mary Tucker and Martha Fiske to help her dress. But today she was alone and struggled for several minutes before she finally got the shoulders and waist in place and the voluminous skirts fell to the floor.

Sighing with relief, Nancy snugged the bodice lacing and then smoothed her hands down the front of her dress. She tugged the lower section of the fitted sleeves down her arms until they circled her wrists. Turning to her dressing mirror, she retrieved a brush from the table and began to brush out her hair. She wanted something stylish and romantic tonight. And she wanted to proudly display the comb that Hal had made for her.

After brushing out her hair, she left a few curls at each side of her face. She pulled the rest of her hair up in a loose cascade of curls at the back of her head and secured it with pins. Then she added the hair pin last as an elegant touch and because she was proud to be wearing Hal's thoughtful gift.

She surveyed the result in the mirror and was pleased. Dressing her hair was another thing she was skilled at. She would forgo a hat this evening and take a parasol so that she could show off her pretty hairpin.

Feeling her excitement build, she pinched the apples of her cheeks to add a bit of color. Then she picked up the glass bottle of eau de cologne from the bedside stand, removed the decorative stopper and inhaled. The scent of bergamot and lemon oil reminded her of home. Wearing the scent had been part of her daily ablution when she lived at home, but the bottle hadn't been opened since she left home. Tonight, however, she was going dancing with her husband and she wanted to smell especially nice for him. She replaced the stopper and shook the bottle before dabbing the cologne behind each ear. With a quick swipe across each of her wrists, she replaced the stopper and returned the bottle to the dressing table.

Just one chore remained before she could deem herself ready. She hurried outside and snatched the two bed quilts off the sagging clothes-line. They were dry, and they smelled wonderfully fresh. It would be blissful to settle into her comfortable bed after a night of dancing and romance. She took the quilts to her bedroom and made the bed.

Pleased that she was finally ready for her evening out, she collected her gloves from the dressing table and hurried to the parlor. The kitchen door was closed, telling her that Hal had come home and was bathing.

"I hope you heated your bath with the water on the stove," she called through the door.

"I did indeed, and the bath felt wonderful," he called back. "Thank you."

True to his word, Hal dressed quickly and was soon striding into the parlor where Nancy sat trying to settle her nerves. She stood as he entered the room and her mouth gaped. His black hair, still damp from his bath, was combed back off his forehead and tangled in a loose wave below his collar. His cheeks were scrubbed to a low shine, and his jaw was smooth from his recent shave. When she met his eyes, they seemed alive with excitement, with anticipation, and something more. Romance.

He reached for her hand and raised it to his lips. "How is it possible that you are even more stunning than you were on the day we married?"

His sincerity made her smile. "I was just thinking the same thoughts about you. You are quite dashing this evening, Mr. Grayson."

"I'm glad you find me a suitable escort," he said, tucking her hand into the crook of his arm. "Shall we head out?"

Gloves on, reticule in hand, her parasol waiting by the front door, Nancy gave her gallant husband a warm smile. "Where are we going?"

"Dancing," he said, and they both left the house laughing because he refused to share his surprise.

Outside she came to a halt on the wide stoop, her parasol half opened. Tied in the shade of the red maple tree was a beautiful chestnut-colored Morgan harnessed to a sporty phaeton. The sleek black carriage sported four large black wheels and an open top, a welcome attribute on the warm summer evening. The harness jangled as the horse gave an all-over shudder to shoo away pestering flies.

"A horse and carriage, Hal? My curiosity is suddenly as voracious as Captain's," Nancy exclaimed, snapping open her parasol and angling it overhead. "Where are you taking me?"

"Tsk tsk," he said wearing a self-satisfied grin as he guided her down the steps. "You know what happens to the cat that gets too curious?"

"Yes, it finds a home, takes over the woodshop, and eats all the table scraps."

Warm laughter erupted from Hal. "Not the point I'd intended, but I must concede you are right on all counts. But don't get your tail in a twitch, Mrs. Grayson. Your voracious curiosity will soon be satisfied."

Nancy twirled her sunshade and faked a pout that made Hal laugh again.

"Come now, darling, anticipation is half the fun of any worthwhile event."

Nancy silently agreed, but anticipation was also creating wild butterflies in her stomach. She had no idea what her husband had in store for the evening, and that left her in a quandary.

Needing to distract herself, she walked to the front of the carriage and stopped within the horse's sight but didn't crowd or touch him. "Hello, handsome fella," she said, blowing lightly toward his flared nostrils, knowing he was seeking her scent. Tugging off her glove, she slowly extended her hand and allowed the horse to sniff her fingers. Within seconds, he nuzzled her palm.

"Oh, he's seeking a treat, and I have nothing to give him," she said, glancing at Hal.

"I've got a couple of treats for him tucked away in this sack," he said, gesturing to a burlap bag beneath the seat. "I brought a few lumps of sugar and a couple of apples."

Her heart melted. "You are such a thoughtful man, Hal."

"Don't give me too much credit," he said. "William provided the sugar. I added a couple of apples is all."

"Well, this fella appreciates your kindness, don't you?" she asked, feeding the horse a lump of sugar, which he promptly ate.

Laughing, Nancy patted the horse's neck. He rewarded her with a nudge of his muzzle.

"Well, I can see that Gus is already in love with you, but I simply cannot afford to feed and house a horse." Hal said, his voice teasing. "So the answer is no, we can't keep him."

"That's too bad, isn't it, Gus?" She eyed the tall beautifully sculpted horse then looked at Hal. "Where did you get Gus and the carriage?"

"I made arrangements with William."

Oh, are we traveling far?" she asked, scavenging for clues to their destination.

"I couldn't have the birthday girl walking tonight, now could I?" Hal extended his hand to Nancy. "Milady, if I may?"

Nancy actually giggled at his play and his skillful evasion of the question. She placed her hand in his and allowed him to guide her to the side of the carriage as if they were promenading around a ballroom.

The carriage sat high above the ground and Hal had to lift her onto the seat. The warm look in his eyes made her stomach flutter. She settled on the black cushioned seat and tucked her yards of skirts in around her legs.

Hal circled around and climbed in beside her. With a wink at her, he took up the reins, clicked his tongue and gently encouraged Gus to cart them out of the driveway.

Gus seemed to be enjoying the outing as much as Nancy was. Instead of heading into the village, they went the opposite direction. They trotted out Liberty Street and turned right onto a road Nancy had never before traveled. A few minutes later Hal turned the sporty phaeton left onto Shumla Road, a place of green fields tucked between heavily wooded areas. The road followed a creek that Nancy could hear but rarely see. The steady clip clop of Gus's hooves and the jangle of the harness mingled with the crunching sound of the large wheels upon the dirt road. Nancy drank in the rhythmic sounds and the fresh scent of pine and grass. The outing felt positively wonderful, and she sat proudly beside her husband, momentarily overcome by her good fortune.

She'd come from wealth, but there were so many other treasures in life that filled her soul: A carriage ride on a summer evening, the rich aroma of a morning pot of coffee percolating in her kitchen, the feel of Captain's warm little body curled in her arms, the sound of her husband's laugh, the spontaneous joy of tumbling into the creek with her playful husband on a hot summer day. She had all of this and more with Hal... *because* of Hal.

She turned her eyes to her husband and found him looking at her.

"You seem to be enjoying the ride," he said, his voice quiet as if he didn't want to intrude upon the peaceful setting.

"I feel ten pounds lighter out here," she said. "I wish we could take a drive or a walk every evening."

He nodded. "We'll be able to do more of this when I can hire a man at the mill."

"Hopefully that will be soon. The furniture you build and the carving you do is stunning, Hal. I wish you could work at that full time."

"I used to wish that as well, but ironically the mill has begun to grow on me. I'm beginning to understand what John had loved about it. Don't mistake me, I'll never walk away from woodworking, but I plan to find a way balance both. Either trade will make a good business for our sons one day."

The fluttering in her stomach started again. The idea of having children with Hal was feeling more possible each day. And despite her mixed emotions about crossing that intimate threshold, she found she was eager to have a child. She could imagine their round-cheeked infants with dark hair and bright eyes. They would become gangly teens and grow into tall, strong men like their father. Hal would teach their sons about honor and integrity, and she would teach them about love. Perhaps their sons would inherit Hal's talent with woodworking or her love of music. There were so many possibilities, and she felt hopeful for the future of her family.

She lifted her face to the refreshing breeze and embraced the moment. The days were becoming humid and sometimes stifling. But tonight the air was lovely, and she closed her eyes for a moment and allowed the breeze to blow across her face.

Hal chuckled. "You aren't napping, are you?"

She smiled and met his eyes. "I'm trying to distract myself so that I don't ask you where we're going."

Hal laughed. "I'll help distract you by asking what you wish for your birthday."

"I wish you would tell me where we're going."

He looked at her with sparkling eyes and the warmest smile. "Your persistence is adorable. Other than wishing to appease your curiosity, is there anything you want for your birthday that I might be able to give you? This is your first birthday away from your family, and I know you miss them. I'd just hoped to make the day a little less sad for you."

An upwelling of tenderness filled her, and she placed her hand over his forearm. "Thank you. I am a little sad and homesick on and off today, but I'm truly glad to be here... with you, and that makes me happy. Today was to be my debut ball with Elizabeth, and I'm sorry she must attend alone. But I'm not at all sorry to be free of the arrangement with Stuart. I can't help but wonder if Elizabeth has been able to convince my father to allow Stuart to court her, or if she's still stuck in a dreadful arrangement with Robert."

"You should write home and ask Elizabeth about all of this and let them know that you're safe and that you've married a *dashing artist* and are blissfully happy."

Nancy laughed at Hal's witty use of her words to describe himself in such a fanciful light. "Perhaps I will write home," she said, but she knew she wouldn't. Not yet anyhow. Maybe when enough time passed, Hal wouldn't be so angry or hate her father so deeply and she could tell him the truth without him also hating her. She couldn't forget the anger in his voice when he described her father's role in repossessing his own father's mill. It seemed unlikely that Hal would ever see her father in a kind light, or that he'd ever forgive her for lying about her identity if he learned she was Lloyd Tremont's daughter.

"All right then," he said. "This is your birthday, and we're going to celebrate and have our own fun tonight."

His declaration turned her thoughts back to the here and now and the dashing, wonderful man at her side.

"We have arrived," he said, turning up a long drive toward a huge gambrel-roofed barn that reminded her of her stables back home in Buffalo. As they approached, she noticed a number of other wagons and carriages parked along the drive and several men in their Sunday best and ladies with parasols and pretty dresses milling about outside the barn.

Four sets of double barn doors were thrown wide, leaving the majority of one barn wall open to the outside. Lanterns were strung across the inside of the barn, illuminating thick rafters overhead and benches that lined the inside perimeter of the barn. Another gathering of people inside captured her attention. Men in dark suits and ladies in all manner of colorful dresses milled about. There must be twenty couples or more visiting with one another.

Nancy glanced at her husband, surprised, and confused by the sight. "I thought we were going dancing this evening, but this is a... a barn, not a ballroom or a public hall."

Hal laughed and parked their carriage under a sprawling oak just off the drive. "We shall be dining and dancing right here."

"In a *barn?*" she asked. She'd never heard of such a thing.

"That's right. You'll need to hike up your skirts to keep them free of manure."

"What!"

Hal laughed so hard it bent him double and drew curious looks from the men and ladies gathered outside on the lawn.

Nancy angled her parasol to hide herself from their inspection. "Are you jesting with me, Hal?"

"About dancing in the barn? No." He wiped his eyes and grinned at her. "About dancing in manure? Yes. The barn is used for wood storage or for occasional barn dances, so there's no chance of soiling your lovely dress, darling." He stepped down and secured the reins to the oak and then reached up to assist Nancy. "Come on down and see how us common folk live."

"Where are we?" Nancy asked curiously.

"This is one of Thomas Drake's lumber buildings. He's the one I told you about who's interested in leasing our mill."

Nancy's heart sank at those words. So tonight was going to be about business as well. Her hopes for a romantic evening were quickly dashed at the thought. She extended her hand, expecting Hal to grasp it and allow her to step down from the carriage. Instead, he clasped her waist and swung her down from the carriage, whirling her in a full circle before placing her on the ground. Her heart raced, and she stared at him in surprise. "That was rather enthusiastic," she quipped.

With a wide smile on his face, he extended his elbow to her. "Shall we?"

Nancy tucked her hand in the crook of his elbow. Hal placed his over hand over hers and together they said hello to neighbors and friends and introduced themselves to several members of their community. Nancy met ladies in stylish hats and women with ribbons woven through their coiffed hair, all of them friendly and welcoming her with such warmth she had to swallow tears of gratitude.

The men quizzed Hal about his mill output, and the women complimented him on the beautiful furniture he was making for Edwards. They confessed their envy of Nancy because, being married to Hal, she must surely have a house full of magnificent furniture. Hal grimaced, but Nancy merely smiled and pointed out the hairpin that Hal had carved for her. The ladies oohed and begged their husbands to solicit such a piece from Hal's skilled hands for their anniversary or for Christmas or some other special occasion. The husbands rolled their eyes and headed for the beverage table. Hal took advantage of the moment and escorted Nancy through the open doors of the barn.

Lanterns hung everywhere, casting a warm golden hue inside the barn. The center of the barn was completely cleared, and a floor of wide pine planks was scrubbed to a rich luster. Nancy assumed it was the dance floor and found it surprisingly suitable. The enormous barn wasn't full of people by any means, but it was filling quickly as many of the couples from the yard made their way inside. Outside the perimeter of benches sat four long tables and more benches.

The barn felt cavernous as Nancy gazed up to the loft above and rows of thick square rafters extending high into the ceiling. The barn wasn't dirty and musty as she had expected. It smelled of wood and food and a mixture of colognes and perfumes from the many guests.

Intrigued, Nancy turned slowly to take it all in. From the back side of the barn, just beyond the dance floor, the discordant strains of instruments being tuned reached her ears. A group of four gentlemen sat on overturned wine barrels, two of them tuning their fiddles and one tuning his banjo. She surmised that the man without an instrument must be their caller. Looking toward the opposite side of the barn, she spied a long table draped with colorful linens. Bustling around it were a dozen ladies and young girls arranging dishes and platters of an abundance of food. The savory scents from the warm dishes wafted through the barn and made her mouth water—and made her stomach drop to her feet. She should have brought a dish to pass!

Mortified, she turned to Hal. "Why didn't you tell me they would be serving food here? I should have brought something, Hal."

"I know, but I wanted to surprise you, so Mary Tucker has brought an extra dish that she'll say is from you."

"What?" Nancy's stomach dropped yet again. "I know you wished to surprise me, Hal, but you shouldn't have asked Mary to do this."

"I didn't ask. She suggested it to help me keep all of this as a surprise. But don't fret, darling. We are going to repay her kindness by having her and William over for supper and to play cards next weekend. I thought you'd like the chance to entertain in our home."

Hearing him refer to his house as *their* home thrilled Nancy. "I would love to have our friends over. May we invite Tom and Martha as well?"

"Already done. Stop fretting over this. Mary was thrilled to do this for you." He smiled down at her. "Happy birthday, Nancy. I thought it only appropriate for you to celebrate your birthday at a dance. Think of this as your own personal birthday ball. And as your husband, I have the added pleasure of showing off my beautiful wife for the evening."

Nancy shook her head, overwhelmed by all she was seeing and hearing, but mostly by her husband's devoted attention.

"Happy birthday, Nancy!" Mary said, greeting her with a wide smile and warm hug. She was stunning in her dress of deep rose. The hem, sleeves, and collar were trimmed with cranberry colored ribbon and the fitted bodice was accented with pretty pearl buttons. Mary had also opted to forgo a hat and had pinned her shiny black hair in a stylish twist and added a sprig of pink baby rosebuds that complimented her dress. Her emerald eyes sparkled as she clasped her husband's hand and drew William to her side. He immediately wished Nancy a happy birthday and begged a dance with the birthday girl.

Before Nancy could return their warm welcome, Hal slipped his arm around her shoulders and said all dances with his wife were his.

And so the four of them spent a minute laughing and joking, and then Hal and William stepped away for a moment, giving Nancy and Mary a chance to chat.

"I'm so sorry that we didn't join you on Sunday afternoon," Nancy said to Mary. "It had just been a long week and I was feeling a bit maudlin thinking about spending my birthday without my sister."

"No need to apologize. I do hope, however, that your day improved."

"Oh, it did, and in the most surprising way," Nancy said. "Hal took me out to the creek, and you'll never guess what happened. We both fell in!"

"You did? Truly?" Mary asked with a smile that became a full laugh as Nancy described how Hal had slipped on the bank and pulled her in after him. She didn't share with Mary the heated moment that followed. She wasn't ready to share those intimate details of her marriage with anyone yet. Besides, they likely thought she and Hal had a traditional marriage and Nancy's excitement over a kiss would seem unusual. But as she told Mary about their afternoon together, she smiled at the thought that she had really gotten to know her husband better during their time at the gorge. "And so we ate our lunch with our shoes off and our clothes dripping."

Mary clasped her hands together in front of her chest and said, "It sounds like a wonderful day."

"It was," Nancy said, her gaze turning to her dashing husband, who was deep in conversation with William and another man.

"I'm so pleased Hal decided to bring you to the dance. William and I have been anticipating this evening for weeks. It's been an age since we've been out dancing," Mary said. "Wait until you see William on the floor. He's quite the dancer and I imagine Hal is as well."

Nancy shrugged. "I honestly don't know." But as she imagined Hal taking her in his arms and turning her about the dance floor, her breath hitched in anticipation. She glanced at Hal and found him looking at her. He winked one dark-lashed eye at her, and Nancy's stomach fluttered so wildly she thought she might swoon.

"The dance is about to start," Mary said, and they quickly joined their husbands.

As the players made their final adjustments to their instruments, the caller greeted everyone and bade them take their positions on the floor for a welcome quadrille. He announced that the evening would begin with nine dances, a set of five quadrilles, a waltz, then two more quadrilles followed by another waltz. They would break for supper and then finish the evening with a set of five more quadrilles and end with a waltz.

Hal extended his hand and executed an exaggerated, sweeping bow.

With a laugh, Nancy placed her hand in his, and he escorted her to the dance floor behind William and Mary. There they exchanged hugs with Tom and Martha Fiske, and Hal quickly introduced Nancy to Thomas and Victoria Drake, a couple about Hal's or William's age. Victoria was a stunning lady with her high cheekbones and elegant silver dress, her ears sparkling with emeralds that matched her green eyes. Thomas was equally attractive in his black suit, starched white shirt, and black shoes buffed to a mirror shine. Within that short span of minutes, Nancy found the Drakes such friendly, wonderful people she felt she'd known them as long as the Tuckers and Fiskes.

Realizing she was among friends, Nancy eagerly lined up in a rectangular formation with Hal and the other three couples. She was intimately familiar with the dance from her many lessons in preparation for her birthday ball. Tonight, however, she would be dancing in a barn—with her *husband*.

As the musicians played one final note on their instruments and then fell silent, Nancy felt the excitement level rise around her. That moment of silence was their cue that the dance was to begin. In the next instant the musicians opened with their first song, and Nancy and the other dancers launched into a variety of rapid, skimming steps filled with grace and gaiety that left them laughing and breathless and set the tone for the evening.

"You are quite accomplished, Mr. Grayson," Nancy said with a bit of coquettishness as her eyes met his and they circled one another.

"It is my graceful and most beautiful partner that makes me appear so, *Mrs.* Grayson." Eyes twinkling, he gave her a merry spin. As she came back to face him, he greeted her with a warm smile and a wink. She laughed as they each moved on to the next partner in the formation. Each time she and Hal met, the great room felt warmer, her breath shorter, her stomach lighter.

Until this evening, she'd had few occasions to touch her husband's hands. But she had studied those long-fingered artist's hands many times. And as she and Hal danced, images flashed through her mind of his tanned hands beneath the cuffs of his white shirt, the precise movement of his fingers and flexing of his muscled forearms as he used his woodworking tools, the relaxed curve of his fingers around a knife and fork while he ate his supper, the manly strength of his hands as he moved timber and stacked firewood and repaired the barn roof, the way he would playfully hand-wrestle Captain, the surprising gentleness in his hands when he cupped her face and kissed her. And now she was experiencing the exciting feel of his firm grip as he spun her out and back several times during the set of five lively quadrilles, each time exchanging flirtatious comments with her and keeping perfect time as the musicians played.

He gave her one last spin as the final strains of the upbeat song echoed into the rafters above. "I don't want to let you go," he said, giving her a playful bow.

Nancy didn't want to let go of his warm hand either, but she stepped back and applauded with the rest of the dancers. Her eyes locked with Hal's, and she knew that tonight was different for them. They both wanted to be here, together, as husband and wife.

The first waltz of the evening began, and Hal fit his strong, warm hand with hers and placed his other hand at her waist. Her stomach twirled just as he swung her into their first sweeping step.

Other couples swept past, some conversing politely, some laughing into each other's faces, some simply enjoying the music and the dance.

But they all faded away as she fell into Hal's dark eyes and he carried her away in his arms.

The warmth of his gaze made her steps falter. He pulled her close, improperly close, and swept her into the next step as if she'd never stumbled. She was out of her depths now, adrift in an ocean of feeling. All sense of play was forgotten as his eyes seemed to drink her in.

In that moment she could see that he was vulnerable, that he cared about her.

The knowledge shook her.

Because in that moment, she knew with sudden clarity she was deeply, desperately in love with her husband.

On their next turn, he pulled her close again and whispered, "If you don't stop looking at me with those beautiful eyes, I'm going to sweep you right out the door and kiss you."

Nancy gasped so loudly it drew the attention of two couples twirling past them. One couple even apologized as if they'd cut too close.

That made Hal laugh. But Nancy's face flushed so hot she felt faint.

"I hadn't meant to shock you," he said, but his smile was back, and he seemed to be enjoying her loss of composure.

"Well you did."

His wide, white smile let her know he wasn't at all remorseful. "I was merely stating a fact."

Gracious, she hadn't been prepared for this flirtatious side of Hal. If he was this bold with her here in the midst of all these people, what could she expect when they were alone?

Every glance from his dark eyes made her breath catch. Outwardly, he appeared to behave himself for the duration of the waltz, but Nancy felt every private squeeze he gave her hands. He disguised his flirtation well, but Nancy was in a near-swoon by the time the waltz ended.

It was time for the musicians and dancers to take an intermission to enjoy a light supper and much-needed refreshments.

"I'm famished," she declared in a desperate attempt to shift her husband's attention to food.

Hal lowered his head and whispered near her ear, "So am I."

Gooseflesh covered Nancy's neck and she sucked in a breath. "I have no idea how to respond to that," she whispered back.

Hal released a delighted laugh and escorted her to the food table. "I enjoy flirting with you, darling."

The overhead lanterns reflected off the stacks of dishes. Together they followed friends and neighbors down the long tables of food. Nancy selected a juicy slice of pork and a small breast of chicken and added a spoonful of roasted vegetables to her plate. She topped it off with two sliced pickle halves and a fluffy roll with a perfectly buttered brown top.

When they reached the end of the table, Nancy gawked at her plate. "I didn't think I'd taken much, but there's enough here to feed both of us."

"I've discovered the same thing, but I still intend to have dessert," he said, and gestured toward a table in the corner loaded with pies and a cake and other sweets.

Nancy glanced at the plates of cookies, cakes, and pies, not one item of which she'd prepared, and felt a pang of discomfort for coming empty-handed. But there was nothing to be done about it now. And really, only she and Hal and Mary knew the truth, thankfully.

They found a spot at a back table where Tom and Martha Fiske were reserving bench space for them and the Tuckers. Hal put his plate on the table and excused himself to fetch their beverages. Nancy placed her plate next to his and then sat beside Martha. While situating her skirts around her section of the bench, she said, "What a wonderful night!"

"It is, indeed," Martha readily agreed.

Nancy took in Martha's flushed cheeks and sky-blue eyes, the same shade of blue as her dress. "You are absolutely glowing this evening, Martha. How are you feeling?"

"Like I can't breathe," Martha said with a laugh. "I'm afraid if I eat anything my dress seams will burst. This will be the last I wear this gown until after the baby is born."

Hal returned with two glasses of lemonade. After he sat, Nancy turned to him. "Thank you for this evening, Hal. I've discovered that I quite enjoy dancing in a barn... and with you."

"Likewise," he said, his words quiet and for her ears only. "When I saw the flyer in the mercantile earlier this week, I knew you would enjoy it. Seemed a perfect way to celebrate your birthday, and so here we are."

"I've never been so happy," she said. "Truly, Hal. Not ever."

He slid his hand over and gave hers a brief squeeze. "I want to make you this happy every day."

She smiled, wanting to turn her hand over and link fingers with him. Instead, she turned her attention to the safety of eating her meal. They enjoyed their supper and chatted with their friends throughout supper. The Fiskes and Tuckers were eagerly anticipating the upcoming weekend and their dinner at Hal and Nancy's home.

Nancy gave up halfway through her meal and watched Hal scoop the last of a buttered sweet potato slice onto his fork. "I see you made quick work of eating your supper."

"I'm eager to get you back in my arms," he quipped.

She was eager, too, but they took time to eat a slice of pie, apple for her, mincemeat for Hal, before the musicians signaled the dancing would begin again.

Martha patted her slightly rounding belly and said that she and Tom would sit out the rest of the quadrilles, so Nancy and Hal followed Mary and William onto the floor.

This time they formed a square with three other couples they didn't know, which gave them an opportunity to make more friends. Nancy found herself laughing and smiling as the four couples danced the compilation of quadrilles. As the lively songs came to an end, she pressed her hand to her heart, hoping to calm its beating and catch her breath before the last dance.

But less than a minute later the musicians filled the cavernous barn with the last song of the evening, and all couples danced alone. As the flowing strains of the waltz filled the air, Hal clasped her hand and pulled her close, perhaps a little too close, and swept her across the floor.

Nancy followed his lead through the sweeping steps and across the floor. This waltz was a popular dance at many of her parent's parties. She and Elizabeth used to watch from the top of the stairs when they were children, but as they got older their parents would allow them to attend for a while and her father would always dance a waltz and a quadrille with each of his girls.

"What's put that frown on your face?" Hal asked, drawing her a little closer.

Something she didn't want to talk about and thoughts that didn't belong in their beautiful evening. "I'm pouting because I wanted another slice of pie."

His eyebrows lifted. "Truly?"

"Good gracious, no!" She laughed. "I was jesting. I won't need to eat again until tomorrow evening."

"Good," he said, "because I plan to dance with you until then."

"I think I could manage that," she said, enjoying their byplay. "I'm sad to know this is the last song of the night and it's almost over."

"It's not *our* last dance," he said. A storm of emotions swirled in his eyes as he held in his arms, dancing to the flowing strains of the waltz. She felt the brush of his knee against her leg as he drew her close. Her heart thumped in her chest, and her stomach fluttered as Hal looked down at her with dark eyes.

"The song is ending," he said, dancing her off the floor. "Let's thank our hosts and hurry out before the drive is congested with carriages. "I slipped out earlier to check on Gus, and he said he's ready to go when we are."

Nancy smiled and felt deeply grateful for Hal's wonderful sense of humor.

With a playful wink, Hal tucked her hand in the crook of his arm and guided her toward the door where Thomas and Victoria Drake stood to bid their guests goodnight.

"It was such a pleasure to meet you," Nancy said to the Drakes. "Thank you both for this lovely event."

"We were honored to have you as our guests," Victoria said, giving Nancy a warm hug while Thomas and Hal shook hands. "We would like to have you and Hal to supper some evening soon."

Nancy and Hal both expressed their delight and appreciation, and then with a final thank you to their hosts, Hal whisked Nancy outside to their carriage. He lit the carriage lanterns and got them on the road home just as the crowd of guests were making their way outside.

The sound of peepers and the rhythmic jangle of Gus's harness created a heartbeat in the warm night. A vast sky of stars twinkled overhead, and from time to time Nancy caught a hint of Hal's warm, spicy cologne.

Never in her life had she experienced such a romantic night. Each look from her husband made her flush. Until meeting Hal, she hadn't known such intense feelings existed.

Sighing, she leaned back against the seat and gazed up at the night sky. "The stars look like twinkling diamonds, don't you agree? They appear so close I think I could touch them if I stood on the seat."

He arched an eyebrow at her. "Shall I assist you up?"

She laughed. "I'm afraid we would hit a bump and I'd tumble off into the shadows and you'd never find me."

"I'd find you, darling. I'd just look for the starlight sparkling in your eyes," he said, looking over at her, his gaze filled with warmth.

"If you're looking for eyes shining in the dark, you might pluck a bear from the field instead of me." She shuddered. "Do you ever wonder what's out there in the woods watching us?"

He laughed, his gaze surveying her face as if thoroughly delighted with her. "Not unless I hear a growl or something large moving quickly through the brush."

"You're terrifying me, Hal."

He chuckled and lifted his arm to the seat back. "Come here." He slipped his arm around her and tucked her against his warm side. "I'll keep you safe, darling. You just enjoy the stars and this nice summer night."

"I am, Hal. This is an evening I'll never forget."

"I intend to make certain you don't."

Shocked, she glanced up expecting to see a teasing grin on his face. But instead, in the glow of their lanterns, she saw dark eyes filled with adoration.

"I've been waiting all night to do this." He dipped his head and kissed her.

CHAPTER TWENTY-ONE

At the Tucker's livery door, Hal climbed out and secured the carriage. William was right behind them and would tend to Gus and the carriage. That was part of the service William provided at his livery and the added benefit he insisted on giving Hal when he'd rented the carriage. So Hal rewarded Gus with a sugar cube and a friendly pat on the neck as he thanked the magnificent animal for his service.

Then he turned to help Nancy out. He held her hand as they cut through the orchard. A sliver of moonlight shimmered on the creek but didn't provide ample light by which to navigate the grassy apple orchard. Nancy hiked her dress higher but continued to stumble over the thick clusters of grass. Hal easily kept her upright, but the third time she caught her slipper in a thick clump of grass, he realized his mistake. "I'm sorry, Nancy. I should have dropped you at the house before returning the carriage."

"And deny me this exciting challenge and a romantic walk beneath the stars? No, thank you." No sooner had the words left her mouth than she stumbled against him. She laughed and glanced up at him. "These slippers work much better on a dance floor."

"Allow me, darling." Hal reached down and lifted her into his arms.

She hooked her arms around his neck, her face close to his. "Is this your tricky way of getting me in your arms, Mr. Grayson?"

"I'm afraid you've caught me."

"I'm glad I did," she said, her boldness surprising and pleasing him.

He stopped and angled her face toward the weak light of the moon. "Are you glad?" he asked, searching her face, needing to know. "Are you happy with me? With our marriage?"

She cupped his cheek. "The only way I could be happier is to know that you don't regret marrying me."

"The only thing I've regretted is not being able to give you more."

"I don't need a thing that we don't already have, Hal."

He kissed her forehead. "Thank you."

"You cannot carry me all the way home," she whispered against his cheek.

"Perhaps not, but I aim to try." He hefted her higher in his arms. "Hold on."

"I'll never let go."

He carried her to the house, up the steps, and into the foyer. He was breathing hard and his arms trembled from fatigue, but he continued straight to their bedroom.

She glanced at him in surprise—and then she smiled.

That unspoken welcome was his undoing. He lowered her feet to the floor and kissed her, tenderly, deeply, their bodies slowly swaying as if they were still on the dance floor.

He would dance with her all night.

CHAPTER TWENTY-TWO

H al smiled as he shut off the mill at the end of the day and secured the building before heading home Saturday evening. During his walk, he marveled that nearly a week had passed since he and Nancy had taken the final step in their marriage. Their love was big and consuming and more wonderful than he could have ever imagined.

And Hal couldn't stay away from Nancy. Even as busy as he was, each day he would head home for a quick lunch with her. Just two weeks ago he wouldn't have left the mill during the day unless the house was on fire. The thought made him smile as he rounded the bend by Tom and Martha Fiske's house. It had been a long day, and he couldn't wait to get home and pull his beautiful bride into his arms.

Hal savored every minute with his wife. Even during their rushed lunches, they held hands and conversed about their day and planned their evening. They would gaze into each other's eyes, and their thoughts would stray to their new intimacy with each other. And Hal would pull her onto his lap for a tender kiss... and their lunch would sit forgotten on the table.

Just thinking about Nancy made Hal take longer strides to get home sooner. He wanted a few minutes with her before the Tuckers and Fiskes arrived for supper.

Nancy was excited about having company over. Hal was, too. He looked forward to an enjoyable evening with their friends. But he eagerly anticipated the end of the night when he and Nancy would cuddle on the sofa together with Captain. As he did each evening, Hal would tease Nancy by groaning and rolling his eyes as if the cat was so much bother and that he was tolerating the little beast for her sake. But she knew he was playacting and had grown fond of Captain. After their family snuggle, Hal and Nancy would wash up, snuff the lanterns, and slip into their bedchamber—it was finally their chamber and not just hers.

Even now, Hal still couldn't believe the reality and wonder of his life. For all the energy he put into fighting John's idea of marriage, Hal had never dreamed it could be filled with such warmth and joy and passion.

But it was—all because he had impulsively taken Nancy Mitchell home instead of putting her back on the train.

As Hal hurried up the drive and climbed the steps of his house, he knew bringing Nancy home with him was the smartest thing he'd ever done. He strode into the foyer and headed to the parlor—nearly forgetting to remove his boots. Nancy would have his head if he tracked up her clean floors, especially when they were expecting guests. He turned right around removed his boots and set them on a tray by the door. He tugged on his colorful slippers and wondered what William and Tom would think of them. Hal decided that what Nancy thought was more important, and he wore his slippers across the house with pride!

Tonight they were entertaining. Although Hal and Nancy had gone to supper and other gatherings at the Tuckers and Fiskes, they hadn't yet entertained company in their own home. Hal and John certainly hadn't entertained the neighbors in the time they lived here. So Hal was looking forward to a night of fun.

When Hal entered the kitchen, he found Nancy standing by the window with two potholders and a pie in hand, angling it toward the light.

"Something wrong with the pie?" he asked.

Her eyes were filled with concern. "I might have overcooked it." She shook her head. "I just got distracted and left the pie in a bit too long and I think the bottom might have scorched."

"Then we'll eat everything but the bottom," Hal said, crossing the room and planting a kiss on her forehead. "Don't fret so, Nancy. We're entertaining friends not entering a pie baking contest. And I suspect we're serving more than pie this evening, and that everything else will be delicious."

"I hope so." She signed and placed the pie on the windowsill to cool. "I just want everything to be perfect tonight. I want to show Mary and Martha how much I appreciate all they've done for me since I came to Fredonia. And I want to make you proud, too."

Hal drew her into his arms and tilted her chin up. "Look at me, darling." Her eyes met his and he could see how anxious she was. "I am more than proud of you. I'm amazed by you. I'm enchanted with you. I'm in awe of you. This evening wasn't meant to add more work or stress to your shoulders. I just wanted to have our friends over for a bit because I thought it would be enjoyable for both of us."

"I feel the same way, Hal."

"Then please take a deep breath and try to enjoy this. I'm sure everything, including the pie, will be wonderful."

He placed a kiss upon her lips to distract her, to give her something more pleasant to think about, and because he couldn't look at her without wanting to kiss her. "I'm going to wash up. Why don't you sit down for five minutes and relax before they arrive?"

"Perhaps that's a good idea. Everything is ready, so I'll cuddle Captain for a few minutes."

"I'm envious, but I'm sure Captain will appreciate your affection."

She laughed, and Hal congratulated himself on putting a smile back on her face. He washed up in the kitchen and then changed his clothes in the bedroom. When he returned to the kitchen he found Nancy lifting a teacup to her lips.

He drank a glass of water and sat at the table with her while she finished her tea. He told her about his day and asked about hers. "Your garden is looking quite healthy," he said.

Her eyes lit up and she pointed to a basket of leafy greens on the sideboard. "I picked some spinach and a few beans today."

He got up and inspected the dark green spinach leaves and crisp beans. "These look delicious. I can hardly wait to eat these. This is the first of your harvest, isn't it?" he asked, already knowing the answer. He knew Nancy had worked hard to plant and to tend their garden, and he wanted to acknowledge her efforts and the commendable results.

"Yes, and we'll have more by early next week."

"Good, because this will be gone by tomorrow night."

She smiled. "I'd planned to cook them tomorrow evening and top them with salt and butter."

"Sounds delicious," Hal said, patting his stomach. "I'm starving, and whatever you've got cooking on the stove smells good."

"I'll butter a slice of bread for you," she said, going to the sideboard.

He caught her hand and drew her against him. "I'd rather have a kiss."

She laughed and raised up on her toes to peck him on the cheek.

"Well, that certainly took the edge off my hunger," Hal said, eliciting another laugh from Nancy.

A sharp knock on the door startled them apart, and they both went to the foyer to greet their guests. Before he opened the door, Nancy patted her hair and smoothed down her apron. He grasped her hand in his. "You look beautiful. Dinner smells delicious. And your pie looks perfect. Let's relax and welcome our first guests." With that, he opened the door.

Tom and Martha were at the door, and just exiting the orchard were Mary and William, both couples with a basket in hand.

And so began their evening as their friends entered their home with warm smiles and easy conversation.

Martha Fiske glanced around the home that used to belong to her father and said, "Your home is lovely." She smiled at Hal. "It looks a sight better than when you first brought Nancy here."

Hal wrapped his arm around Nancy's waist and gazed down at her. "It absolutely does. Nancy has made us a wonderful home here."

And she had. As Hal observed his friends visiting in his home, he stood a bit taller and a bit prouder.

William and Tom stood near the door snickering over something. Hal followed gazes to his feet. That's when he realized he had forgotten to put on his shoes and was still wearing his slippers. Tom and William were biting their lips, much like he was doing. Finally, he grinned. "I see you fellas are admiring the slippers Nancy knit for me."

Tom and William choked trying to hold back laughter.

Hal shrugged. "They're comfy and so colorful they're easy to keep track of. And my reward for keeping the floors clean is that my lovely bride can spend time with me instead of cleaning floors."

"That's right," Nancy said, linking her arm with Hal's.

The women joined in the laughter, and Hal wondered if Tom and William would be sporting similar pairs of slippers in the future.

"Well, shall we all head into the kitchen? Supper is ready," Nancy said.

"Tom and I brought cornbread and a jar of honey," Martha said, lifting her basket.

"And William and I brought some elderberry wine," Mary added, and the three couples headed into the kitchen.

Supper was filled with conversation and laughter, and the meal was delicious, which went a long way in easing Nancy's anxiety. Mary said the chicken was moist and the vegetables were perfectly seasoned. Even the rolls were light and perfectly browned. Hal shot Nancy a smile, hoping to calm her nerves, but he thought that the oohs and ahs coming from their guests was confirmation enough. He watched as her smile grew with each scrumptious bite their guests took. And he smiled right along with her. He was so proud of the woman she'd become. To think that only a few short weeks ago she had arrived expecting to direct a *staff* instead of doing these tasks herself. Yet she'd taken to this life and she was blooming with as much strength and splendor as the plants in her garden.

As the women cleared the dishes after supper and the men took out the cards, Hal thought of the first day Nancy tried to cook in his kitchen, now *their* kitchen, and had nearly smoked them out of the house. If it hadn't been for that one mishap, she wouldn't be here now. He would have sent her back to Buffalo. But the smoke-filled house, and her subsequent illness, had kept her in Fredonia and set them on a course to where they found themselves today, happily married and in love. The way she'd given so fully of herself in every aspect of their marriage had melted him. The sassy, compassionate, and fiery woman had broken through his angry, grieving heart and saved him from drowning in despair. From the minute he met her, his emotions had been in a whirl, and yet he knew without doubt he loved her.

Laughter from the ladies drew his attention. Nancy was showing Mary and Martha the tabletop pie safe Hal had made for her. She ran her hand over the smooth lines of the piece and pointed out all the intricacies in the carving. It wasn't the first time he'd seen her admire his work. He had been so pleased the day he'd presented it to her. She had been disappointed all week because he wouldn't let her help in the woodshop. He said he needed solitude to carve a special piece for Edwards, which was partly true. But he finished the piece early and was able to make a small pie safe for Nancy. When he'd finally presented her with the piece Nancy squealed with delight and promptly whacked him with her dish towel. She chastised him for hoodwinking her and then lavished him with affection for the gift.

He was pleased he could make something she was so proud of and touched by how much that gift meant to her. He wanted to give so much more. He knew she had grown up in wealth and had been forced to sacrifice so much. But she seemed genuinely happy with what little they had. A look around the kitchen again reminded him how she'd taken so little and made his house into a home.

And how she filled his days with joy and nights with love. He smiled at the thought and watched her return to the table with the apple pie she thought she'd burned. Just two bites in and Hal caught her eye and tapped the pie crust with his fork. *It's perfect,* he mouthed.

I know! Nancy mouthed back, her eyes filled with happy surprise.

"If you two are done making eyes at one another, I'm ready to play cards," William joked.

Nancy's cheeks flamed, but they all laughed.

Mary said to her husband, "You men scoot out of the kitchen until we get things cleaned up, then we'll play cards."

"Come on, fellas," Hal said getting to his feet. "Let's clear out." He popped a quick kiss on Nancy's cheek as he passed her and then headed to the parlor with his friends.

NANCY SMILED as she and the ladies worked quickly to get the dessert dishes cleared from the table.

"You two certainly look happy," Mary said.

Nancy paused while washing a plate, her dishcloth still submerged under water. "I am happy. I never expected this life when I got off the train from Buffalo, but I don't think I could have chosen a better man for myself."

"Well, that handsome husband of yours obviously feels the same if those loving looks he was giving you during dinner are any indication," Martha added.

Nancy felt her cheeks warm and she ducked her head. She wasn't used to talking like this with women or with anyone actually.

"It's wonderful to see you and Hal laying a solid foundation for your life here together."

Nancy hoped that was so, but their foundation had a crack in it— one fat lie that created a fissure that could bring down everything they were building.

Sounds of the men's voices coming from the parlor interrupted any further thoughts she had. Hal strode into the kitchen, tall, lean, and utterly charming in his ridiculous slippers. "Are we ready to play some cards?" he asked, wrapping his arm around her waist.

"Yes, the table is cleared. I just need to wipe off the stove and I'll be over."

"What are we playing?" Mary asked, retrieving a jug of elderberry wine from her basket.

"How about Four Jacks," William said, and they all agreed as they took their places around the table.

As Hal shuffled the cards, Nancy took a seat to his right. She had just settled in when Captain trotted into the kitchen and leapt into her lap. "Hello, sweetheart," she said, stroking his ears and down his back. Captain hunched his back and rewarded her with a loud purr that made the entire group laugh.

"That cat has completely taken over the house," Hal said, but Nancy knew he wasn't complaining. Hal loved having Captain in their lives. She'd even seen him hand-wrestling the cat when Captain decided to make Hal's tools his playthings.

As Captain settled on her lap, Hal dealt the first round. Nancy checked her cards and wanted to groan.

William played the first card, and Hal wound up having the highest card and taking the trick, which meant he'd earned himself a penalty point.

"Oh boy, that wasn't wise," Hal said, and everyone laughed. He led the play and Nancy followed suit.

"Argh," she said as she laid a Jack on the table, realizing she would take the penalty point when the rest of them quickly played lower cards, leaving her holding the bag, so to speak. She scooped the cards and started the next round.

While they laughed and chatted and played cards, Nancy ran her hand down Captain's back, soaking in the comfort of her surroundings and the feeling of her home. She had good friends, an adorable cat, and a loving husband in a cozy home. What more could one want or need? Even while living in the luxury of her father's wealth she hadn't felt this content or happy.

Play continued with each of them dragging tricks and laughing and sipping wine, except Martha who drank tea. As the hands piled up, Nancy continued to collect more and more penalty points.

"I'm dreadful at this game," she exclaimed after one hand where she collected not one but two penalty points. Her outburst elicited laughter from their guests and startled Captain, who jumped down from her lap, clearly done with the periodic disruptions. She watched him meander into the parlor where he would likely curl up on the sofa to avoid the noise.

They played cards long into the evening, and Nancy observed their guests. She watched as William placed his hand over Mary's at the table or popped a kiss on her cheek when she celebrated a good hand. They shared a playful and deeply respectful love that was clear in their marriage. But Nancy had also witnessed their private glances and the deeper intensity they shared. She was pleased that she no longer had to long for that type of relationship with her husband—because she had the same wonderful romance and passion with Hal. Taking the final step in consummating their marriage had created a deeper connection between her and her husband—one she felt each evening when they slept in each other's arms.

She also observed Martha and Tom. They were equally as loving, but Tom showed an additional tenderness and protectiveness toward Martha and their unborn child. When he thought no one was looking, he would place his hand gently over Martha's rounding belly and she would place hers over his. And the secret, tender glances that they shared told a story of love and devotion to family. Nancy couldn't help but wonder if all men became tender and protective of their wives when they were pregnant. She placed her hand on her stomach and wondered what it would feel like to have a child growing in her womb and if Hal would be equally protective of their unborn child when she conceived.

As the candles burned low around the table and the wicks grew short in the lanterns, Martha finally said she must take her child home to bed. Tom stood and pulled out the chair for his wife, helping her to her feet.

"We need to head home, too," Mary said, and everyone stood.

Hal wrapped his arm around Nancy, and together they walked their guests to the front door.

"Thank you so much for a wonderful evening," Mary said. She leaned in and clasped Nancy's hands before whispering, "I'm so happy for you and Hal. I knew you two were a match the moment I saw you together."

Nancy smiled. "I'm glad you were right."

Laughs were shared, and final goodbyes were said, and Hal finally closed the door behind them and sagged against it with a loud groan. "I thought they'd never leave."

"What!" Nancy laughed. "You had a wonderful time and you know it."

He grinned. "I did. But I couldn't wait to have our privacy back."

"Privacy for what?" she asked.

"For snuggling on the sofa with my wife and our rascal cat."

CHAPTER TWENTY-THREE

As Nancy heated leftover baked chicken for lunch, she marveled that two weeks had already passed since she and Hal had taken the final step in their marriage.

In all her fantasies of married life, Nancy had never dreamed it could be filled with such warmth and joy and passion.

But it was—and she couldn't be more content.

The sound of the kitchen door opening told her that her husband was home. He'd started using the back door at lunchtime, so he didn't have to remove his boots. Taking them on and off took up precious minutes they could be sharing, and so Nancy gladly swept up after he headed back to work.

"Something smells good," he said, entering the kitchen and filling the room with his presence.

Sawdust covered his clothing, and perspiration stains wet the underarms of his shirt. His hair stuck out around a dirty old cap. But to Nancy, Hal was utterly handsome. He was so different now from the angry grieving man who'd met her at the train station. Despite his heavy workload and painful grief, Hal had softened and learned how to laugh again. His natural disposition was playful and funny and romantic, and now he brought that charming side of him home to her each day. And that made him even more dashing and positively irresistible.

Wearing a warm smile, he crossed the kitchen, the spark in his eyes telling her that he was as eager to see her as she was to see him. This tall amazing man was here to see *her*.

He slipped his arms around her waist and drew her close. She went willingly and even arched her neck to receive his gentle kiss and playful nuzzle.

"You smell like vanilla and peppermint," he said, his voice close and warm against her ear.

She replied, "That's because I've been working in the garden this morning, so I rubbed peppermint leaves on myself to keep the bugs away."

"That doesn't explain the vanilla."

She laughed and directed his attention to a plate of cookies cooling on the sideboard. "I used vanilla in the cookies I baked for you this morning. I put a touch of vanilla behind my ears to make me smell better."

"You smell good to me." He growled and nibbled her neck.

She laughed and eased back in his arms. "If you keep dallying, Mr. Grayson, your lunch will burn. Unhand me so I can remove it from the oven."

With an exaggerated sigh, he released her. "I suppose I can eat while you read your letter." He withdrew a paper from his shirt pocket and handed it to her. "It seems one Elizabeth Tremont has sent you a letter, and I must confess that I'm rabidly curious."

Nancy squealed with excitement as she plucked the letter from Hal's hand. "I can't believe my sister replied so quickly!"

"Your sister?"

Nancy nodded. "I sent her a letter a week ago," she said, already fully engrossed in opening, and reading the letter. She couldn't wait to hear what Elizabeth thought of her marriage to Hal and to also receive news of home.

My Dearest sister,
I cannot express how relieved I am to have received word from
you and to know you are well. Father is desperately ill, and I beg
of you to return home immediately. I miss you terribly and we
will speak of your marriage and other topics upon your return.
Come quickly!
With deepest affection,
Elizabeth

NANCY CLAPPED the letter to her chest and sank onto a kitchen chair, her knees too weak to support her. "This can't be," she whispered in disbelief. Her father couldn't be ill. He was strong and... and, oh dear, he had collapsed once before, and his health had been so precarious those few weeks.

Hal cupped her arms and knelt in front of her. "What is it?"

"My father is ill, and I need to return to Buffalo immediately," she said, her voice flat, her thoughts sliding sideways. Images of her dear father on his death bed spun through her mind. She'd been with him during his last collapse, and it had been terrifying... he'd nearly died. He could die now. Before she got home. She had to hold his hand and tell him she was sorry and let him know how much she loved him, that she hadn't meant to hurt him.

"I'm sorry, Nancy. I don't have funds to take us both to Buffalo, but I'll find a way to secure passage for you. I didn't think Elizabeth was married," Hal said.

"What?" His words barely registered in the swirl of memories and worries muddying her thoughts.

"Did your sister marry a Tremont?"

"No." Nancy shook her head, more to clear her thoughts than as an answer. "She isn't married yet."

Hal's forehead creased, lowering his dark brows. "Your *sister* is a Tremont?"

Nancy nodded, wondering how quickly she could pack and if she could catch the afternoon train. The heat from the oven nauseated her, and she wanted to leave the kitchen.

Hal tapped the tabletop, startling her.

"How can Elizabeth be a Tremont if you're a Mitchell?" he asked, the suspicion in his eyes becoming eerily reminiscent of when Nancy had first met him.

Suddenly her thoughts crystalized and became clear. Ice filled her veins and her heart beat wildly in her chest. She froze as if she'd suddenly found herself caught in the sights of shotgun. Hal was staring at her, disbelief filling his eyes. There was no way out of the truth. She had unwittingly revealed her secret. The warmth that had been in Hal's expression only moments ago was gone now, leaving behind stark eyes filled with questions and embers of anger.

"You are twins, which means you have the same father," he said, and she could see the dawning horror in his eyes and that he already knew the truth. He shoved himself away and back-stepped as if she'd suddenly become a poisonous snake. "You're Lloyd Tremont's *daughter?*"

Nancy rose to her feet, her legs quaking beneath her. "Yes, and he's terribly ill. I'm sorry, Hal. I hadn't meant to deceive you—"

"But you did."

"I had no choice... that is... my father spoke of your family a number of times and how tragic it was that the Graysons had come to despise him and his bank and—"

"With good cause," Hal snapped. "He's heartless and greedy and—"

"Not the man I know!" She pressed a hand to her stomach, queasy from emotion and from hearing her husband speak such unkind words about a man who had given her everything. "I won't defend myself, but I will defend my father because he is a good man. I know firsthand that he has helped a great many people. I don't know what transpired between our fathers, but I know without doubt my father would never intentionally destroy another man or his business. You need to get both sides of the story before you make a wholesale judgement about a man's character, Hal. Because the Lloyd Tremont I know is a kind and loving father and a generous man. Whatever problem stands between you and me is of my own doing, not my father's."

"Your father's hand is in this whether you see it that way or not. You had to escape his unjust demands, and so you ran off and made up a name to hoodwink my brother."

"Mitchell is my mother's maiden name and I... I couldn't tell your brother my real name or he wouldn't have accepted me."

"Darn right he wouldn't have!" Hal jabbed his finger her direction. "You lied to him and you lied to me. And knowing all of this, you let me marry you."

"I had to," she said, quietly. "I had no other place to go. I wasn't being entirely self-serving, Hal. I knew John was from a good family. Regardless what you think of my father, he thought highly of your family. I fully intended to be a good wife to John. And when circumstances changed, I found myself with you and... and I desperately wanted a real, loving marriage with you."

"You let me come to care for you," he said, hurt thick in his voice.

"Hearing you say all of this aloud makes it seem so much worse, so dreadfully underhanded, but that was never my intent."

"But it was underhanded," he said, his voice hoarse with emotion. "What else would you call it?"

"A mistake." Sizzling sounds and wisps of smoke came from the oven. The lunch she'd lovingly prepared for him was burning... just like his hatred of her.

He snorted with disgust. "It's far more than a mistake, Nancy. It's a betrayal of everything I thought we were building. And what I find most appalling and—" He pinched the bridge of his nose as if willing himself not to lose his temper. "—and *unforgivable*, is that you betrayed my brother."

Her heart banged in her chest and her body trembled. "I can imagine how you must see this, Hal. An apology seems insignificant in the face of so much injury, but I'm truly sorry."

"Do you realize that the legality of our marriage might be questioned because you married me under a false name?"

A rush of moisture filled her eyes and she could barely squeeze words from her thick throat. "It's legal to me."

Fists clenched, he glowered at her, his face red with anger and disbelief and... hurt. "Pack your bag. I'll return in an hour to take you to the station." In a two long, angry strides, he'd crossed the kitchen and slammed out the back door of the house.

Nancy sagged against the table, her heart pounding, regret, tears, and the smell of burning chicken clogging her throat. What had she done?

AN HOUR after he'd stormed out of the house, Hal returned home, no calmer than when he'd left. He could understand what had provoked Nancy to misrepresent herself to John Radford. Desperate circumstances led to desperate measures. Hal could fathom that. What he couldn't understand, what he would *never* understand, is how she could have withheld the truth from him knowing he was falling in love with her. Hal had opened his heart and shared everything with her, his dreams, his regrets, his *grief.* Had none of that had been sacred to her?

Had she felt anything for him at all? Or was that a lie, too?

Nancy's deceit outraged him and left him trembling with anger and hurt. It appalled him to think that he had married the daughter of the man responsible for putting his own father in financial jeopardy. But the thing that cut the deepest was that she'd known all of this while lying in his arms, while he whispered words of love and they made promises and created dreams together.

Clamping down his outrage, Hal strode inside to get his deceitful bride and put her on a train as he should have done the day he met her.

He went to the kitchen, retrieved a tin cup from the cupboard and filled it from the water jug on the sink. Gulping the cool liquid, he let it soothe his hot throat. Turning, he leaned against the sink expecting to see Nancy entering the kitchen.

But the light sound of her footsteps was absent.

A paper lay on the table beside a roasting pan of badly scorched chicken. Curious, Hal picked up the paper and realized with dread that it was a letter from Nancy.

Dearest Hal,

Knowing how you feel about my father and perhaps me as well, I am having Mary take me to the station. I hope your love for your brother will help you understand why I took the course I did. My intent was never to lie, defraud, or betray anyone. I only wanted to protect my sister. I hope over time you will find it in your heart to forgive me. As for whether or not our marriage is legal or binding, I will leave it up to you. In your arms I have found joy and love that I never expected and that I never want to lose, but I understand if you feel differently.

I will await your reply to know whether or not I should return to Fredonia, and to you, upon the resolution of my father's illness. Whatever you decide, please take loving care of yourself and Captain.

With affection and deepest apology,

Nancy

WITH A CURSE, Hal slammed the tin cup onto the scarred tabletop. Water splashed across the table, the place he and Nancy had shared so many meals and conversations and plans. She had rolled her pie dough here. Hal had offered to sand and stain the top smooth and varnish it to a luster, but she'd begged him to leave it because it had character. She claimed the divots and scars in the table told a story and that they would add their own marks to the tale. And someday their children and grandchildren would become part of the tabletop legend. And so now he'd left his own mark in the top, one of anger and frustration and heartbreak.

Tossing his cup in the sink, Hal strode out the back door, rounded the house and headed across the orchard to visit Mary Tucker.

When Mary opened her door, she nodded as if she knew he wasn't in the mood for tea and a cordial chat. "I see you have something on your mind, Hal. Come in," she said, inviting him into her cozy kitchen where Hal and Nancy had shared joyful meals with Mary and William.

He took a seat at the table across from her. "Did Nancy tell you what's happened then?"

Mary nodded. "She's dreadfully concerned about her father."

"You took her to the station, I presume?"

"Yes, after a visit to the watchmaker, we went straight to the station."

Hal's jaw clenched. "Did she say why she needed to stop at the jeweler's?"

Mary shook her head. "She didn't say, but I admit I thought it odd for her to take the time to shop when she was in such a hurry to catch her train."

Hal knew why she'd stopped at the jewelers. It wasn't to shop. It was to sell another piece of jewelry. But she said she'd sold off every-thing, so what could she have offered the jeweler that—oh, no. Hal's gut clenched with anger and hurt. She'd sold her mother's ring... her *wedding* ring. It was the only piece of valuable jewelry she had left. He'd told Nancy he would find the funds to send her to Buffalo, so why did she sell a ring she held so dear to her heart? Because she hadn't wanted to ask anything of him while he was so angry with her? Because she feared he wouldn't let her travel to Buffalo? Or because she no longer wanted to be married to him?

Mary reached across the table and squeezed his clenched fist. "I don't know what's going on, but I suspect it involves more than Nancy's father. I think you should know, Hal, that she was extremely

219

concerned with your well-being. She asked me to look after you and Captain."

Hal closed his eyes and shook his head. Regret, anger, outrage, and a myriad of emotions swirled through him and made him sick to his soul.

She was gone. He had no idea what to do with any of it, and so he did the only thing he knew how to do—he got up and went back to work.

For days he worked around the clock, his mind turning over the mess with Nancy. Time in the house was painful. The rooms were empty. Dishes were piling up in the sink again, and he didn't care. The house was unbearably silent, devoid of Nancy's presence and the sound of the out-of-tune pianoforte she loved playing. Even Captain wouldn't come inside, preferring to hide in the barn rather than subject himself to Hal's misery.

The emptiness consumed Hal. It seemed forever ago that he and John had shared the house. The minute Nancy set foot inside, she'd filled it with light and love. It seemed even the house was missing her presence. When Nancy left, all sense of home left with her.

Her absence cut a gorge through Hal's chest. He missed her in the deepest part of his soul. But what she'd done was unforgivable—and he just couldn't get past that.

CHAPTER TWENTY-FOUR

Granted a brief respite from her father's bedside, Nancy wandered in the garden at her childhood home. Only she found no comfort there because the sprawling estate didn't feel like home anymore. She'd been here eight days... eight long and painful days fraught with worry and heartache and regret. The large house was quiet, and everyone's focus had been on her father, allowing Nancy time for reflection without being barraged by questions. She'd given her mother and Elizabeth a short account about finding *Mr.* Grayson's advertisement and that she'd found it preferable to her arranged marriage. She assured them that her decision had been a good one as she was quite happy with Hal Grayson.

For the most part she had told the truth. She'd left out the part about John Radford, allowing them to think it was Hal who placed the advertisement in the newspaper. It wasn't that Nancy was trying to cover up the truth but rather that she was too weary and heartsore to divulge the painful details.

Thankfully, Nancy's father was improving a bit each day, and the grip of terror was easing in her gut. But part of her heart was dying. She hadn't heard a word from Hal. Not one.

Mary Tucker had sent a short letter, however, and Nancy was eager to read it. Anticipating word from home, she sat on a wrought iron bench beneath a young pear tree to read the letter. Birds twittered overhead, and sunlight splashed down through the tree branches and warmed her shoulders.

Mary shared news of her visit with Hal and her hope that whatever burdens Hal and Nancy were carrying would soon be lifted. She was keeping an eye on Nancy's boys, as she referred to Hal and Captain, and taking Hal a hot meal each evening. She had taken in the clothes Nancy had left on the clothesline and placed them on the kitchen table for Hal. She had watered Nancy's garden during the last two hot days and encouraged Nancy to hurry home as the vegetables were ripening and weeds were sneaking in.

The thought of weeds taking over her little garden made Nancy cry. She didn't know if that forty-foot stretch of tilled earth would ever again be her little garden. She missed Captain so badly it caused physical pain in her heart. And Hal... any thought of him, any memory of their time together sliced through her like one of his sharp gouges digging through a piece of basswood.

She had found so much and had lost it all.

The feel of her sister's arm circling her shoulders startled Nancy, but only because she'd thought she was alone in the garden. She and Elizabeth were so attuned to each other and had comforted each other so many times over their years together that Nancy didn't have to lift her head to see who was at her side.

"What's burdening your heart?" Elizabeth asked.

"There are weeds in my garden." A flood of tears rushed out and Nancy buried her face in her hands.

"What?" Elizabeth rubbed Nancy's back. "What's going on?"

Nancy shook her head, unable to talk.

"You're frightening me."

"I can't talk here," Nancy whispered. She pushed to her feet and headed away from the house where her mother could see into the garden.

Elizabeth easily caught up with her and again circled her arm around Nancy's shoulders. "Come on. We'll go to our place."

Without protesting, Nancy allowed Elizabeth to lead her down a path they'd walked from their earliest memory. The garden was blooming with purple petunias, pink hibiscus, and vibrant clusters of scarlet zinnias tucked into well-tended beds. They passed high trellises where bushes of red roses climbed high, spreading their sweet perfume through the garden. They wove their way through groomed hedges and perfectly clipped leafy green rhododendron and azalea bushes. They passed garden beds filled with peppermint, basil, and other herbs. Nancy had planted rosemary in her little garden back home. She had broken off a stalk of the fragrant herb and shredded it into a dish she'd prepared just days ago. She'd added some to the chicken stew she'd made for Hal just two days before he'd learned the truth... before the warmth in his eyes had turned to ice.

Nancy gripped her sides, literally aching inside.

"Are you ill?" Elizabeth asked.

Nancy shook her head, but she did feel ill... with regret.

"Come on," Elizabeth said, moving them off the path. "We'll sneak into our nest and talk just like we used to do."

They rounded a cluster of bushes and ducked into their private sanctuary. They'd spent countless hours playing and talking together in the hidden cove of honeysuckle bushes. Inside, where it was shaded and cool, they sat at the edge of a small stream that cut through their mother's garden and meandered across the large field at the back of their property. Nancy and Elizabeth had shared many heartaches, secrets, and dreams in this place, so it felt natural for Nancy to pour her heart out to her sister. She told her everything.

"This is utterly heartbreaking, Nancy. To know you did this for me... it pains me deeply." Elizabeth's eyes were moist. "I would have rather married Robert and watched you marry Stuart, the man I love, than to see you suffer such heartache."

Nancy knew Elizabeth meant every word. Her sister would have borne her own heartache to spare Nancy the same. That was exactly why Nancy had left home and agreed to marry a stranger. She and Elizabeth looked out for one another. They always had. They always would.

"I wouldn't have let you do that," Nancy said, drying her eyes on the handkerchief clutched in her hand. She sniffed and straightened her shoulders. "I missed you terribly, Elizabeth. So many times I wanted to write to you, but I couldn't. Not until I was sure."

"Sure of what?"

Sunlight poked through the vines overhead and created a pattern across Elizabeth's red hair. Her cheeks were rosy from the warm day and enhanced her soft features of her small jaw and full lips. Elizabeth was beautiful. They were twins, but Nancy had never seen herself as she saw Elizabeth. Nancy felt ordinary and unremarkable, but suddenly she wondered what Hal saw when he looked at her. Did he see her as she saw herself, as an ordinary girl? Or did he see the beauty that Nancy saw in Elizabeth when she looked at her twin?

"Sure of what?" Elizabeth asked again.

"That Hal really wanted to be my husband... that he wanted a real marriage with me."

"You sent a letter to me so I'm assuming he demonstrated his desire?"

Nancy nodded, too choked by emotion to answer. He had demonstrated his feelings in so many ways. Every word he'd spoken, every gesture and action had been truthful and laced with good intentions. Laughter and singing and working together...dancing and sleeping in his arms, gazing at each other across the supper table or while playing cards with their friends or when working in his cluttered workshop... so many memories and every one of them broke her heart.

As if Elizabeth understood the path of Nancy's thoughts, she sighed and leaned back on her hands. "If your husband is the kind of man you say he is, he'll think all of this through and want you back."

"Maybe," Nancy whispered, but it seemed impossible at the moment. He was too angry. Too hurt.

"Give it some time. Every wound heals eventually."

Nancy nodded, knowing there was truth to Elizabeth's words. But wounds left scars and some scars remained tender for years.

Hiding out and sharing secrets and heartaches with her sister gave Nancy a sense of home, and for that small comfort she was deeply grateful.

"What are you going to do?" Elizabeth asked.

Nancy shook her head. She had no idea. What *could* she do?

"Will you go back?"

"I don't know." A rogue tear rolled down her cheek and she brushed it away, irritated by her loss of control. "Hal was really angry... and hurt by my deceit. I don't know if he can forgive that."

"Surely he understands why you answered the advertisement and used Mother's maiden name?" Elizabeth asked.

"I don't think Hal condemns me for why I ran off. He's hurt because I allowed him to open his heart, to make himself vulnerable to me, and that's why my lie has wounded him so deeply." Nancy sighed and peered through the undergrowth into the field where she'd raced horses. She'd been a reckless girl who embraced the thrill of danger. She'd approached becoming a mail order bride with the same wild abandon. Only now the danger wasn't just physical. It was emotional, and her heart would pay the price. Hal already was suffering from her reckless decision.

"Perhaps you should write to him," Elizabeth suggested. "Maybe if you apologize—"

"No," Nancy said, cutting in. "I owe him more than a letter. I love him and never meant to hurt him, but I did." Lifting her chin, Nancy said, "As soon as Daddy is well enough to travel, the two of us are going to Fredonia. We both have business with Hal Grayson." With that, Nancy got to her feet and whacked debris from her skirt.

Elizabeth grinned and stood beside her. "Now that's the sister I remember."

Nancy knew she would go back to Fredonia, with or without her father, but for all her bravado she found no comfort in her decision because Hal might not want her back. The thought of a life without him was too awful to contemplate.

THREE WEEKS HAD PASSED since Nancy left for Buffalo, and Hal hadn't heard a word from her. He thought she might have at least let him know how her father was faring, but Hal had made it clear he loathed the man, so why would Nancy bother? He sat in his workshop staring at a decorative frame he was carving for a mirror on a lady's dressing table. Captain was flopped on the bench watching as Hal worked his gouge, roughing out the pattern of oak leaves and acorns around the outer edge of the piece.

It was well past midnight and the lantern wick was burned to a nub.

An occasional scurry or flutter from the barn loft was the only sound to break the deep silence. Captain lifted his head, perked his ears, and listened for minute or two. Then he sighed, lowered his nose to his paws again and stared at Hal with sad, accusing eyes.

"I don't blame you for holding a grudge, Captain. This woodshop is one sad place these days."

Hal didn't know when he'd started talking to the cat, but Captain seemed to understand every word. He wondered if Captain was also plagued by images and memories from the many nights Nancy had helped in the woodshop. Despite managing her own chores, she'd gladly joined him here each evening. She played with Captain and flirted with Hal while tending his ledger and helping him build furniture. She brought laughter and light to his shop and to his life.

If there was any little job Nancy could do to ease Hal's burden, she would roll up her sleeves and dig in. At every turn she had been there to offer comfort and assistance and tender passion. The void her absence left in his life had carved a canyon of grief in his chest. Hal missed her so deeply he ached. He couldn't eat the meals Mary Tucker and Martha Fiske delivered each evening. He couldn't sleep in the bed he'd shared with Nancy, so he spent sleepless nights on the sofa. He couldn't enter the kitchen without expecting to see Nancy tending to meals or her kitchen chores. But the worst thing, the absolutely most painful reminder was the silent pianoforte, the one treasure she'd loved and he'd been able to give her.

Thoughts of their last conversation dredged up memories and turned Hal's thoughts to his father. His dad had told him that Lloyd Tremont was not responsible for their hardship, but Hal had seen Tremont's bank repossessing the sawmill their family depended on. What other conclusion could Hal have drawn? To Tremont's credit, the man had apologized, but he'd refused to listen to reason. Hal had presented his savings, had promised to send additional payments to the bank each payday, had offered to work for Tremont until the debt was paid. But Tremont insisted it was too late and he had no recourse but to repossess the mill.

Perhaps that was true, but the man hadn't needed to sell the mill to their competitor. That was the final injury that Hal couldn't accept. But it was too late to do anything about it, and so Hal had walked away.

It had been too late for him to help save the mill, to repair his relationship with his father, to remain in Buffalo another day. And so he'd returned to Fredonia to work and to think and to come up with a way to help his family.

But John's death and Nancy's arrival had turned Hal's life upside down.

Nancy's leaving had stirred up a lot of painful memories and even more questions. Hal needed answers and knew he would find them only in Buffalo.

For a long while Hal sat on the milk churn that Nancy had used as a stool, petting Captain, and thinking. Finally, as the lantern wick flickered, warning it was in its final minutes of lighting the shop, Hal planted his hands on his knees and stood. "All right, Captain, Mary Tucker will be taking care of you for a few days. Behave yourself and stay off my tools."

Captain sprawled across several chisels, eyes mere slits as he peered indifferently at Hal.

Hal shook his head. "Well, there's no need to be so upset about my leaving. I'll come back."

Captain didn't bat an eye. He stretched out one back leg and sighed as if bored with the whole conversation.

Hal snorted, ruffled the cat's ears, and wondered when he'd grown so protective of the little rascal. "Don't eat anything that's going to make you sick."

Hal knew he didn't need to worry about Captain. He could come in and out of the barn through a small hole in a broken wall board, and Mary Tucker would spoil Captain with table scraps.

With a final round of petting for Captain, Hal then stashed his tools and left the barn.

As soon as he got inside, he packed his valise. At first light the next morning, he strode out Liberty Street toward Thomas Drake's house to do what he should have done weeks ago.

CHAPTER TWENTY-FIVE

It was the second day that Nancy's father had felt well enough to sit in the family parlor. He was fully alert and much stronger, which relieved her mind considerably. But the look in his eyes concerned her.

"Are you comfortable, Daddy?" she asked, after tucking him into his favorite chair and covering him with a blue and gray lap quilt she and Elizabeth had made for him last Christmas. His pallor still matched his gray hair, and his eyes were ringed with dark circles, but the strength in his voice assured Nancy that he was improving.

"Sit down, Nancy." Her father gestured to the large padded footstool his feet were resting on. "We need to talk."

The command in his voice turned Nancy's knees to water, and she sagged onto the footstool. Even at seventeen years old and a married woman, she still felt a rock in her gut when her father used that steely tone of voice with her.

"Do you have any idea the worry you put me and your mother and sister through?"

She did and deeply regretted it. "I never meant to be so inconsiderate, Daddy. I never meant to hurt or worry you."

"Then what were you thinking running off like that?" he asked, his voice cracking with intensity.

"Daddy, I know you're upset, and rightfully so, but please don't get yourself worked up." Nancy sat on the edge of the footstool and took her father's hand in her own. He'd always been a robust, strong man, but today his hand trembled and his grip was weak. "Elizabeth told me you collapsed after reading my letter. I'm... I'm so sorry." She paused a moment and swallowed the emotion pushing up her throat. She couldn't cry. She was here to comfort her father, not the reverse. And she deserved his anger. So she choked back her feelings and said, "I thought I was doing something kind and loving for Elizabeth, but I can see now that my actions caused immeasurable pain and heartbreak for the people I love most."

Her father's eyes welled up and he squeezed her hand, surprising her with his strength. "Your disappearance scared me to death. We searched the woods and fields and outbuildings numerous times. When we found no sign of you, Elizabeth suggested you'd run off to avoid marrying Stuart. I had officials and my own men looking for you everywhere. Each day that passed was another twenty-four hours your mother and I spent living in panic. I couldn't imagine where you'd gone off to. Why didn't you just talk to me?"

"I tried, Daddy. I believed you wouldn't change your mind, and I just couldn't break Elizabeth's heart. I couldn't imagine being Stuart's wife knowing that every family event would subject Elizabeth to the pain of seeing Stuart and me married. And I couldn't bear to know that my husband would never be able to love me because he already loved my sister."

Her father shook his head, his gray hair shining in the parlor lanterns. "I had no idea."

"I couldn't break Elizabeth's trust. I was afraid that telling you she had feelings for Stuart would land her in trouble and perhaps even get Stuart banished from calling here. You're quite protective where your daughters are concerned."

"And too indulgent with you, I fear." Disappointment filled his expression.

"No, Daddy. You taught me to be honest and live with integrity. I used my love for Elizabeth to justify a couple of lies, but I was wrong and those lies hurt people. I'm terribly ashamed and remorseful and would never again use such poor judgement. You had nothing to do with my bad decisions."

"Yes, I did. I let my girls down. I thought I was providing a safe and good future for you and Elizabeth. I didn't realize I was breaking your hearts." Tears beaded up in his eyes. "You don't know how deeply that pains me."

In the face of his emotional struggle, Nancy bit her lip and fought her own emotional battle. She'd never seen her father cry. He was a man in charge, a man in command of all around him. He was a leader for the men who worked for his bank. The highly paid household staff catered to his needs with a sense of honor and respect. Lloyd Tremont was a pillar of the community and a man of great love and strength to his wife and daughters. He wasn't a man who cried.

And yet he did.

He opened his arms, and Nancy leaned into the warmth and security of her father's embrace. The scent of his cologne and laundered shirt was the smell of home, love, and security,. She felt the familiar and deep comfort of her father's arms, and yet she recognized she was no longer a girl seeking solace but rather a daughter comforting her father. And she was a woman in need of her husband's arms. For a long minute her father held her, and when his arms trembled, Nancy held him. "I've made such a mess of things, Daddy."

"It certainly appears that way," he said, easing her back in his arms, and then putting a handkerchief to his nose. "Tell me about this man you've married. I'm surprised Hal Grayson would marry my daughter unless it was to hurt me." He frowned. "He didn't hurt you, did he?"

"Of course not, Daddy. He didn't even know I was your daughter."

He froze with the handkerchief over his nose, his brown eyes wide. "How could he not?"

"I lied about my name."

His hand fell to his lap, the handkerchief forgotten. "You did what? How did you meet and marry then? I thought the young man had left the area."

Nancy felt sick inside. "He did leave the area, Daddy." And so Nancy spent the next several minutes catching her father up on her travels, trials, her lies, and ultimately the demise of her marriage. "Our marriage problems are my fault, Daddy. I wasn't truthful with Hal. He's understandably angry now, but he is truly a kind and wonderful man."

"Oh, Nancy...." Her father shook his head, disappointment in his eyes. "In all my days I'd have never expected this behavior from you."

His chastising hurt. Her sinuses stung, and she had to bite her lip to hold back her tears of remorse and regret.

"So your young man is rightfully upset by your deceit?"

She nodded. "And my lie is made even worse because Hal believes you treated his father, Daniel, unfairly when you repossessed his mill. Is that true, Daddy?"

His frown deepened. "I can assure you I dealt fairly with his father. That young man better not have filled your ears with half-truths or hurt you in any way."

"Of course he didn't, Daddy. It was I who hurt him. And that is precisely why he was so hurt and angry. I'm not sure he can forgive me." Saying the words aloud made them more real. To her horror, her eyes welled up and she clamped her teeth down on her lip. "I... I'm giving him some time to accept the truth of our situation and think things through. But I need to go home... back to Fredonia and try to fix this mess I've created. I need you to go with me, Daddy. You and Hal need to talk about your dealings with his father."

"Of course I'll take you back. Because if you can't get that husband of yours to come around, I will. You're responsible for your lies, Nancy, and for rebuilding trust in your marriage. But getting your heart broken or your pride hurt doesn't mean you walk away from a commitment. Whether that young man likes me or not, he married my daughter and

I'll see that he stands by his promise to you." Her father patted her hand. "Where's my girl who could outfox this old fox?" he asked, chucking her beneath the chin as he'd done numerous times. "You can work this out."

"Maybe. But one thing I've learned is that Hal isn't a man to be outfoxed or coerced into anything."

"Well, the two of you have a mess on your hands that needs to be resolved. If you can't set things right, I'll be having a talk with the boy."

Nancy didn't want her father's intervention or to outfox her husband to get him back. She wanted their love to be enough.

HAL HAD PREPARED himself to feel emotional at John Radford's gravesite. He hadn't, however, expected the sight of his brother's name carved on a small wooden cross to take him to his knees.

On the day they buried John, there had been no marker with a name to identify a body or to remind loved ones who they'd lost. It was just a dirt-filled hole covered with wood shavings.

Today, however, the name *John Radford Grayson* was etched into a thick piece of oak that stood at the head of the grave. This is where John's body was. *John* was here, in this spot right beneath Hal's knees. Hal's beloved brother was *here*.

But he shouldn't be!

Hal's gut cramped. John shouldn't be here. Searing emotions whipped wildly through Hal, stinging like a lash. He clenched his fists, trying to hold onto his composure.

John had loved this place. He'd wanted to grow old here, and when he died, he wanted to be buried at the mill, beneath a mountainous pile of pine shavings. No one could have imagined they would be faced with the painful task of carrying out John's wishes. And yet here they were, only weeks after John's death, still shocked and disbelieving that he was really gone.

As John had wanted, Hal and his family buried John at the farthest edge of the sawmill. They filled his coffin with pine shavings and laid him to rest on a grassy knoll overlooking the small pond where Hal and John and their siblings swam as kids. They'd had family picnics beneath the maple trees and had played numerous games in the surrounding fields and woods. Ever present in the background of their lives had been the whining sound of their father's mill and the fragrant scent of fresh-cut pine and oak and walnut.

John had been happiest here. For John, this fifty-acre parcel of land was home. Hal had been selfish and shortsighted in asking John to leave a place he loved so deeply. Now it was little comfort to know John would never leave home again.

Regret and wrenching sorrow surged through Hal, closing his throat, stinging his eyes. The leafy trees and grassy fields of his childhood blurred, his vision flooded by tears and images of his past. Memories flashed through his mind like lightening bugs, illuminating moments for a fraction of a second... Hal and John nailing boards in a tree, lying on the wooden platform on their stomachs to spy on the world around them, John throwing a stick in anger and clocking Hal in the head, hunting field hens with their father in the woods, hot summer days of rushing to the pond for a cool dip during their short breaks at the mill, John eager to return to work, Hal wanting to linger and whittle his next piece of art. So many moments. So little time.

Hal buried his face in his hands. If only he'd have known.

He wanted to apologize to his brother, to sling his arm around John Radford's shoulders and continue their adventures in life together. But John was gone. Forever.

Crouched at his brother's grave, the sound of his own wracking sobs sliced through Hal, a painful confirmation that his beloved brother was dead.

"Come on, son."

Hal felt himself being raised up and pulled into his father's arms, a place he hadn't been in years.

His father's presence momentarily stunned him. For an instant Hal thought to pull away, to straighten his shoulders and act a man as he'd been taught. But intense love and sorrow surged through his heart, and Hal fell into his father's arms and sobbed like a child.

In that moment of overwhelming emotion, Hal clung to his father. He wanted to say, *I'm sorry, father... Please forgive me... I miss my brother...* But words were impossible.

In their fierce grip, father and son supported each other, two men wounded to their souls, giving what they had left. Apologies and memories and healing mingled in that moment. Hal recalled the numerous times he'd been lifted in his father's strong arms or carried on his wide shoulders. And it seemed Daniel Grayson was still a robust, strong man capable of holding and comforting his son. His wide palm thumped Hal's back as if to say, *It's all right... we'll get through this... time to pull on our boots and keep moving...*

Hal stepped back and backhanded his eyes, feeling weak and ridiculous, like a boy instead of a man.

But his father stood unashamed of his own tears. His broad shoulders, the home of so many heavy burdens of which Hal had added his share, were beginning to round now. But there was fierce resolve and deep love in his father's eyes. "There's no shame in loving or grieving, son."

Hal nodded, but he did feel shame for thinking only of himself. He could only imagine the pain his father felt over losing a child. "I've been unforgivably selfish, Dad. I should have never asked John to come to Fredonia. He'd still be alive if... if he had stayed here with you."

"You can't know that, Hal. And if I recall properly, it was John Radford who encouraged you to take the job with Edwards and move to Fredonia. You might have asked him to come later on, but it was John who started you on that path and who made the decision to join you there."

"But I knew the wagon he was driving wasn't safe." Hal kicked a cluster of grass, furious with himself. "I *knew* we should have left the wretched thing sitting in the field."

"I suspect your brother knew that as well," his father said. "If anyone is guilty or responsible for John's death, it's me. I lost the mill and that forced John to make other decisions that took him to Fredonia." Releasing a weary sigh, he dragged a worn handkerchief from his pocket. He wiped his eyes and blew his nose, then stuffed the red square in his shirt pocket. "Give your brother more credit, Hal. John was a smart man capable of making his own decisions. You aren't responsible for his decisions or his death, even if you feel otherwise. Your brother loved you and wouldn't want you to carry this burden of guilt on your heart any more than you'd want him to if the circumstances were reversed. It was just a tragic, heartbreaking accident. Don't make me lose two sons over it."

Hal cast a sweeping glance around him, seeing fields and woods and the sawmill with long timbers lying on the hard-packed ground waiting for the saw, stacks of lumber ready to ship, and mountains of sawdust that would be sold for insulation around homes when the weather turned colder. Beyond the mill, nestled in a copse of towering white pines, sat his childhood home. His mother and father now lived there with four of their children... and one son buried on the hill.

Hal shook his head, weary and heartsore.

"What's on your mind, son? I suspect you didn't come back just to visit John's grave?"

Hal had come back for Nancy, for answers, and now it seemed he'd come back seeking forgiveness. Releasing a hard sigh, he spoke to his father man to man. "I need to understand what happened with the mill. Why did you buy it when you knew you couldn't pay for it?"

"I was foolish." His father reached down and plucked a long blade of grass. He stuck one end in the side of his mouth as if clamping a cigar in his teeth, a habit of his when mulling over difficult task or situation. Finally, he said, "I anticipated getting the steamer contract again. We've had it for five years and I had no reason to suspect we wouldn't win the next bid. My mistake was in purchasing the mill before I had the new contract in hand. It was a foolish thing to do, Hal."

"Why'd you do it then?"

"I wanted to provide you and John with your own business."

"Owning a sawmill was John's dream, not mine," Hal said.

Their eyes locked, and his father nodded. "I know, but I hoped owning your own mill would be tempting enough to keep you here. I couldn't bear the thought of losing my boys. Unfortunately, that's happened despite my efforts."

Hal shook his head, a rock of regret in his gut. "I've been so foolish. I should have stayed and run the mill for you."

"I'd have still lost it, Hal. Without the contract I couldn't earn enough to pay for it."

"Lloyd Tremont shouldn't have been such a heartless businessman. He should have given us a chance to work things out and save the mill. John and I might have found more work for the mill."

"You're using your talents exactly as you should be, Hal. And my failure here has nothing to do with Lloyd Tremont. He suggested I wait to purchase the new mill until I had the contract in hand, but I assured him I'd win the bid. By all rights he shouldn't have given me that loan until I could prove myself capable of paying for it. But he took me at my word, and I let him down."

"Then he should have trusted you to make things right."

"No, Hal." His father shook his head. "Lloyd knew I couldn't make things right. Not without the contract, which I won't get another shot at for a year. He did the right thing."

"The right thing? He sold the mill to our competitor!"

"He auctioned the mill. Our competitor had the contract and could afford to make the highest bid. Lloyd couldn't control that. I tried to tell you that before you stormed into his office."

Hal's eyebrows shot up in surprise. "He told you I called on him?"

A half-smile tilted his father's mouth, a sign he was amused. "He did. I confess I was right proud of you for looking after your family, Hal, but you made unfair accusations to a man who has helped us on a number of occasions. Lloyd Tremont is the reason I'm still able to operate my mill at all. He could have taken both saws and everything we've got. Instead he wrote off the loss on my unpaid loan and that enabled me to keep the other saw operating. You should have thanked the man instead of condemning him."

It was as if his father punched Hal in the gut. His breath sailed out and he stared in disbelief. "All this time I thought he was a heartless blackguard and..." Hal raked his hands through his hair and stared at his father. "I've been such a fool."

A grin tipped his father's mouth. "Being a grown man doesn't mean you won't make mistakes, Hal. I know from repeated experience."

The idea that Hal had unfairly accused a man who had gone out of his way to help his family burned like acid in Hal's gut. But knowing he'd wounded Nancy with his cruel and unfair words about her father was a thought too painful to bear.

"Come on, son." His father clapped his strong, work-roughened hand over Hal's shoulder and turned him toward the mill. "Your mother will singe our ears if we're late for supper."

They had walked three paces when Hal suddenly stopped.

His father took another step and then looked back. Their eyes met, and Hal could see the question in his father's dark gaze.

"Dad, you aren't responsible for John's death or for driving me away. We both made our choices because that's what we wanted to do. You need to know that. And you need to know that there's not a man in this world I respect or love more than you."

CHAPTER TWENTY-SIX

Tuesday morning, Nancy and her father were playing chess in the library. Her father chided her for letting him win, but Nancy assured him she was simply being kind in consideration of his infirmary. He laughed and said he was glad to see her getting back to her old self.

But Nancy wasn't her old self at all. She was no longer a willful girl chasing every challenge. She was a married woman who was growing increasingly heartbroken and missing her husband. She couldn't sleep. She could barely tolerate food. She couldn't think of anything but Hal and the fact that it had been nearly a month since she'd left him. She knew she'd hurt him, but she thought she might at least receive a letter from him. She had heard nothing but silence.

"Shall we put the game aside and go to the music room?" her father asked. "It would make me happy to hear you play again."

"Perhaps Elizabeth will play for you, Daddy. I don't feel like playing today." Nancy couldn't bring herself to touch the ivory keys of the beautiful instrument because it reminded her of her old out-of-tune pianoforte and her big love for her small home back in Fredonia.

"Your melancholy is wringing this old heart. I want back my sassy, willful daughter, not this quiet and weepy woman you've become."

"Weepy?" Nancy met her father's eyes in surprise. "When have you known me to be quiet and weepy, Father?" She pushed to her feet and paced to the window. "I'm quiet because I'm growing impatient to return to my husband. I know you're not yet well enough to travel, but I intend to return to Fredonia this week." She folded her arms across her chest and faced her father. "When you're fully back on your feet, Father, I want you to come to Fredonia and talk with my husband. He needs to know what really happened between you and his father."

"I wish you'd wait then," he said leaning back in his chair. "I think another day or two of rest should see me well enough to travel."

"All right, Daddy, because the two of you need a proper introduction and to settle whatever issue stands between you."

With or without her father, Nancy was going back to Fredonia this week. To her home. To her husband. And he was going to listen to her apology and realize he has more to think about than his own feelings. If it wasn't just emotional upset delaying Nancy's monthly, then Hal Grayson had a child on the way.

———

AT THE TREMONT ESTATE, Hal took a moment to admire the intricate crest that he and his father had carved in the heavy oak door. He had learned a lot from his father during that project, and Hal gave himself a minute to appreciate their work, and the irony, before he lifted the metal knocker and gave a sharp rap on the door.

A manservant approximately twice Hal's age, dressed in a black suit and black tie, answered the door with great flourish. He introduced himself as Bramwell and invited Hal inside to wait in the ornate foyer. It was a grand home with open hallways leading to many rooms from what Hal could see from the open foyer and recall from his conversations with Nancy.

Bramwell tipped his haughty head. "Miss Tremont is—correction, sir, *Mrs. Grayson*—is in the library with her father. I'll let them know that Mr. Hal Grayson is calling."

Hal found the formality silly, but merely nodded his understanding as he watched the man stride from the foyer with an air of importance. Nancy had told Hal bits and pieces of her life and about the home in which she'd lived. She'd spoken about the expansive ballroom that could hold Hal's small house, and of morning and sitting rooms, of which he had no clue as to the difference in their function. She'd mentioned the family library and the music room and numerous other rooms that made Hal wonder how one family could possibly make use of such space.

This explained why Nancy had expected a household staff to be part of her marriage agreement. Being raised in such luxury, she wouldn't have known any other way of living. What a shock it must have been for her when Hal picked her up at the station. And yet rather than complain or condemn Hal for failing so miserably at providing for them, she'd rolled up her sleeves and created a warm and loving home. For him. For them. Without asking for anything but his love. She'd even taken in a stray cat and befriended the wildlife living around their home. She'd traded in her expensive baubles to purchase food for their table and given herself to him with warmth and passion.

Bramwell seemed to appear silently out of nowhere, startling Hal from his thoughts. With a crook of his gloved fingers, the butler gestured for Hal to follow along. Hat in hand, Hal was taken to the library where Nancy and her father sat with a magnificently carved chess set between them. Nancy rose to her feet and stepped to the far side of her father's chair, as if placing the man between them. Hal's first thought was that her father had already come between them, but it wasn't true. Hal's foolish misunderstanding was what stood between them, and he meant to clear that up posthaste.

The interior felt dark after spending the morning outside at his father's mill. Heavy drapes hung over tall windows, dark wood bookshelves and gray patterned wallpaper covered the walls. Two ornate tabletop lanterns illuminated the space around Nancy and her father and cast a warm golden glow across the hardwood flooring.

Nancy's pearly skin and gorgeous red hair were beacons in the dark, her eyes full of emotion as she gazed across the room at him. Hal ached to pull her into his arms, but etiquette—and unanswered questions—held him back.

Tremont sat in a high-backed padded chair, a woven blanket across his legs, but his power and wealth were undeniable. "The last time I saw you, young man, you were shaking your fist and telling me that I am a ruthless man who doesn't care about crippling businesses or destroying families." Although Tremont's words were blunt, his eyes seemed to hold amusement instead of anger. "I suspect this visit might be more difficult than you anticipated."

"Perhaps, but I hope that won't be the case. The last time we met, sir, I was a hotheaded, ill-informed young man," Hal stated just as bluntly because he had been wrong and needed to admit that to Tremont and to let Nancy know that he was to blame. "I've since been educated and have come to apologize for being unreasonable and unforgivably rude. My father has set me straight on the facts."

Tremont arched one white eyebrow as if mildly surprised. "Well, I'm glad to hear that. I should find it incredibly awkward to have my daughter married to a man who hates me."

"As would I," Hal said, because there was no way to gracefully dance around the issue. "I can assure you, sir, that I do not hate you. In fact, I've gained great appreciation and respect for you. Thank you for enabling my father to carry on his business. I understand how difficult it must have been for you repossess the mill from a man who was becoming your friend."

"In all my years in banking, it was one of the hardest things I've had to do," Tremont said, his shoulders lowering a couple of inches on a sigh. "But I have investors and board members, and the decision wasn't wholly mine to make. Keeping a business alive can often require hard decisions."

"I understand," Hal said, and he truly did. He'd made a few of his own before leaving Fredonia. Tremont was a good man, and a very wealthy man, but that didn't mean he didn't have to conduct business in a manner that would keep his investors happy.

"I'll tell you another thing, Mr. Grayson. It's nearly impossible to watch my girls marry and move away." With that, Tremont reached up and clasped Nancy's hand, his eyes still on Hal. "There's nothing in my life I value more than my daughters. Imagine my surprise when I learned Nancy was married to the hotheaded Grayson boy who had vowed to make me pay for my unfair treatment of his father." Tremont shook his head, his eyes filled with concern. "All I could imagine was you being harsh with Nancy because of your hatred for me. The shock and worry nearly killed me."

"I can assure you that it was a complete and utter shock to me as well. And I've done my best to be a good husband." Hal swung his gaze to Nancy who was looking on with a sense of uneasy anticipation. "The real irony, sir, is that Nancy is everything I would have chosen in a wife and far more than I could have ever hoped for."

Nancy's lips parted on a small gasp, her eyes filled with surprise and a mix of other emotions he couldn't sift through in that instant.

Hal hoped she could see the sincerity in his eyes as he spoke his first words to her. "We need to talk, Nancy."

Before she had an opportunity to respond, her father said, "Hold on, young man. I'm sympathetic to the situation you and Nancy are embroiled in, but I must caution you to tread carefully with her, or I'll become every bit the ruthless man you thought me to be."

Hal's mouth quirked in appreciation. "I'd be disappointed if you were anything less than ruthless in that case."

"Then state your intentions."

Undeterred by Tremont's demand, Hal said, "I intend to have a private conversation with my wife."

While Tremont sat with his mouth open, Hal closed the distance to Nancy in two strides and presented her with her mother's ring.

Her lips parted in surprise.

"This belongs to you."

Outside, Nancy directed Hal down a worn carriage path toward the stables. They walked in silence until they were away from the house and halfway to the enormous gambrel-roofed barn that housed the horses.

"I'm surprised you came," she said, glancing up at her husband and noticing his hair had grown. The breeze flipped one wavy lock of hair around his collar and made her fingers itch to touch it. "Daddy and I were planning to head to Fredonia the end of the week."

Hal looked at her, his black brows raised as if astounded. "You were coming back? With your father?"

"Yes. I needed to see you, Hal. I owe you an apology."

He sighed and glanced across the paddock behind the stable where four of her father's six horses were being exercised by her cousin. "I don't understand, Nancy. Why couldn't you have told me before I... when the truth would have mattered less?"

"Was there ever a point in our relationship when that was true? I thought you hated my father."

His eyes met hers.

"Hal, if I had thought for one minute I could have told you the truth without hurting you, I'd have done so. It tortured me to deceive you." She pressed her palm to her chest. "I cannot express how deeply I regret my bad decisions."

"Am I one of those bad decisions?" he asked, and she could see the pain in his eyes.

"Oh, Hal..." Nancy threw her arms around his neck and hugged him. "I know you might never forgive me," she said, "but I want you to know you are the best thing that's ever happened to me."

He stood stiff and unyielding. "I need to know something," he said, grasping her arms and gently setting her away from him.

An icy rush streamed through Nancy's veins. Was he pushing her away because he was still angry? Because he couldn't forgive her? Because he didn't want her or their marriage?

"I need to know if there are any other secrets that you're keeping from me—or lies you're telling me."

Tears sprang to her eyes and a small sob burst from her throat. She clapped a hand over her mouth and inhaled, fighting her tears and the pain of his insulting question. "No," she whispered. He had a right to ask, but it hurt that he felt the need to do so. "The only thing I didn't tell you was my real name. Everything else I've said, including *I love you* was the truth."

As if he couldn't bear her pain, he cupped her face and looked into her eyes. "I'm sorry, darling, but I need to know that you'll never again deceive me."

"Of course I won't. I know I hurt you, and I regret that more than I can express. As I live and breathe, I will never again betray your trust or our love."

"Thank you," he whispered, as if greatly relieved. "Because everything we will ever have together will be built on trust." He pulled her into his arms and held her tight. "I love you, Nancy Tremont Grayson, and I want you back in my life."

"Oh, Hal..." Nancy rested her cheek on his chest, feeling his warmth and hearing his strong heartbeat. "I've missed lying my head on your chest and hearing your heartbeat. I've missed the feel of your arms and the sound of your laughter. I've missed you and Captain and our house every minute of every day."

"I can't tell you how glad I am to hear that." He eased back to see her face. From his shirt pocket he withdrew a simple gold band. "Now that I've seen all of this..." He gestured to the sprawling estate with stables and guesthouse. "Part of me thinks it might be kinder to walk away and allow you to live an easier, more comfortable life here than to take you back to the one of toil and struggle you'll have with me. But I can't walk away, Nancy. My life is empty without you in it. Our small house is only a home with you in it. I can't offer any of this, but I can offer you a life filled with love and laughter and all the animals you wish to rescue. This simple band is all I can afford, Nancy, but I want to put my own wedding ring on your finger tomorrow and take our vows with our families present."

Speechless, Nancy looked at the simple band and the remarkable man standing before her professing his love—and she felt like the most fortunate woman in the world.

"You bought a ring?" she asked, her voice trembling with emotion. "You came here planning to marry me and take me home?"

"Yes, darling. Captain has called me every kind of fool and refuses to speak to me until I bring you home. So if you're willing, we can marry tomorrow and head back to Fredonia... to Captain and to *our* home... together. The choice is yours. Will you stay with your father? Or will you return to Fredonia with me?"

Nancy shook her head and laughed as if he was pitifully ignorant. "If you even have to ask that question, then you've been blind and deaf this past three months. That you could even question my love wounds me deeply."

He clasped her hands and she felt his reassuring squeeze. "I wasn't questioning your love, Nancy. I was questioning your desire to return to a hardscrabble life with a hardheaded man."

She released a small laugh and gazed up at him. "You are most definitely hardheaded, Hal, but I admire that you're your own man. I'm sure Daddy would like to help make our lives much easier, but I suspect you would never accept his aid or my dowry. Would you?"

She saw Hal's shoulders tense, and she knew the answer before he spoke.

"Nancy, I realize you might not want to live without the comforts your father can provide, and I don't want my pride to keep you from those things, but... I can't live on the coattails of another man." Hal sighed and released her hands. "Better we have this conversation now, however difficult it might be. Are you asking me to accept assistance from your father? Do you want more than I can provide?"

She linked her fingers in front of her skirt and cocked her head to study him. "I need days filled with laughter and nights filled with passion. I need to tend my house and garden with my own hands. I need to be able to put a meal on the table each day for my family. I need to know that my husband wants and loves me." She shrugged one shoulder. "That's my list of needs. What I *want* is your love."

Relief flooded his eyes and he exhaled hard. "Those are all things I can provide you, Nancy."

She smiled. "I know. I was just waiting for you to figure it out."

He cupped her elbows and drew her close. "Are you sure this is what you want?" he asked. "I need to be certain we understand each other."

"Yes, I like living simply without all the obligatory events and posturing that comes with my parents' sort of life. I like filling our kitchen with the aroma of a meal I've made with my own hands. I like dancing in a barn rather than a ballroom. I love the challenge of making music on our out-of-tune pianoforte instead of sitting for music lessons and playing for a roomful of my parents' friends. Simple, loving, joyful living is what I want, Hal. That's more than enough for me." With that she placed a kiss on his warm cheek. "Any other questions?"

"What time would you like to marry tomorrow?"

"Five o'clock, if that suits you."

A slow grin tilted his mouth. "Any time suits me."

"All right then. I have much to do before tomorrow, so unless you have more questions, you should go tell your family that they'll be attending our wedding."

"No more questions, just an intense desire to kiss your sassy mouth," he said, slipping his arms around her, and dipping his head.

Nancy laughed and pushed him away, leaving him standing with his lips pursed and his eyes wide. "You shall get your kiss tomorrow, Mr. Grayson, at our wedding ceremony. Now be off with you, and let me tend to my business."

CHAPTER TWENTY-SEVEN

At five o'clock the next afternoon, Nancy stood in a small clearing in her mother's garden where she and her family had enjoyed many casual lunches on a blanket spread beneath a large red maple tree. But today, in her pale pink gown adorned with white lace, it wasn't a casual lunch she was sharing with her family. Instead, she stood beside Hal Grayson, ready to speak her vows with all of the love she felt in her heart for the man beside her. Unlike their first wedding, there were no nerves, no worries, and no apprehension. Her love for Hal was all consuming, and she was never more certain of her decision than she was in that moment.

The two of them were surrounded by their families seated on shiny, black wrought-iron benches that her father's staff had collected from various nooks throughout the garden. The scent of roses wafted through the garden on a light breeze. Butterflies flitted among purple petunias and blooming sedum. Seeing the two plants growing and flowering side by side told Nancy that summer was fading and making way for fall.

Nancy embraced her wedding day and spoke her vows with love

and confidence. She saw that same certainty in Hal's eyes, heard the love in his voice as he promised her forever. This handsome, amazing man loved her. He wanted to marry her again and build a wonderful life together. He offered all he had, his strength, his passion, his love—and it was everything she needed and treasured.

They kept the ceremony brief, but it was touching and beautiful with both of their families gathered together to witness the two of them commit their lives and their hearts to one another. This time they had chosen each other, and that joy was reflected in their eyes and their smiles—and the fact that they couldn't bear to be more than a step away from each other.

As they visited with their families, the sun moved from behind the pine trees that lined the garden and cast a bright light over Nancy and Hal. In that moment of warmth, she felt the presence of John Radford watching over them and blessing their marriage. She looked up at her husband and wondered if he might have experienced the feeling as well, but all she could see in his eyes was joy—and love.

They enjoyed an informal supper in the garden, giving their families an opportunity to get acquainted socially and as in-laws. It warmed Nancy's heart to see her father, a robust wealthy man with silver hair, laughing with Hal's father Daniel Grayson, a dark-haired and strikingly handsome man. It was obvious they were enjoying their chat and that there was no discord between the men. Hal stood near his father talking with his two brothers, their resemblance strong. The Grayson men were tall, breathtakingly handsome men with their dark hair and finely chiseled features. They brought an air of royalty to the garden never before present despite the caliber of people her parents had entertained here. The Grayson men possessed an inherent currency other men couldn't buy... integrity... dignity... strength and a fierce resolve to protect the caliber of their character at all costs. This was why Hal had such difficulty forgiving Nancy's lie. He would rather forfeit his life than sacrifice his honor.

Hours after their wedding ceremony, Nancy was most happy to slip away with her new husband. Hal had removed his suit jacket and rolled up his sleeves. He carried his jacket over one arm and presented his other arm to Nancy. "Shall we head to the guesthouse?"

"I thought you would never ask," she said with a laugh.

He arched an eyebrow. "I thought you were enjoying the visit with our families."

"I was... for the first hour."

Laughing, they strolled the cobblestone path that took them through the groomed shrubs and bushes of the garden to the back gate. The shadows were lengthening, and the sky was painted with the light pinks and oranges of the setting sun. It would be a while yet before night fell, but the day's end was an hour or less away.

They stepped through the wrought-iron gates at the rear of the garden and walked into the field beyond. Ahead of them, a well-worn path wove through the grassy field separating Nancy's parent's house from the guest cottage where Hal and Nancy would spend their second wedding night.

The path was wide enough for two lovers snuggled close to each other. Still, Nancy felt her dress sweeping through the tall grass and had to stop briefly to gather her skirt. When she hefted the yards of material high on her arm, Hal glanced at her legs and grinned.

"Would you like me to carry you?" he asked.

"No, I would not," she said, laughing at his intentionally lascivious gawking. "I'm simply protecting my dress." Although she would be taking the rest of her personal items home with her, which would greatly enhance her wardrobe, they wouldn't be able to afford material for new dresses for some time, and therefore she needed to protect the clothing she had.

Despite revealing an indecent amount of her legs, her stride was much easier, as if she was freely moving forward with her life, finally leaving behind the heavy secrets that had burdened her heart and wounded Hal's. She knew that married life wouldn't always be an easy walk on a level path. Their journey together was bound to be filled with all manner of events, some they would celebrate, some they would grieve, and some they would simply have to work through together. She squeezed Hal's hand, silently promising to be his playmate and his strength for the rest of their days.

"Does this walk after our wedding feel at all similar to you?" Hal asked.

"It feels similar and different at the same time."

"Exactly." He stopped and faced her. "When I spoke my vows the first time, Nancy, I meant every word. But today, knowing how deeply we love each other, our vows felt different, as if they meant more."

"I know. I think it's because we're different now. We've both grown so much since the day we met at the station. We know what we were promising each other."

Regret filled his eyes and he cupped her face. "I'm sorry I wasn't kinder that day at the station, darling. I had no idea of the burden you were carrying. My eyes were so blinded by grief I couldn't see the treasure standing right in front of me. But I see you now, sparkling and beautiful and absolutely enchanting... and I feel like the luckiest man alive."

He drew her into a kiss so tender and so filled with devotion it made Nancy's eyes tear. How could such a strong man be so gentle?

She leaned into his warmth and cupped her free hand over his cheek and square jaw. They let the kiss fall away like a flower petal on a summer breeze, but their gazes held.

"I will always remember the first time you kissed me—on our wedding day," she said. "That day I was running away from something. Today, I'm running toward something wonderful and completely amazing. *You.*"

"We sure took a long and winding path to get where we are today. I have no doubt that we'll face more challenges ahead, but I'm confident now that we'll face them together."

"I'll be at your side every step of the way—wherever our path takes us." She raised up on her toes and placed a gentle kiss on his lips. In the cocoon of his arms, she felt safe and protected—and liberated. She felt passion and desire. She'd enjoyed making love with Hal, but something special had developed and deepened through their wedding today. With no secrets coming between them, she was finally free to love him fully.

"I could stay right here kissing you all night," he said, his voice dreamy sounding. "But we should get to the cottage before dark, don't you think?"

"What cottage?" she whispered as if snared in a dream she couldn't wake from.

He laughed and playfully nipped her nose. "Come along, darling."

Laughing, they turned and finished the walk to the cottage.

The guest cottage was a one-story fieldstone structure tucked beneath the large, sweeping branches of a copse of oak and maple trees. It sat several yards away from the creek that ran through her father's property. A front porch made of stone and oak and trimmed with white railings looked inviting with its two wooden rocking chairs. Windows with bright white trim sat beneath a shingled roof and flanked a stone chimney. No smoke rose from it tonight, though, for it was too warm outside for a fire. Colorful flowers in bright reds and pinks covered the well-manicured beds that surrounded the porch and butted up against the wooden lattice beneath the porch.

Nancy stopped in the yard for a moment, dropping her skirts and eyeing the small glade. "I'd forgotten how peaceful it is in this corner of Daddy's property."

Hal slipped his arms around her from behind. "This guesthouse is larger than our home."

She angled her head to see him. "Not quite, but we might get some good ideas here about adding more room to our own home. The cottage has a lovely loft."

His lips pursed. "The pitch on our roof isn't steep enough for a loft. But I could build us a loft bedchamber in the barn."

She laughed. "Captain would love that."

They were in no hurry to move, both seeming to enjoy a quiet moment to simply breathe.

"Is this the field where you and your cousin raced your father's horses?"

"It is," she said, grinning at the memory.

Hal chuckled. "Why is it that I no longer find it so hard to picture you racing through the fields with reckless abandon?"

"Perhaps it's because you know my true nature now?"

"You mean because I've learned that you're willful and daring and sassy?" he asked. "Yes, perhaps that's why I can easily see you disobeying your father and racing the wind on your horse."

"You don't sound disappointed by that revelation."

"That passionate spirit is what I love about you," he said, pressing a kiss to the side of her head.

Nancy stood there wrapped in his arms for a long while. The shadows were lengthening, and the pinks and oranges of the sky were being consumed by twilight.

With Hal's hand at her back, they entered the cottage.

Polished wood floors and natural oak walls with exposed overhead beams greeted them. On the opposite wall, a huge fieldstone fireplace stretched to the ceiling. Polished pewter candlesticks sat on either side of the large portrait of a Tremont ancestor that hung over the fireplace.

She looked at Hal who was taking in the cottage with a bit of amazement. "Do you know that I used to step completely into the fireplace when I played here as a child," she said.

He eyed the massive fireplace. "I don't doubt that you could or that you did although I'd certainly not encourage it. Please don't share that with our children when we visit."

The thought of staying here with her husband and children while visiting her family brought a sense of peace and healing to Nancy's heart.

She could already imagine her dark-haired boys darting around the two high-backed wing chairs that sat to one side of the fireplace or playing with their toys at the small round side table between them.

Opposite the chairs was a cushioned high-backed sofa which Nancy knew was quite comfortable from the numerous naps she'd taken here as a child. But no one would be sleeping on the couch tonight, she knew that for sure. Nancy looked forward to snuggling with Hal on that sofa on future visits to see her parents. The idea that she could visit her family now, and that they in turn could come to visit her, filled her with joy.

"There's even a kitchen here," Hal said, gesturing to a small stove and sideboard in the far corner of the room. "This is all quite spectacu-lar." He pointed to a wide-rung ladder. "I suspect that leads up to the loft? Is that where we'll be sleeping?"

"Yes it leads to the loft, but we'll be sleeping in the bedroom tucked beneath the loft. You can peek inside. I think you'll like the four-post canopy bed and appreciate the carving in the headboard," she told him.

He took a quick look and agreed that the quality of the carving was very good and that the bed looked quite comfortable.

"Hal, would you please open some windows? It's dreadfully stuffy in here," she said. "While the cottage airs, we can go sit by the creek while it cools off inside."

"Good plan." He hung his coat over one of the chairs and set about opening the windows. He crossed to the fireplace and opened the windows on either side as well. A refreshing breeze blew through the room as Hal removed his tie and unbuttoned his collar.

Nancy hurried to the bedroom and opened the chest at the foot of the bed, pulling out a red and blue brightly colored quilt before closing the lid.

Quilt in hand, she and Hal headed outside. She led the way to the creek, and as soon as they spread the quilt on the creek bank, they sat with a sigh. "Did you know that this creek meanders like a serpent all the way to Lake Erie?" she asked.

Hal cocked his head. "That right? Well, did you know that Canad-away Creek empties into Lake Erie as well?"

"I didn't, but I find the similarity rather ironic and intriguing."

Hal leaned back on his hands and stretched his long legs out in front of him. They sat on the blanket in comfortable silence, listening to the babbling creek as night fell and moonlight cast a soft golden glow across the field.

"I have to tell you that Captain has been asking after you ever since you left," Hal said, breaking the silence.

Nancy laughed. Then she sighed. "I've missed you and Captain and our house so much, Hal, I honestly thought my heart would break in two halves. I can't wait to get back to Captain and our cozy little home."

Hal scrunched his face as if he'd just gotten caught dipping his spoon in the stew pot before supper. "I'm afraid our cozy house is a disaster at the moment. And I might as well confess that I haven't picked any vegetables or pulled a single weed in our garden either. I'm sorry, Nancy, but I just couldn't bear to set foot in it. All I could see when I looked at all those green leaves is you kneeling in the middle of all those plants... And when you weren't there it was... unbearable. I'm sorry."

Nancy bit her lip but couldn't hold back her laughter. "Oh, Hal, I know about the garden. Mary sent me a letter and told me the weeds were overtaking the plants. And I have to tell you, I cried over it. I cried on my sister's shoulder about the fact that my garden had weeds. How silly is that?"

Hal clasped her hand. "It's not silly. You worked so hard on that garden, and I'm ashamed that I let it go. I will clean my mess in the house and help you tend the weeds in the garden as soon as we get back home."

"You have your own work to do, and I'm eager to take up my chores again. I miss them. I miss knowing I've accomplished something at day's end. But do you know what I missed most of all?"

"What?"

"I missed looking after and loving you and Captain."

With a groan, Hal wrapped his arm around Nancy and drew her against him. "I can't express how empty life was without you, darling. All I can say is I never want to live without you again."

She leaned into him, drawing strength and comfort from his words. Still, there was one question remaining that simply wouldn't leave her alone. "Hal, there is something that I need to know," she said, but she was afraid of the answer, and she didn't know how to ask the question. She lowered her gaze to their clasped hands, searching for words. She was afraid to ask, afraid of what she might see in her husband's eyes. But she forced herself to look... and to ask. "What would you have done if my father had been guilty of treating your father unfairly? Would you have wanted to stay married to me? After everything that happened?"

"Is that what's had you worried?" Hal asked, disappointment in his voice. "I came to Buffalo to get you *before* I knew the truth. I had decided that I couldn't live another minute of my life without you." Their eyes met. "I was hurt and needed time to get my thoughts sorted and my feelings untangled. But there is nothing in this world more important than you. Not one thing, Nancy. I just needed to know that you loved me in return and to make sure there were no more secrets between us."

She let out the breath she didn't realize she'd been holding. "The only thing between us is love, Hal. I will love you *always* and *forever*."

"As I will love you." He leaned in and placed a gentle kiss on her lips.

She drew back and smiled. "Would it be terribly inappropriate of me to remove my shoes?"

He grinned and reached for her foot. "No, darling. In fact, that's a grand idea. I'll remove mine, too." He helped her off with her shoes and then removed his own.

She tried to imagine doing this with Stuart and burst out laughing.

Hal arched a quizzical eyebrow. "Are you laughing at my big feet?"

"Gracious, no!" she said. "I just had the most absurd thought." She told him about Stuart and how mortified he would be by her behavior. "I'm so grateful I can be at ease with you. It's divine to play and love and be myself with you."

"I will admit that you shock me on occasion."

She leaned in and nibbled his bottom lip. "You like it."

"I love it," he said, pulling her into the warmth of his arms.

And as they snuggled in the moonlight on the bank of the bucolic creek, there were no secrets between them, only love, passion, and the promise of forever.

CHAPTER TWENTY-EIGHT

Two days later, Hal and Nancy returned to Fredonia. For the first time, Hal's trip to Fredonia felt like he was coming home instead of running away from something. He had finally buried the demons surrounding his father's circumstances and his brother's death, and he could now enjoy building a life here in Fredonia with the woman he loved at his side.

"Are you ready to go inside?" he asked. And before Nancy could answer, Hal carried his bride into their little home in Fredonia. He never thought to be crossing this threshold with such a feeling of joy in heart. He had never even considered that he would be crossing this threshold with his wife in his arms. Until Nancy came into his life, the house had simply been a place where he and John Radford would camp out between work hours. After John's death, it had become a cavern of grief. But Nancy had brought light and love into his house and made it a home. For Hal, for them both, and for Captain who was at his heels yowling for attention.

Hal twirled his bride in a slow circle, loving how her laughter filled the foyer. The instant he set Nancy on her feet, Captain paddled her skirt with his paws and demanded the affection he had been denied for nearly a month.

"Hello, baby boy," Nancy said, lifting the demanding little tiger into her arms. She hugged him to her chest. "I missed you so much, sweetheart." She buried her face in his fur, talking to him, hugging him, loving him in a way that made Hal's eyes tear.

Captain rooted in her neck, kneading with his paws, and pushing and trying to get closer until Nancy laughed and kissed his furry head.

Unable to help himself, Hal scratched Captain's ears and said, "You're beginning to embarrass yourself, young man."

Nancy whispered to Captain, "Your father was exactly the same way, so don't listen to a word he says."

Hal laughed, loving her sense of humor and his unexpected and deeply desired family. "Welcome home, Nancy."

"It's so unbelievably good to be here!" she said, her wide smile confirming her words. "I can't wait to tend to my chores. I'll have the house in order and the garden cleaned in no time."

Hal laughed. "This from the woman who thought she would be directing a staff and who couldn't build a fire when she first arrived?"

She arched a haughty brow. "I've learned a thing or two since coming here, you know."

"And what might that be?" he joked, knowing full well the many important things she learned and skills she'd acquired.

But instead of teasing him, her smile faded, and her eyes grew serious. "I've learned that in risking everything, I was able to find the love of my life."

Hal drew her into his arms and kissed her but was shortly interrupted by sharp claws piercing his chest. "Ow, Captain, you little rascal!"

Nancy grinned. "I guess Captain is telling me to get him some supper and get busy with unpacking." She lowered Captain to his favorite sleeping spot on the bench.

"There will be plenty of time for your chores, Nancy. There is something else in this house that has missed your touch."

"The stove?" she asked.

Hal laughed. "Yes, definitely, but also your pianoforte. Would you play a song for me and bring some music back to our home?"

"I would love to!" she said, rushing to the parlor. She ran her palm over the instrument. "I missed this old out-of-tune darling so much I couldn't bring myself to play for my father."

Hal watched as Nancy sat on the bench and placed her fingers on the keys. He bit his lip to hold back a smile. He couldn't wait for her to play her first note.

With a saucy smile, Nancy ran her fingers up the keyboard as she used to do in jest, making them laugh when she'd hit the badly tuned keys. But this time the keys rang out in perfect tune, filling the house with beautiful music. Nancy turned to him in surprise, her smile illuminating the room, her eyes glistening with tears. "Did you figure out how to tune this?"

Hal shook his head.

"You hired someone to tune it?"

He nodded. "Please don't stop. I've longed to hear you play on a tuned instrument."

Although she faltered briefly, Nancy continued to the end, finishing the song with a happy flourish and tears in her eyes.

She stood and threw her arms around him. "Thank you for such a meaningful gift. I can't express how much I love this. But I worry that you spent money on something unnecessary when we have so little to spare."

"It wasn't unnecessary, Nancy. You deserve this. And hearing you play is a gift to me." Hal eased back to look at her. "This will mean, however, that we will have to wait awhile before I can purchase a feather-filled tick for our bed, I'm afraid. We'll have to suffer a while without one."

A smile tilted Nancy's mouth. "I do believe that I'll need a rocking chair and a cradle before I need a new mattress."

Hal looked at her, momentarily confused. But then he saw in her eyes what she was telling him.

"Really?" He asked, emotions of love and joy and disbelief all tangled together.

"Yes, Mr. Grayson," she said. "You are going to be a father next spring."

Hal's throat tightened, and he choked up, completely and utterly overwhelmed by his love for his wife and their unborn child. He glanced at her flat belly where their child was growing. He placed his hand over her belly, and she covered it with her own. And for that moment he stood in wonder, realizing he was holding his wife and child.

Hal gazed into Nancy's beautiful brown eyes and said, "I think I'd like a little girl with your fiery spirit, your stubbornness, your loving heart and beautiful red hair."

"Well, I'm sorry to disappoint you, but we are having a son. And he's going to be tall and dashing like his father. And he will be named after his uncle, John Radford."

Completely undone by her words and her news, Hal pulled his wife into his arms, unable to speak. Tears filled his eyes. He would always feel the loss of his brother, but Nancy had shown him how to move past grief and find love. In all of his grand plans for his life, he never once dreamed his heart could hold so much joy and love or that he would know such deep contentment as he held his wife and child in his arms.

EPILOGUE

Five Months Later

Nancy placed two loaves of baked bread on the kitchen sideboard and sighed, thankful that job was done. She placed her hands on the small of her back and arched backward, her belly protruding as she did. She wasn't sure how she would survive the last three months of this pregnancy. She already felt huge and her hands and feet were starting to swell. Feeling a nudge to her side, just under her ribs, she rubbed her hand over her belly, settling the foot or elbow that insisted on protruding. "Settle down, sweetheart. You have a while yet before it's time for you to begin your own story."

Nancy went to the foyer, scrubbed a peephole in the frosty windowpane, and peered outside at the snow-covered orchard. The snow had been falling for several days, only letting up yesterday evening and allowing the bright moon to shine off the fresh snow. This evening was clear, and it was bitter cold outside. Even Captain, ever the fearless adventurer, had stayed close to home during the past few days while the storm had buried the fields and roads in snow. Nancy was content to stay inside. In her present condition, she was happy to bundle herself in her home and sit in front of a warm fire.

Loud stomping outside drew her attention to the steps. She'd been so lost in thought she hadn't even seen Hal leave the barn. But he was outside, climbing the steps and struggling with a piece of furniture.

She opened the door, and he carried a beautiful rocking chair inside. He set it down in the foyer as she closed the door, shutting out the cold and blowing snow off the porch.

"Whew, it's bitter out there," Hal said as she shook the blown snow off his hair. He removed his coat and hung it on a hook before wrapping Nancy up in a hug. "Warm me up. I'm freezing."

She laughed and wiggled in his arms. "Hal, your hands are freezing!"

"I'm just trying to cool you off, darling. You say you're hot all the time now."

"Well your son doesn't like the cold!" Her laughter bubbled out as she twisted in his arms.

Laughing, he kissed her neck and turned her toward the chair. "Maybe our son will like your new chair. Will this suffice to rock our children?"

An intricate carving of maple keys and leaves adorned the top of the dark walnut rocking chair. Six fashioned flat rungs formed the back of the rocking chair. Smooth curved arms framed the wooden seat and turned spindle legs connected it to long curved rockers. "It's absolutely beautiful, Hal, but it looks so fragile. I don't dare sit in it. I'm so heavy I'm afraid I'll break it."

"What? You can't weigh over a hundred pounds."

"I can assure you I'm at least twenty pounds over that mark."

He laughed and sat in the chair, pulling her onto his lap and wrapping his arms around her. "Darling, this chair is solid enough to hold our entire family." As if to prove it, Captain jumped onto her lap and joined them.

And as Nancy sat there in Hal's lap, she realized he was right. This sturdy rocking chair, this work of art crafted by her husband's loving hands, would hold their entire family for generations.

SECOND CHANCE BRIDES SERIES

*These books are the Clean & Wholesome editions
of the Grayson Brothers series
(The same stories without love scenes)*

---

*Always and Forever
Twice Loved
Then Came You
Only You
My Heart's Desire
The Greatest Gift
My Forever Love
Chances Are*

Subscribe to Wendy's NEWSLETTER

WWW.WENDYLINDSTROM.COM

Exclusive offers and behind-the-scenes scoop at Wendy Lindstrom's private Rustic Studio.

The one newsletter that readers highly anticipate!

"ALWAYS ENTERTAINING!
NOT YOUR USUAL NEWSLETTER."

"I open it the minute it hits my inbox.
It's like having coffee with a friend at
Wendy's beautiful rustic studio."

ABOUT THE AUTHOR

New York Times & USA Today Bestselling Author Wendy Lindstrom is known for the riveting emotional power of her work. *Romantic Times* has dubbed her "one of romance's finest writers," and readers rave about her enthralling characters and "masterfully crafted" stories. She is the creator of the "original Grayson Brothers" series that includes RITA award-winner *Shades of Honor*.

Professionally produced in audiobook format—and Whispersync ready—her Grayson Brothers series captivates listeners and is fast becoming an Audible 5-star favorite.

f facebook.com/authorwendylindstrom

Made in the USA
Monee, IL
13 August 2020

37882994R00163